THE ANNUNCIATION

"But at the beginning of creation God 'made them male
and female. For this reason a man will leave his father and
mother and be united to his wife, and the two will become
one flesh. So they are no longer two, but one. Therefore
what God has joined together, let no man separate."
Mark 10: 6-9

a novel by

RON TEACHWORTH

WESTBOW·
PRESS
A DIVISION OF THOMAS NELSON
& ZONDERVAN

WestBow Press books may be ordered through booksellers or by contacting:

WestBow Press
A Division of Thomas Nelson & Zondervan
1663 Liberty Drive
Bloomington, IN 47403
www.westbowpress.com
1 (866) 928-1240

ISBN: 978-1-4908-4030-7 (sc)
ISBN: 978-1-4908-4031-4 (hc)
ISBN: 978-1-4908-4029-1 (e)

Library of Congress Control Number: 2014910555

Printed in the United States of America.

WestBow Press rev. date: 08/07/2014

For Zojilia, Julian Scott, Marisol Bien, and Analisa Bien

1

Olivia Gianetti waited in the kitchen with her mother while her grandmother, Eleanor, hung her coat and hat in the hall closet. Eleanor walked into the kitchen wearing an expensive dark blue dress and a string of eye-catching Mikimoto pearls around her neck. She had just arrived at the house after a long breakfast with the university president.

Olivia and her mother were nervous as they sipped the last of their morning coffee. They never knew what to expect from Eleanor, but she seemed in an unusually good mood.

"Well, did you get the application in?" she asked. Her tone was friendly but serious. Eleanor was referring to Olivia's application for the art restoration project fellowship in Florence, Italy that coming fall. It was an opportunity of a lifetime. Olivia had never worked so hard in her life as she did on the application, and she was anxious.

Olivia looked to her mother, and then answered, "I hand-delivered it to the Dean's office myself yesterday before I left school. I did my best."

Helen did not make eye contact with her mother, but she took her daughter's hand and smiled.

"Don't worry yourself to death Livi. We will all pray for the best."

Olivia glanced at her watch and saw she was running late. She had to leave if she was going to get to her next class on time. She stood up and grabbed her sweater and book bag.

"We'll just have to wait and see," Olivia said. "They said we'd get a letter in a week or so. Wish me luck, Grandma," Olivia said giving Eleanor a quick peck on the cheek, and then said to her mother, "I'll be home for dinner, Mom." And she was gone.

There was always tension with Eleanor that went in all directions, but at the moment she was unusually calm, as she already knew her granddaughter would be selected for the fellowship. Helen stood and offered to make another pot of coffee, but Eleanor declined and quickly got up from her seat.

"Thank you, but no dear. I have a board meeting to prepare for. I spoke to the Dean last night, and Olivia will be part of the fellowship. But let's wait for her to get a letter. Then we'll celebrate. In the meantime, you can plan on it and don't worry about the cost. I'll take care of that."

Eleanor Rose Grandville, Olivia's grandmother and the matriarch of the family, had been instrumental in getting Olivia into Madonna University. For years, she'd worked hard for the church and now sat on the Detroit Archdiocese Board of Directors. The Archdiocese of Detroit employed Eleanor, from an early age, first as an elementary school teacher, and then a school principal. Now, at seventy-five, she was retired and worked hard to raise money for the church. As a reward, she was asked to serve on the Madonna University Board of Directors, and before long she rose to the position of Vice Chancellor. It was Eleanor's influence that led to a full scholarship for Olivia through the Felician Sister's Foundation. Olivia's mother, Helen, was a single parent, struggling financially, and was grateful for her mother's support.

2

On its final approach before landing, the United 747 jumbo jet banked right, allowing Olivia an aerial view of Florence from her window seat. Although tired from lack of sleep, Olivia felt a rush as she viewed the ancient city for the first time.

Also on the flight with her were a group of ten young seminarians from the Detroit Major Sacred Heart Seminary and Olivia's group of ten young women who were in their first year of study to become Felician sisters. The seminarians and Felicians from Detroit had been selected to take part in an eight-week fellowship to be administrated by the Archdiocese of Florence.

They were the best and brightest devout Catholics from southeastern Michigan who would assist on fresco renovations in the San Marco Convent and study art history as part of their stay. They had been selected based on extensive biographical checks, scholastic achievement, and lengthy essays. After all the scrutiny and intensive orientation classes, Olivia was honored to be included in a program that had been formally approved and funded by the Vatican.

As Olivia looked at the ancient city from her window, sunlight covered half of the tile roofs below, awaiting the cover of dark rain clouds that were moving in from the west. The large jet landed at the Amerigo Vespucci Airport just northeast of the city. Olivia breathed a sigh of relief at the sound of the wheels touching down. She crossed herself gratefully as the plane taxied to the gate and was connected to the gangway that would allow the passengers access to the terminal.

The students soon found themselves in baggage claim on the ground floor. The young women from Madonna College waited patiently for the single suitcase each of them had been allowed to bring. The young seminarians took the initiative of pulling off the luggage as it came by on the conveyor belt. Each suitcase had a small red tag in the shape of a church. Even surrounded by the hubbub of the baggage area, Olivia could hear thunder outside.

When the students finally gathered on the walkway in front of baggage claim, rain pelted the taxicabs and shuttles that were queued up to carry people into the city. The tourists seemed to gravitate to the taxis and buses, but the students had been provided with vouchers for the train that would take them to the Fortezza da Basso. As the train sped towards Florence, the students looked over their instruction sheets and talked quietly.

Olivia sat next to her friend, Vanessa. They had known each other a little back in Detroit, but sitting next to each other on a long flight to Italy had drawn them closer. Although they were both in training for the sisterhood at Madonna, they were in different areas of study. Olivia was an art history major with a minor in philosophy, and Vanessa was a theology major with a minor in art history.

As the train pulled into the station downtown, they could see the skyline of Florence from the Palozzo delle Mostre and the rain was now coming down much harder. September was known for being a wet month throughout northern Italy. People sheltered under their umbrellas while waiting for buses or taxis that would take them to their final destinations in the city. Many of the tourists were there for the upcoming visit to Florence by Pope Paul II in celebration of the role Florence played in the arts. Olivia stood inside the bus station holding her small, black, cloth suitcase and scanning the information sheet. She turned to Vanessa.

"It says here we're supposed to catch a bus to San Marco." Olivia looked around and then pointed to a small, green bus. "Is that it?"

By now, the rain was coming down steady and hard. None of the students had thought to bring rain gear. The girls sloshed through puddles in the piazza to the bus, holding their instruction sheets over their heads. The young men flipped up their collars and followed.

The bus driver did not speak English, but waited patiently with a checklist as each passenger put a check mark next to his or her name.

By the time everyone was on board, two young seminarians were without seats and had to remain standing, holding tightly to stainless steel pole supports above their heads. Finn McNelis, a young Irish-American from the Sacred Heart Seminary, almost lost his balance as the bus made a sharp turn left. Instead of heading south toward the downtown area, the bus turned and headed east toward the fifteenth century convent.

The rain had thinned to a drizzle, and everyone was surprised to see many shops closed with their shutters drawn. Large granite stones that had been laid in a checkerboard fashion to form the streets were washed clean to a dull glow. Olivia and Vanessa sat together and discussed their expectations.

"Do you have any idea what the rooms will be like?" asked Vanessa.

"I'm sure they'll be simple and clean. They used to be called cells. Makes it sound like a jail. I know they're all on the second floor. I hope they have a window," said Olivia as her eyes wandered to the two nice-looking seminarians who stood not far away.

Vanessa said, "I read that they'll issue us their traditional blue garments, white blouses and matching headwear for our stay in honor of their Dominican roots. It'll be a nice break from brown. I wonder what the guys will have to wear?"

"Who knows," Olivia said, still distracted. "They'll probably have to wear work clothes while working on the restorations, but beyond that, black I guess…Like what they have on today."

Olivia was watching the tall, slender boy with thick, dark hair. She could not hear their conversation but could tell the young men were entertaining each other with stories as they laughed sporadically. The tall young man's smile reminded her of the movie star, Hugh Grant. What is he doing in the priesthood? She blushed and looked away.

Because of the rain, there were fewer people out and about in the streets. Streams of water flowed down the sides of the slightly arched stone boulevard, carrying debris, straw, twigs, and litter to the Arno

River. Off the main streets were smaller side streets that appeared like dark caves winding off into the blackness, lined by buildings so close together there was only room for pedestrians or possibly a motor scooter.

There was an air of excitement on the bus, as this new experience was many things: independent study, fellowship, but most of all an adventure for many young people who had never traveled abroad. The workshop fulfilled six college credits and a fellowship citation on their vitae. Everyone began to realize their experience in Florence would likely form professional relationships that could last for years, and they were all excited by the recent news of the visit by Pope John Paul II during their stay.

3

The bus pulled around the Donatello statue and stopped in front of the thirteenth century convent facade. White columns rose three stories high, each capped by a white cross. The students entered the vestibule of the San Marco Convent, which was now also designated as a museum.

Upon their entrance, Ana Maria Sutara, the acting Mother Superior in charge of the convent, immediately greeted them. Mother Ana Maria was a large, heavyset woman dressed in an all-white habit. Standing next to her was a young Sister who did not speak and kept her eyes down. With a commanding voice, Mother Ana Maria addressed the group.

"Sorry about the dreadful weather, but thank God you're all here, safe and sound. Welcome to San Marco. It is a long trip from Michigan, and you must be tired. We will get you into your rooms after a short tour. I am Mother Ana Maria, and this is Sister Julia. You can leave your suitcases here, as we will be coming back this way before you get your room assignments in the chapter room. I will provide you with my formal remarks at dinner. Okay then, everyone. Right this way."

Mother Ana Maria led the group with Sister Julia in tow. She had only recently been put in charge of the convent and museum, and this would be her first group staying at the convent for an extended period. Mother Ana Maria Sutara had been a sister at San Marco for ten years before being promoted to Mother Superior upon the passing of Sister Mother Superior Angelica.

Beyond her role as Mother Superior, Ana Maria was a woman yearning to do good work. When the opportunity to head up the fellowship came along, she was beside herself. The work would go beyond being the gatekeeper at San Marco, and when she was told that Pope John Paul II might be visiting, the idea went far beyond her expectations. Mother Ana Maria was both maternal and dedicated to duty and service. She initiated contributions to the local soup kitchen and the mission for battered women, but if there was one thing she had in common with her sisters, it was the desire to be loved. It was hard for her to be open, vulnerable, and accept affection when she had to be a disciplinarian.

She proceeded to give the students a quick tour of San Marco. They went first to the church, a gothic design with large frescoes that portrayed the Stations of the Cross and The Altarpiece fresco. After a short prayer, the group headed to the large refectory, the washrooms, and the kitchen area, all of which surrounded a magnificent square outdoor courtyard. The walkways around the courtyard were covered with high, vaulted ceilings supported by Roman columns.

On the second floor, they were shown the dormitory corridor and the library, and they stopped occasionally to view the famous Fra Angelico fresco paintings. Mother Ana Maria was well schooled in the history of the convent, something that would become more evident in their Art History classes. After the tour, the group gathered again in the entryway to reclaim their luggage. Mother Ana Maria gave a few more instructions.

"Everyone needs to check in with Sister Julia and get their room assignment. Mass will be held at five in the church, followed by dinner at six in the refectory. So, welcome again to San Marco and the new fellowship program. I hope you all enjoy your stay. In the name of the Father, the Son, and the Holy Spirit, may the Lord be with you."

As Finn grabbed his suitcase and headed toward the chapter room to get his room assignment, his suitcase latch caught on the edge of a chair and opened, spilling its contents onto the marble floor.

"Whoa," Finn said, staring at the empty suitcase in his hand.

The closest student to him, Olivia, bent to help him retrieve the spilled contents. She could hear other seminarians laughing softly. She kneeled to help the young seminarian fold his clothing and get it back into the suitcase.

Olivia was handing him several pairs of folded underwear as Sister Julia approached.

"What happened?"

Finn's face flushed hot as he took the underwear from Olivia's outstretched hands.

"The catch on my suitcase got caught on the chair, and this young lady is trying to help me... repack." He looked at Olivia directly and held out his hand. "I'm Finn, by the way."

Olivia had no choice but to shake his hand. "I'm Olivia. I think you're all set."

Finn smiled. "Nice to meet you, Olivia. Thanks for your help."

Olivia glanced nervously at Sister Julia, and then at Vanessa, who cocked her head and smiled.

The students dispersed to their rooms. Olivia and Vanessa had been assigned to a double room with two single beds, a dresser, a sink, and a window overlooking the courtyard. The young men were in one corridor, and the women were in an opposite corridor in the U-shaped wing of the convent. The walls of the convent were much thicker than usual, and there were frescoes everywhere.

When Olivia and Vanessa got to their room, their uniforms were laid out on their beds. Each had two sets of dark blue tunics, white blouses, dark blue short headpieces, and white socks. They would wear one while the other was to be washed. They had enough time to unpack and rest before Mass.

4

That night, it was raining in Bucharest. In the darkness, it was hard to see the two men who escorted Daresh Oldani to a backstreet grill just off Strada Delfinului in the Sector 2 part of the city, not far from the train yards. He did not know the two men beside him. Petrov had said only that he was to meet with Gravil, the leader of a small Piagnoni cell.

When they reached the hole-in-the wall grill, one of the men unlocked the steel door, allowing all three to enter without turning on the light. Behind the counter, Daresh could see a room at the rear of the kitchen lit by a small light. As he entered the room and watched the two men who brought him disappear, he saw Petrov seated at a card table with another older man he assumed to be Gravil. Daresh recognized an emblem on the older man's dark jacket as the insignia that represented the work of the zealot extremist, Girolamo Savonarola. Petrov gestured at a flimsy folding chair, and Daresh sat down. Finally, Petrov broke the silence. "Daresh, this is Gravil. We are here to talk with you about a new assignment. This is highly confidential. Understood?"

"Of course. As you say. What is this about?"

But it was Gravil who answered Daresh's question.

"Daresh, I know your father. We fought together against the Communists as part of the underground, and we share the same religious commitment." He was referring to the secret society of fanatical Catholics known as the Piagnoni, who militantly opposed the modernization of Catholicism in 1962. "I am pleased that you've joined our efforts. I have heard good reports of your work in and around the city."

"Thank you sir," Daresh said, peering intently at the older man. He was smaller than Daresh had imagined. His short white hair and thick eyeglasses made him seem timid, but when he spoke, his voice was anything but meek.

Gravil continued, "This will be a very different assignment. It will go beyond surveillance and the protests we have waged against the Roman Catholic Archbishop here in Bucharest. We will work diligently to place you in proximity to the Pope."

"Is he coming to Bucharest?"

"No. We have learned that he will be in Florence this fall. We are now working to learn more of his itinerary."

"Why have you selected me?"

"You are unknown, and we will be able to create a clean and undetectable identity, one that will go unnoticed by the Vatican security force, and your military experience with weapons is an asset."

Daresh was beginning to understand the terms of his assignment. He glanced away, noticing his two escorts outside huddled under a small awning to protect themselves from the rain. Daresh could hear the sound of a freight train close by. Inside, a single light bulb hanging down from the plaster ceiling flickered as he made his decision.

"I need to discuss my terms," he said nervously."

The two men looked at each other with expressions of relief. After a long pause, Gravil responded slowly. "There will be time for all of that. And there will be much to do preparing you for the trip. The purpose of this meeting is only to propose the assignment and get your agreement. Petrov will be your contact, and he will oversee your preparation for the work we are asking you to do in Florence. Let me tell you this: there are only four people who know of this high profile assignment. That would be you, Petrov, myself, and our photoengraver who will prepare the documents. You are sworn to secrecy. Understood?"

"Yes. I understand."

With that, Gravil rose and reached out his hand to Daresh, who extended his hand in return. The two men embraced. As Gravil held him close, he spoke softly in his ear. "We have a lot riding on this, Daresh. If you are successful, the Piagnoni will celebrate your accomplishment for decades to come. God bless you, my son."

As Gravil left the room, the two escorts returned and looked to Petrov for their orders. "Take him back to his house," Petrov said. Turning to Oldani, he said, "These two men will act as bodyguards until you have left for Florence. Do not take offense. It's for your protection." Daresh nodded and shook Petrov's hand. The sound of yet another train could be heard in the distance as the men disappeared into the Romanian night, completely unnoticed.

A week later Daresh Oldani stood under the tall metal canopy at the Gara de Nord train station in Bucharest waiting for the eight p.m. train that would take him to Florence. Rain pelted the thin, metal roof like a snare drum and made him nervous. He had a light dinner earlier from the same run-down grill where, in the backroom, he was given his ticket, a sealed envelope, and some cash.

Now he paced the platform, anxious to be on his way. He eyed the trash lying between the tracks with disgust. The cleanliness of the Bucharest streets and trains was always below acceptable standards, and it reminded him of the neighborhood where he was raised.

This was his first big assignment, and he was experiencing a combination of indigestion and free-floating anxiety. After Daresh was discharged from his military obligation, the Piagnoni had spent more than a year training him. The small Piagnoni cell that operated out of Bucharest was part of a larger network of conservative Catholics who organized in secrecy. Their goal was to return Catholicism to the ways of the fifteenth century. Made up of mostly radical Dominican priests and friars, a few members were direct decedents of the Medici dynasty. They held tightly to the pre-Vatican II views on the role of the Catholic Conscience and felt that the Catholic Church had lost its spiritually transforming effect in the United States and throughout the modern world. The crisis was relatively clear-cut: There was a basic lack of commitment among Catholics to the teachings of the Church. As a result, the small, secretive group held vehement protests when Pope John Paul II appeared in public.

Daresh got in line to board the older third class train as it pulled into the station, steam belching from its screeching wheels as it finally came to a stop. The wooden bench seats held three passengers, and there was little room for luggage. Fortunately, Daresh carried only a small canvas bag containing a single change of clothing and a few necessities. Before leaving, he had cut his hair short and made sure he was clean-shaven. Of average height with short, dark brown hair, he now looked like a thousand young men walking the streets of Bucharest looking for work.

As soon as he stepped into the train car, he rushed to find a seat next to a window where he could rest his head and get some sleep. The distance to Florence was almost a thousand miles, and the train would travel through the night, crossing the borders of three countries before reaching Italy sometime in the morning.

In the middle of the night, the train came to a stop just south of Belgrade in the small town of Lazarevac. Daresh woke up and rubbed his eyes. Only a few passengers got off his car while many more boarded. Day workers and poor families packed themselves into the car with extra luggage and an occasional pet. Daresh was thankful for his seat.

He put down his small Italian language booklet and pulled an envelope from his pocket and opened it carefully. The Piagnoni encrypted all their written communication using a one-time only, word reversal pattern. After he removed the contents, he opened his wallet and removed a small, circular cardboard decipher key that was used to change the first letter of every other word with more than four letters. The decipher key was designed to be used only once and then discarded. Daresh was instructed to decipher each instruction at various time-sensitive intervals. The first instruction was to be read before reaching Florence. He glanced furtively at the two children next to him to see if the hubbub had awakened them, but they were still asleep. He twisted around to make sure nobody was paying attention before he proceeded to decode his first instruction.

He sensed this trip to Florence was important just by the nature of the written communiqué. It was no secret that the Pope would be in Florence sometime during the month of October to celebrate the festival of the arts, and Daresh assumed his trip was related to the Pope's visit.

He had attended one protest before. He slowly began the painstaking process of deciphering the first of two instructions. The train was well on its way and daybreak on the horizon when he finished the first instruction.

Upon arrival, get off in the Rifredi part of the city. There you will find a single room accommodation at 306 Via Galeno. Make sure your room is on the first floor and has a window. Open your second directive after you have confirmed the Pope's visit. Purchase a prepaid cellphone and two SMS cards. Call your contact once you have your phone working. We will find you employment.

As the train sped through the countryside, Daresh could see the conductor coming down the aisle and carefully checking everyone's ticket and passport. Daresh reached into his jacket pocket and removed both his ticket and his newly issued passport. The photo had been taken at the Bucharest grill after he cut his hair and shaved his beard. The name read Josef Dvorsak.

5

Mass at San Marco began promptly at five o'clock and was led by Father Stephen Paggi who served the convent from St. John Fisher, his parish across the street. A tall, thin man in his late thirties, Stephen Paggi had lost most of his hair by his mid-twenties. His father had given him eyeglasses for his birthday. The frames were made of turtle shell found only in South Africa. Their expense and distinctive design were in stark contrast to the things most men of his station were likely to have. Otherwise, he always wore black slacks, shirt, and coat, as well as the typical white collar that always caught peoples' attention.

Stephen Paggi loved the relationship with the San Marco Convent just across the street in the area of Florence known as centro storico. He was attracted to the long, quiet streets of shops fronted in creamy yellow plaster, and the traces of old Roman ruins, much of which were rebuilt after World War II.

His parents ran a wine distribution company that sold Tuscan wine to most parts of the world. Mr. and Mrs. Antonio Paggi could easily be described as upper class. They had offered to buy Stephen a car. Instead, he insisted on a bicycle. When the Bianchi bike was delivered to the church office one spring afternoon, he had wished it were more modest. Something black with a basket for groceries was what he had in mind. The beautifully designed Bianchi Milano was a piece of art with a price tag that exceeded his yearly salary.

The relationship between St. John Fisher and San Marco was symbiotic. The nuns took care of Stephen and his staff by providing meals. In return, he provided mass to the sisters and acted as a liaison to the office of the Archbishop of Florence at San Lorenzo, where Stephen was frequently invited when Americans were visiting. His years spent in graduate school in the United States made his knowledge of Americans valuable to the Archbishop and his staff.

His analytical skills helped him manage the parish finances and provide a safe environment for school children. It was a lot of responsibility. Running an elementary school as well as the church required him to be both a pastor and a principal. His closest friend and confidant was his sister, Madera, who he would often invite to lunch at their favorite eatery, the Café Rivoire off the Duomo court. Madera always included Stephen in family activities, and he often visited for dinners where they enjoyed recounting stories of their teenage years.

Fr. Stephen Paggi did a lot of writing and publishing for the church: a weekly bulletin and articles on education for the Florence Catholic Journal. The teachers in his school were a mixture of San Marco Sisters and lay people, all with teaching degrees. The fourth grade teacher was Derek Girodano, who doubled as soccer coach and was Stephen's running partner. Stephen attended film screenings and concerts with Derek and his wife, and they often did some camping north of Florence. The work at St. John Fisher, along with a close relationship with San Marco, provided Stephen with a life he loved.

The six nuns who lived in the active convent, along with a few volunteers in the neighborhood, attended the Mass at San Marco each day. The church was simple in design, a single nave with two side chapels created in the sixteenth century by the Flemish sculptor, Jean de Giambologna.

As the young American students entered the church for Mass, they stood momentarily to observe *The Crucifixion,* which was scaffolded to the ceiling and prepped for restoration. The church was cleaned and cared for by a small staff of local elderly women and was now often visited by tourists. The young Felician sisters continued on their way in their new ensembles, followed by the young men in black suits with white collars. In addition to the students, there were clergy from St. John Fisher, and an important Monsignor from the Dioceses of Florence.

As Father Paggi entered with Mother Ana Maria, the Archbishop Giuseppe Gellini of Florence followed them and took his seat behind the altar. Surrounded by twelfth century stained glass and Renaissance frescoes, the Mass got underway as the nuns held tightly to their rosaries. The Latin Mass was conducted only on special occasions, in this case, to honor the students. The Dominican monks who headed up the restorations chanted the response psalms. With flowers, incense, and candles, a special Mass set the stage for the fellowship to get underway.

The Archbishop sat at the head refectory table dressed in a black suit and a cape edged in red. The huge room was dark, except for light from the windows arched high near the ceiling. Each table had multiple candles that gave off a warm light and softened the edges on everything in the room.

As Finn looked around the room, his eyes found Olivia. He couldn't help staring. Her light and clear complexion was framed by dark hair pinned under her headpiece. Rich green eyes seemed to fill the upper half of her face. *She's so beautiful,* he thought.

When the meal finished, all eyes shifted to Mother Ana Maria, who made formal Italian introductions, leading up to the final introduction of the Archbishop of Florence, who requested that each of the students stand and introduce themselves.

This caught the young students by surprise. The first student chosen was Olivia's roommate, Vanessa, who blushed, paused to collect her thoughts and stood up.

"I am Vanessa LoDuca, and I am studying in the Order of The Sisters of St. Felix of Cantalice, more commonly known as Felician Sisters. We are an active-contemplative order that was founded in Warsaw, Poland. We seek to harmonize a deep spiritual and community life with devotion to diverse acts of mercy. I was raised in the Detroit area and study theology and art history at Madonna University. I feel privileged to be selected as part of the fellowship." And with a bow, "Your Excellency."

With that, Vanessa sat down. She had set a model for everyone else and given everyone time to prepare his or her remarks. The two sitting next to Vanessa were seminarians from various parts of Michigan studying to become priests at the Major Sacred Heart Seminary. Then it was Finn's turn. He was tall, athletic, and flashed his beautiful smile around the table. His demeanor was so casual and friendly, even Mother Ana Maria couldn't help smiling back. It was hard not to like Finn.

"My name is Finn McNelis, and I am an Irish American from a suburb of Detroit. I attended Brother Rice Catholic High School, and I'm in my second year of study at Sacred Heart Seminary where I major in art history and theology. Well, maybe in reverse order. I write for our school magazine, "The Mosaic," and I am also a big Detroit Tiger Fan. The Tigers are Detroit's baseball team, Your Excellency."

At the mention of baseball, there were snickers from Finn's fellow seminarians, but Mother Ana Maria looked down and frowned. The introductions continued around the table until finally it came to Olivia, who by now had made some notes on her napkin. All eyes shifted to her as she stood and not just because it was her turn, but because they saw what Finn saw. She had large green eyes, dark, long hair, and larger than normal lips that gave a balance to her face. Often and repeatedly, she had been asked to model for the Detroit Archdiocese when they needed attractive young women for their brochures. All of which she had respectfully declined. She stood and bowed to the Archbishop.

"My name is Olivia Gianetti, and let me first say it is an honor to be here this evening and to be part of this selected fellowship. As described by others before me, I am studying to become a Felician Sister. Our order was founded in 1843 by Sophia Truszkowska and named for a shrine of St. Felix, a 16th Century Franciscan Saint who was especially devoted to children. I live in Livonia, Michigan with my mother. My father lost his life in the Vietnam War. My major is art history with a minor in philosophy at Madonna University. And if I may say so, this is the most beautiful place I have ever seen. Your Excellency."

There was applause led by the bishop as he rose and walked to a small podium set atop a wooden table. The back of his head was covered with a small, red kippot. Each side of the podium provided space for candles and flowers. The Archbishop removed a piece of folded paper from a pocket inside his suit coat and began his remarks.

"Good evening and welcome. Let me start with a verse from the prophet Isaiah.

Although the Lord gives you the bread of adversity and the water of affliction, your teachers will be hidden no more; with your own eyes you will see them. Whether you turn to the right or to the left, your ears will hear a voice behind you saying, 'This is the way.'

This will be your way. It is an honor to meet all of you from Michigan, and we are excited to see the fruits of your labor and instruction. As you may know, this convent has a rich history that we all want to preserve. During the 15th century, it was home to the Order of the Dominicans and a famous friar and painter, Fra Angelico, who lived most of his life within these walls and completed what are now forty-three famous frescoes. He lived in one of the cells, in the dormitory corridor, right above our heads. In addition, this convent is now partially a museum under the order of the Museo nazionale di San Marco and also houses the manuscripts of Girolamo Savonarola. Originally, these grounds were a Vallombrosan monastery beginning with the Medici family who renovated the entire complex in 1435. We attended Mass this evening in a church consecrated in 1445 by Pope Eugene IV. The fresco that greeted you at the entrance at the top of the staircase is the famous *The Annunciation*. As you ascended the staircase, you probably asked yourself how many times you have seen that image in your studies. And now you find yourself here, standing in front of the original fresco. There is so much here, and I could go on all night, but I just wanted everyone here to know how excited we are to have this project underway. And we just found out about the Papal visit by Pope John Paul II during your stay. His Holiness is familiar with the project, and it has his full support. We are now working on a special meeting here at the convent during his brief stay in Florence. So there is much to look forward to, and I will come by from time to time to meet with you and observe your progress. Father Paggi and Mother Ana Maria will oversee the daily routine designed for you and your endeavors. Let me close with a passage from Proverbs: 'A good name is more desirable than great riches. To be esteemed is better than silver or gold. May the Lord be with you, in the name of the Father, The Son, and The Holy Spirit.'"

6

The San Marco Convent was renovated as recently as 1962 and heated by way of boilers that forced hot water through radiators on the first floor, the idea being that the heat would rise and keep the second floor warm. Once back in their room, Olivia and Vanessa realized why they were issued thick cotton pajamas, because the room was bone cold. As the young women undressed and made ready for bed, they could hear the nuns making their rounds. Lights out was at nine p.m., and tonight there was a reminder that there was a light breakfast served at seven a.m. The announcement also served as a bed check. It was Sister Julia who seemed to be the sergeant at arms for Mother Ana Maria as she poked her head into the room shortly after they were in bed.

"Good night girls. There are more covers in the linen closet across the hall if you need them."

"Thank you Sister," said Vanessa as she wrapped herself in a large cotton comforter.

The door closed and they heard Julia move down the hall. Moonlight from the small window lit the room dimly, and they could hear frogs in the distance. Unlike the girls in the dorms in Michigan, the nuns who lived in the convent observed traditional daily routines that had existed for centuries. There were lauds at daybreak, terce during work hours, sext while sharing their main meal. nones during more work hours, vespers at sunset, compline before retiring, and matins at two a.m. The students were not expected to follow that routine, but to observe and learn the way of the Dominican Order.

Olivia lit a candle and whispered quietly, "I am so glad I wasn't sitting next to Mother Ana Maria when she called on us to make an introduction. You did such a great job. It was helpful for all of us."

"It reminded me of high school debate class, when Sister Janet would force us to do extemporaneous responses. The meeting with the Archbishop was impressive. I have never met an Archbishop before, not even in Detroit. The dinner was delicious. It had to be special for everyone, don't you think?"

Olivia nodded. "I'm sure. Finn was funny mentioning the baseball team. Did you see the look on Mother Ana Maria's face? I thought she was going to say something."

"Speaking of Finn, you folded his underwear so nicely when it fell out of his suitcase…how was that?" Vanessa tried to resist it, but couldn't help laughing.

"I know!" Olivia said. "Did everyone notice? I mean they just happened to be right there in front of me. What could I do?" Laughing hard now, Olivia covered her mouth with her pillow. When she regained her composure, Olivia continued. "Vanessa, had you met Finn before the trip?"

"You know he looks familiar, but I can't place him."

"Where do you live in Michigan?"

"I lived in Madison Heights, but I was born in a rural part of Oakland County. Have you heard of Holly?"

"Just south of Flint?"

"Yeah. It's mostly white farm kids like me. My parents had a forty-acre farm, and we raised some animals and a large vegetable garden. My father worked for General Motors and did some truck farming on weekends, but when GM pulled out of Flint, he was transferred to the Detroit area. We sold the farm and bought a house in Madison Heights. I went to Marion High School. When I was a senior, one of my teachers introduced me to the Felician Order."

"Boyfriends?"

"I dated in high school. In fact, I dated a boy from Brother Rice. Maybe that's where I saw Finn, at a football game or something. I had a boyfriend for a short time, and he took me to my senior prom. I kissed him a few times, but nothing serious. He went away to college, and that was that. Where did you go school?"

Olivia rolled onto her back.

"I went to Ladywood High School in Livonia. We lived so close; I had to walk to school. I almost froze to death in the winter. Luckily I had a friend who had a car, and she would pick me up. I played violin and was an altar girl at St. Maurice Parish, where everyone was used to altar boys. My grandparents helped us financially because my mother was a single parent. I took an art class in high school, and the Sister who taught the class loved art history, especially the Renaissance period. She helped me with my fellowship application."

Vanessa wanted something more from Olivia. "Did you have any problems in school?"

Olivia paused, but knew she wanted to have a close friend during this time, someone in whom she could confide. "I was really overweight in elementary school. Kids made fun of me and called me tubby or fatty, sometimes chubby. It made me insecure. When I hit puberty, I lost the weight gradually, and by the time I was in high school, I was thin…go figure."

Olivia glanced over and could see in the dim moonlight that Vanessa was sound asleep. She blew out the candle. The Italian fall nights were chilly, and it was an exciting feeling to be in Florence at the convent of San Marco. Everyone had waited patiently to use the phone that evening to call home and let their families know they arrived safely. There were no cell phones allowed in the convent, but laptop computers were allowed as part of their study. In addition, the library provided a bank of networked workstations with printing capability.

Dogs barked when the bell tower at St. John Fisher rang on the hour, and the sound of distant motor scooters provided a buzz that was new to the ears of the young students. The city of Florence was ancient, yet modern. The Duomo and the large central piazza were less than a fifteen-minute walk, and the students would be provided with free time on the weekends.

As everyone in the convent settled in for a good night's sleep, Mother Ana Maria worried about the responsibility of looking after the new arrivals. The bishop had told her how important this project was to the Vatican and the Diocese of Florence. Before her eyes closed for the night, she used her last waking moments to ask God for strength, and then she prayed the rosary.

7

In addition to their assisting with the restoration and attending classes, all students were assigned to a work detail. Olivia was up early working in the kitchen where she was being introduced to cutting vegetables and helping prepare bread dough. It would be another hour before the refectory would start serving breakfast.

A delivery truck pulled up to the rear of the convent and backed up to the double doors that led directly into the kitchen storage. The young Italian deliveryman was new, and he jumped down from the driver's seat to look for the cook who was stirring soup in a large aluminum kettle. The young man took the liberty to say,

"Buongiorno, Can I get some help unloading the food supplies? There are a lot of boxes. I am Nino from Giuseppe Foods."

The two men exchanged handshakes and small talk, and then the cook yelled out, "Kyle, Olivia. Help this young man unload the truck."

Kyle and Olivia stopped their prep work. Olivia pulled her hair net back and followed the deliveryman to the rear of the building. He pushed back his black hair and muscled open the heavy steel storage bay doors and then propped them open with boxes. Opening the back of the truck, Nino climbed up and grabbed a box and handed it down to Kyle.

"All the boxes are labeled, so if you could stack the boxes together, it will make it easier for the cook."

As Kyle moved away, Olivia stepped up to the truck. Nino stood holding the box with a smile on his face.

"Such a beautiful girl," he said, clicking his tongue. "You can't be studying to be a nun."

Olivia reached for the box. "We are students here. I am part of the Felician order from the United States."

She was hoping that would stop his flattery and smiles. It took about fifteen minutes before the truck was empty. Kyle and Olivia started walking back towards the kitchen when Nino jumped down from the truck and tapped Olivia's shoulder.

"Can you tell me where I can find the front office? I am new to San Marco. May I ask your name?"

Olivia turned to Kyle for help, but he kept walking. She sighed. "My name is Olivia, and I can show you the way."

Nino followed Olivia through the kitchen and down the hallway towards Sister Julia's office trying to stay ahead of him and avoid conversation, but it didn't work.

"I wish all my help were as beautiful as you," he said behind her. "Do you have some free time in your schedule? I could show you some of the sights here in Florence if you like."

Olivia kept walking and refused to respond to his pitch. By this time, a few students were making their way to breakfast, as Olivia could now see Sister Julia working at her desk in the office. She knocked before opening the door.

"Excuse me Sister Julia, but this man needs to talk with you," Olivia said before turning to make her exit.

"Thank you for the help, Olivia," Nino said smiling. "Maybe I'll see you before I leave?"

Julia watched, frowning, as Olivia quickly made her way back towards the kitchen. When she returned her gaze to Nino, he handed her an envelope. "This is the invoice. My boss said you pay by check on the delivery. Is that right?"

"Yes, we always pay on delivery. Let me write you a check."

Nino sat down in the leather chair, and when he stood up, he intentionally brushed up against a picture hanging on the office wall just above the sitting area. Julia looked over startled, as he stood straightening the framed print.

"Here is your payment. Have a good day."

Nino smiled and took the check, "Perfecto. See you next week."

What Sister Julia did not notice was the small listening device Nino so carefully attached to the back of the picture frame. It would scan all telephone conversations from the office and send them to an offshore server set up by the Piagnoni.

8

The Ancient Art in Italy Fellowship was divided into three general parts: work in the morning, classes in the afternoon and a seminar in the evening. Everyone shared a light morning meal consisting of coffee, juice and fresh baked bread. Breakfast lasted from seven to eight, and each student had his or her individual work schedule.

The students were assigned to restoration projects in two locations: San Marco and the Santa Maria del Fiora located in the center of Florence. A couple of Sisters volunteered at the St. John Fisher Elementary School across from the convent because it was their minor area of study, and there was one small fresco in need of cleaning. The remainders of the religious students were divided into two groups for each location and were trained carefully in assisting the restoration procedures. They learned to record every step of the operation using state-of-the-art digital photography. Repairing cracks in the plaster, removing layers of candle soot, and removing crystalline accretions of salt that had whitened areas where water had leaked were the main focus of the work.

In addition, some mural surfaces were showing signs of bubbling and flaking plaster. Four monks who were temporarily housed in the residence of St. John Fisher headed the restoration project. They had been trained in Rome and had worked on the restoration of the Sistine Chapel. The first days of training exposed the students to the use of a variety of solvents. Whenever possible, distilled water with a very small amount of detergent was used to remove soot and water-soluble gums. Only the highly trained monks engaged in the actual retouching of the painting by using acrylic resin sealed in a polymer.

After the work in the morning, a light lunch was served cafeteria style in the convent refectory, usually a bowl of soup or a sandwich. The afternoon was spent attending two three-credit classes at the convent. Early Fifteenth Century Religious Architecture, and Theology and Philosophy. These classes were held in the chapter room and the small refectory. The ten students in each classroom would switch mid-afternoon. Mass was held every day at five p.m., and dinner was at six. From seven to nine there was a general seminar for everyone on The Art History of Fra Angelico in the chapter room.

After an extensive interview process, Dr. Mariana Morelli had been hired to deliver the Art History lectures. Her great grandfather, Giovanni Morelli, was a famous art historian from Verona. A medical doctor by trade, he had later shifted his work to art history and politics. As an art historian, he had developed the Morellian technique of scholarship, identifying painters by scrutinizing minor details that revealed the artists' unconscious shorthand for portraying certain physical features. Dr. Mariana Morelli had done her dissertation on Fra Angelico and was known by the Sisters for her time spent studying the frescoes at San Marco.

The students worked on Saturday morning but had free time in the afternoon and again on Sunday after the ten o'clock Mass. Some used the time to do laundry, study, and complete homework assignments, but occasionally there would be time to explore Florence. Everything seemed so different from Detroit. Many of the students felt intimidated, but everyone was excited to get started and to participate in such genuine work.

9

The office of Monsignor Franco Delsoni, deputy to the Archbishop of Florence, was located in the San Lorenzo Cathedral on the second floor next to the Biblioteca Medicea Laurenziana. The huge, solemn cathedral located in central Florence had a conventional grandeur so frank and inventive even locals couldn't help noticing it.

When the phone rang at Monsignor Delsoni's desk, it was the receptionist telling him he had a call from Father Jonathan Fitzpatrick at the Vatican. Monsignor Delsoni sighed. As the designated liaison between the Vatican and the fellowship activities at San Marco, he would be overseeing arrangements for the Pope's upcoming visit. Delsoni picked up the phone.

"Prego, Father Fitzpatrick. I have been expecting your call. How are you?"

"Ah, you know. Some good days now and then. It's been raining here in Rome, and it's damp. Puts a chill right through me."

Apparently the rain had moved south from Florence to Rome because sunlight now filled the Monsignor's fifteenth century office, brightening the high ceilings, dark red walls, and hand carved oak furniture.

Father Fitzpatrick asked, "Have the students arrived?"

"Yes," Delsoni said, putting his feet up on an ottoman. "They arrived yesterday and settled in at the convent. They were all very excited to hear about the Papal visit. How are the arrangements progressing?"

"The security team hasn't cleared his itinerary. They are meticulous when it comes to the background checks and it takes forever, but we're hoping he will still be able to meet with the students, even for a short time.

Can you send me photos of the students? We have their applications, but photos will give us some visual information to work with."

"Of course, Father. And we have a bottle of single malt Irish whiskey here for you, a small token from the Archbishop. I hope we can share a drink."

"I'll count on that," Fitzpatrick said. "May the Lord be with you."

"And also with you, Father."

10

The students could not wait. Their energy exploded that first morning as they focused on their assignments. There was little talk at breakfast, except for the monks who used the time to provide an explanation of the background work that had been underway for months. Students were shuttled off in groups of two or three to their respective work assignments at Santa Maria del Fiore, leaving half of the students to gather in the San Marco chapter room. The first topics covered that morning was safety, including the use of scaffolding. One large fresco in the refectory had been scaffolded, and within minutes the monks led them to the restoration of *The Crucifixion*.

The blue metal scaffolding extended upward, attached with three distinct and interconnecting sections. The long metal struts were set on eight-inch wheel wells that locked automatically. The monks explained the bracing, as well as the planking that supported the worker. On the platform high above the marble floor was a small table that held the materials they would be using, and next to that was a stool for sitting. Jeremiah, the lead monk, demonstrated the safe way to climb the scaffold from inside the structure.

"Always climb from the inside of the framework. That way, your weight, pulls toward the center of the scaffold... like this. Never climb from the outside as it could cause the scaffold to tip. Use both hands, placing your feet on these braces, like so, and climb upward. It takes a while to feel comfortable, but always take your time. Once you're up here, you can see bracing surrounds you, so there is little chance of falling. The same procedure is used for descending. Any questions?"

The students stood in awe of the large fresco in the shape of a half moon, flat along the bottom and arched at the top. The image was of Christ on the cross surrounded by angels as his Mother knelt below. Along the top of the fresco was a banner design that was badly damaged by water. Along the bottom were portraits of seventeen saints inside connecting circles about thirty inches in diameter. These too were damaged over time from contact with people and furniture.

Once back in the chapter room, the Monks reviewed a history of restoration projects throughout the centuries that ranged from using linen clothes to rubbing the fresco with bread, mostly executed in the early part of the seventeenth century. Later, in the eighteenth century, there had been an attempt to clean the fresco using sponges dipped in Greek wine. The monk explained that today, with the assistance of the Restoration Laboratory of the Vatican Museum, conservation and restoration was elevated to a high technological art, and their work ahead was careful to follow the procedures outlined in a copy of the manual they had each received.

Olivia sat with her notebook, which contained a flood of information about the materials, as the monks continued with their instructions. Friar Jeremiah insisted they refer to him by his first name, and that everyone should follow his example. Everyone in the room wore off-white muslin protective suits that zipped up the front, latex gloves and head coverings that resembled food service caps.

As a starting point, Friar Jeremiah gave the students a definition. "Fresco painting is a method of painting using water-based pigments on freshly applied plaster, usually on wall surfaces, but not always. The colors, which are made by grinding dry-powder pigments in pure water, dry and set with the plaster to become a permanent part of the surface. Fresco painting is ideal for making murals because it lends itself to a monumental style and is extremely durable."

For the next hour, he explained the substructure of the convent walls and went into detail describing the plaster and cement that was used in the fifteen century. His power point presentation gave a cross section diagram of a typical fresco, always pointing out where there were variations.

He explained that, in preparation for the project, he and his team had been consulting with Dr. Mano Cerisano, who ran Editech, a Florence-based company focused on the "diagnostics of cultural heritage." They were currently working on locating a lost mural allegedly painted by Leonardo da Vinci. Most of the equipment they were using had been adapted from medical devices. Infrared, thermal graphic, ultraviolet and other kinds of scanners allowed them to see images behind the fresco's layers of grime and dirt. Jeremiah said that over time, cracks in the terracotta roofing had allowed moisture to seep into the frescos, causing instability in the plaster that contained the embedded pigment.

Olivia glanced around the table and observed Finn taking notes. Sunlight from a window touched his hair, and she could see hues of dark brown mixed with black. The length of his hair caused him continually to use his fingers to comb it back from his face. She watched the movements of his hands as he carefully took notes. These were hands more likely to belong to a writer than a laborer. Underneath his muslin suit, she could see his black satin jacket that bore the embroidered insignia of his favorite baseball team and its name: Detroit Tigers. She waited for his eyes to come her way, but they did not.

The days that followed were hectic. Students were adjusting to a new and challenging schedule. Many were used to staying up late and sleeping in when they could. Here at San Marco, there was a lot of structure that included meals, work, study, and attending Mass. In addition, the training was intensive. Although the monks did the heavy lifting, all of the meticulous cleaning and preparation was to be done by the students. Under the supervision of Friar Jeremiah, they worked at both sites assisting two groups of experienced monks. There were minor injuries, cuts, bruises, and one young seminarian fell from the first rung of a scaffold, resulting in a trip to the emergency room. James was scraped up and sprained his wrist, but was released the same day.

There were constant visitors from all parts of the clergy and weekly visits from the Archbishop's office. The Florence press did some student interviews, all of which were controlled by Father Paggi. They worked hard at making the public relations very positive. The part of the Pope's visit with the students was yet uncertain and not made public. All in all, the students worked hard and studied hard with a high level of enthusiasm. Gradually, the students became friends and developed relationships with Father Paggi, Mother Ana Maria, the friars, and the Convent Sisters.

11

Finn McNelis was the first born, with two younger brothers and two younger sisters. He had shaped the path for all the kids in his large Irish-American family.

His parents had met in New York City and moved to Detroit looking for work in the auto industry. His father landed a job at the Ford River Rouge facility where he worked the assembly line, joined the UAW, and eventually was promoted to foreman at the heat treatment plant where the temperatures got up to 120 degrees Fahrenheit.

The McNelis family soon outgrew their small two-bedroom bungalow and moved to Livonia, where they bought a four-bedroom, two-story house in a subdivision. Finn learned to play trumpet in the sixth grade, joined the Cub Scouts and had a paper route that had over a hundred customers, which earned him over ten dollars a week. The family joined the St. Clément's Catholic Church where his father became active in the Knights of Columbus.

Finn's father had one love, and that was baseball. He had grown up ten blocks from Shea Stadium in New York and played baseball in high school. When Finn was very young, his father enrolled him in T-ball, and later in little league teams, but Finn did not have a true competitive spirit. He preferred reading, being in the middle school band, and later in the school orchestra.

By high school, Finn dropped all participation in sports and tried out for theater productions and sang in the choir. Still, Finn loved to watch baseball games. He loved the culture, the lush green field, the hot dogs, the cheering, and the drama on the field. His father took Finn and his brothers to as many baseball games as he could afford. He often worked overtime to buy tickets for Saturday afternoon games at Briggs Stadium to watch the Detroit Tigers play the New York Yankees. Finn wore his Tiger baseball cap proudly and jumped and yelled as loud as anyone when a line drive went over the left field fence.

While at school, he took art classes and excelled in his AP English class.

His mother provided all the emotional support Finn needed. She came from a middle class family in Brooklyn where her father played cello in the Brooklyn Symphony. Finn's mother was tall, with very long hair and had studied dance at an early age. She played oboe in high school and then switched to clarinet in college. She was in her second year at New York City College when she met Finn's father and had to drop out to give birth to a nine-pound baby boy. If anyone did the math, Finn was born about eight months after a big Irish wedding.

Finn was slightly introverted and, because of his innate intelligence, he was double promoted after second grade. It was when they moved to Detroit that he was tested and placed in fourth grade, so he never saw the inside of the third grade classroom. The academic part of the school came easily to the lanky young boy who was always younger than his classmates. It was for this reason that he was socially behind the others and didn't date girls in high school.

In the last semester of his senior year of high school at Brother Rice High School, his mother could not keep him in clothes. He grew nearly six inches, and by the time he walked across the stage and got his diploma, Finn was starting to get the attention of his young women classmates, attention that came too late.

Finn's local priest, Father Donovan, had encouraged him to consider a full scholarship to the Sacred Heart Seminary in Detroit with the priesthood in mind, but that was played down during the recruitment period, which focused on a fully paid college education with the option of becoming a priest in the final year. His parents were thrilled at the offer. Without any other way to get to college, Finn accepted.

During the first year of Seminary, he studied Art History and wrote an outstanding paper on the early Renaissance period in Florence,

Italy. It was his writing and knowledge that got him accepted into the fellowship program.

Finn's roommate, Kyle Larson, was the polar opposite of Finn. He had gone into the seminary after a troubled youth that included a dysfunctional home life, attendance problems in high school, and some close calls with local law enforcement. He had plenty of innate intelligence that assisted him in his acceptance to the seminary, not to mention the church's dire need for new priests. He was a quiet, introverted young man, slightly overweight and very studious. It was as if the structure of the school helped him organize his life.

Kyle assumed that his acceptance into the fellowship was the result of a letter of recommendation written by one of his teachers. Kyle had done extremely well in his theology class and was excited to find out that they were to be roommates. He was not into athletics but admired those who followed their own sports teams, and he was fascinated with Finn's baseball jacket. Their group of ten seminarians all wore black or grey plain jackets, except Finn. His satin baseball jacket set him apart, and Kyle wanted to get the inside scoop. A few days into their stay, Kyle had a chance to ask Finn about his family.

"I come from a large family, with two brothers and two young sisters. My dad worked for Ford Motor Company at the Livonia Stamping Plant, and my mother worked as a nurse's aid at Henry Ford Hospital. My dad was a foreman on the assembly line and had to quit college to support his family. He told us he bought his first house on the GI bill and did some of the construction himself. We never had much for extras, but there was always enough food on the table. Both Mom and Dad came from big Irish families, and that meant a lot of potatoes, cabbage, maybe some bacon, occasionally some corned beef, and always Mass on Sunday. My dad loved baseball, and he would take us to Briggs Stadium to see the Detroit Tigers play their home games. We always sat in the left field bleachers, and Dad would order hot dogs with sauerkraut, peanuts, soda, and cotton candy for my little sisters. I caught a baseball one time that bounced off one of the bleachers right in front of us. I grabbed it in mid-air. My Dad was so proud; he built a wood base and put it in the front room. I tried out for baseball in high school, but I didn't make the team. A lot of the kids had families who could afford to send them through the little league system, and by the time they reached high school, they were developed. So, I just became a fan, and it's probably better because I like to write, and athletics is just not my thing. Maybe I could do some sports writing."

The sounds of pedestrian traffic from outside the convent walls were gone, and the St. John Fisher bell tower rang ten times before the two young seminarians fell asleep.

12

Sister Julia and Sister Mary walked the hallways, and helped a young girl who had a stomachache and trouble sleeping. As they continued their walk in near darkness, Sister Mary asked Julia, "Have you ever thought about leaving the order?" Sister Julia was taken aback.

"Why would you ask such a question?"

"Because I have a friend who has just left her order. In a letter, she told me she wants to re-evaluate her vocation, so she took a leave of absence from her religious life and moved to Chicago. She says she left with only the clothes on her back and some small savings from high school employment that her parents kept in her name. She told me her parents were very disappointed, and they talk to her less and less. Her story lingers in my mind, and I have wanted to tell someone."

Julia said, "I think the idea is there in all our minds, but very few act on it. I have had some difficult times in the past, but being here at San Marco has helped, and now I think I have found a place where I can carry out God's work. I'm glad you told me, Mary. Let me think about what you have asked, and we'll talk about it more when we have time."

The smell of church incense seeped into the convent from the five o'clock Mass and worked its way up the stairs to the second floor rooms. Sister Mary said it helped her sleep.

13

Finn had asked Jeremiah if he would be able to work at the Santa Maria del Fiora, so he was assigned to the monk who was renovating a balcony wall in the cathedral. The renovation required some light demolition, and Finn was provided with heavy-duty work clothing, leather gloves, protective eye gear, and a hard hat.

It was a real contrast to the sensitive and careful work at San Marco. The Basilica di Santa Maria del Fiore was the cathedral church of Florence, Italy. The Duomo, as it was ordinarily called, was begun in 1296 in the Gothic style to the design of Arnolfo di Cambio. It was completed in 1436 with a dome engineered by Filippo Brunelleschi. The exterior of the basilica was faced with polychrome marble panels in various shades of green and pink bordered by white and had an elaborate 19th century Gothic Revival façade designed by Emilio De Fabris.

The cathedral complex, located in Piazza del Duomo, included the Baptistery and Giotto's Campanile. As the cathedral came into view, Finn knew why the basilica was one of Italy's largest churches. Until the development of new structural materials in the modern era, the dome was the largest in the world. From his reading, Finn recalled that it was still the largest brick dome ever constructed and was considered even now to be the mother church of Florence.

When he reached the Duomo, the church was closed, and the work area was cordoned off, but his ID gained him access. He recognized David, the monk who was heading up the wall demolition. The small wall was so old it had started to deteriorate under the weight of the balcony. A special company had been brought in to provide hydraulic jacks to shore up and provide support during the removal of the wall. David and Finn worked all morning removing the small wall and had finished by midday. Just before the lunch break, Finn was taking the last wheelbarrow of debris to the industrial dumpster, when he noticed a small wooden box partially exposed in the rubble covered in mortar dust. *How did that get there? It must have been placed in the wall,* he thought.

Before he dumped the debris, he removed the ancient box and wiped off the dust. The box was about ten inches long and four inches wide with a hinged top that was clamped shut. When he wiped off the box, he could see a set of symbols that he did not recognize. As he walked back into the building to find brother David, he remembered that he had just left for lunch, so Finn stuck the box under his arm and headed back to San Marco. As he walked along, Finn realized how the Renaissance Era utilized the classical ideas and art forms, following the cultural ideals of continuation with the ancient world. Over a period of a few short years, the architect Brunelleschi and Donatello the sculptor carried out work in Florence that would revolutionize the world.

The Piazza surrounding the Duomo was crowded with people from all parts of the world. There were tourist groups huddled together where the leader waved a small flag, encouraging members to stay close. Some of the tour guides had small microphones, reciting the facts and figures of Florence. Finn stood behind a group from Japan, looking at the ornate work on the Battistero, before heading up the Via Ricasoli on foot. As he passed the restaurants and coffee houses near the Palazzo Medici Riccardi, he imagined himself sitting at one of the colorful tables, sipping espresso and talking with a beautiful woman.

He took a different route back to San Marco so he could see a different part of the city. Crossing Via dei Pucci he could see a small crowd of people gathering, and he picked up his pace.

By the time he shouldered his way through the crowd, he saw two young men fighting. The crowd was watching as if two roosters were going at it, and no one seemed interested in breaking up the fight. Finn's instinct was to break up a fight, but he didn't know what to do with the wooden box. He turned to a middle-aged woman with a white scarf and a red cross on her lapel standing next to him.

"Could you hold this for me?"

She backed away, afraid to take the box until she noticed the small ID badge on his belt. Once she'd taken the box from him, Finn stepped into the circle. Both young men were muscular, over six foot and probably two hundred pounds each. Finn was intimidated, but he pulled the two apart, shouting, "OK, stop…enough." The men stood separated by Finn's outstretched arms, eyes blazing, still plotting their next swing.

Finn yelled, "It's over. Go home before the police come."

The larger of the two reached around Finn and took a swing at the other, but missed, hitting Finn full in the face.

The next thing he remembered was lying on the sidewalk while a couple of young people stood over him. The crowd had disappeared, and the two combatants were long gone.

The young people helped Finn up as he wiped the blood from his lip and tried to get his bearings. He was a little dizzy. One of the young people grabbed his arm to steady him.

"Are you all right?" she asked.

"I think so. What happened?"

"You got hit trying to break up the fight."

Finn blinked his eyes and looked around. "Where is the woman with a white scarf?"

"There's no woman. Just us. Are you okay?'

"But she was right here. I asked her to hold something for me. She was short…Glasses, black jacket and wearing a white scarf."

Finn looked around, but the street was back to normal. The two young people walked away, and there was no sign of a woman. Finn looked in all directions and tried to get his bearings. He started walking north, holding his hand on his face. He was worried he had lost the box.

Again, Finn stopped and looked in all directions, but there was no sign of a woman. He crossed the street and walked another block and started to recognize where he was. The buildings looked familiar, and he noticed a small park. He could see the woman sitting on the bench with the dusty box in her lap. When Finn walked up, she smiled and said.

"There you are. I was wondering what happened to you. Are you all right? Here is your box. I was afraid someone was going to take it during all the commotion, so I slipped away and came up here. I saw your ID badge that told me you worked at San Marco, so I knew I could find you." She frowned as she noticed the injuries on his face.

"Oh my. You're hurt."

Finn took the box and smiled. "No…Just a scratch. Thank you for taking care of this."

The woman handed Finn the box. "You're a nice looking boy. You remind me of my son, Gianmarco. You be careful and take care of yourself."

Finn took the box and thanked the woman before he headed off, as he could now see the church bell tower of San Marco. He needed to get back to the convent, clean up and do some laundry.

14

The laundry room was located on the first floor, at the end of a long corridor of ten guest rooms, making it somewhat isolated from the main convent activity. It was late that night, past compline, or bedtime. Olivia had agreed to do Vanessa's laundry when she did her own, but there were so many demands on their time, it was long overdue. She left the room in the dark and quietly made her way downstairs carrying two nylon laundry bags. Once in the laundry room, she groped the wall for a light switch.

Once the lights were on, she loaded several machines and set them going before she sat on a bench and took out her art history notes. When Finn walked in carrying his black nylon laundry bag, Olivia was startled. She hadn't expected anyone else to come down this late.

"Hey, Olivia. I didn't think anyone would be here, given the time. We must have the same idea, trying to catch up."

Olivia smiled and nodded nervously. She was not expecting to see anyone, and the way she was dressed made her feel uncomfortable. She was not used to being seen in old jeans and a borrowed T-Shirt that should have been a size larger. She tugged down the bottom of the shirt in an attempt to cover herself and crossed her arms to cover herself even more.

Finn was barefoot, wearing cut off jeans and a Detroit Tigers T-Shirt. He loosened the tie on his laundry bag and dumped the contents into the washing machine. Before she looked away, she noticed the scratches on his face.

Olivia tried to make conversation. "Some of the students say you know how to use a computer to listen to baseball on the Internet. Is that true?"

Finn laughed. "I try to find the broadcasts on the Internet, but the time zone changes make it a little tricky. With all the work, I am lucky to find time to do laundry. Hey, I wanted to ask you, how do you like the Madonna campus? I have some friends there."

Finn measured the detergent into the machine, selected the appropriate settings, and then leaned against the dryer nearest her.

"Madonna's a great school," Olivia said. "There's a lot of school spirit. How do you like Sacred Heart?"

They both made attempts at keeping direct eye contact at a minimum, but something kept pulling their eyes together. Finn noticed the beautiful shape of Olivia's mouth.

After minutes of uncomfortable silence and glancing at each other, Finn said,

"Hey, I think your clothes are dry."

Olivia hadn't even heard the ding or seen the light go off.

"Oh, thanks. Did you hear something…Like someone walking around? I should get going. I don't think we're supposed to be here doing this so late. I mean, Vanessa probably wonders what happened to me."

Olivia opened the dryer door and pulled a huge amount of clothing into the rolling basket, which she then rolled to the table used to fold clothes on. Finn loaded his clothes into a rolling basket and joined Olivia at the counter.

Olivia worried that Sister Julia would walk in at any moment and find them after curfew. As Finn folded his clothing, he took his time and was very precise, folding each item neatly from edge to edge. She looked again at his hands: strong, gentle and well kept. As they finished, they packed everything back into two laundry bags.

Finn asked, "What do your friends call you, like, as a nickname?"

"My mom calls me Livi."

"I like that. It suits you. I don't think I've ever met a Livi."

"It's just a nickname my father gave me when I was born."

"Okay, well, goodnight, Livi. I'll see you tomorrow."

"Goodnight Finn."

As they quietly walked upstairs with their laundry bags in tow, they could see Julia walking down the west corridor with her back towards them. They smiled goodnight and slipped into their rooms unnoticed.

15

As Daresh Oldani lay in a single bed, he looked at the dirty window facing the alley. He wished there was more sunlight, but it was the only room available on the first floor. He thought back to the first night he arrived. It had been late and raining hard. By the time he reached the doorway of the small pensione, he was drenched as well as exhausted from the long train ride. There was no signage on the pensione door, which opened to a small, dingy office where an elderly man, a foreigner himself, looked carefully at Daresh's passport.

"Someone just left this morning," the man said. "It's the only room I have available on the first floor...near the end of the hallway. There is a group lavatory about halfway down the hall. Would you like to see it?"

"No need. It will do."

Oldani reached into his wallet and paid for the room, two weeks cash in advance, and took the key.

When he got to the room, he had checked to see if the window would open and, after applying some excessive force, the window finally broke free from where it had been glued shut by many coats of paint. He poked his head into a narrow alley where street debris and garbage cans lined the stone and brick walls. Although the drop to street level was a little less than six feet, he knew that, in an emergency, the door deadbolt would hold long enough so that he could be out and onto the street within a minute or two.

He had found day work by waiting early each morning at a location where men would gather to be picked up by local farmers or construction contractors. It was manual labor force that mostly loaded trucks with farm goods or unloaded construction materials. There had been a week of this kind of work that kept him busy until finally the call came from his contact who told him that there was an ad in the St. John Fisher church bulletin for a part time prep cook at San Marco Convent and that he should apply as soon as possible.

Daresh had made the call to San Marco, and Sister Julia scheduled him for an appointment with Mother Ana that next day. This was the break that his contact said they were waiting for. The convent was a hub of activity, and information about the comings and goings of the Archdiocese was readily available.

Oldani showered and shaved that morning, hoping that his appearance would be acceptable, and his broken English would not present a problem, but he was nervous. This was his first real assignment, and he could tell from the tone of his contact's voice that this was what they had been waiting for. He put on his dress shirt, looked into the small mirror, made the sign of the cross and double-checked his passport before leaving the rooming house and heading in the direction of San Marco.

Mother Ana Maria sat behind her desk searching for her employment folder while Daresh Oldani sat quietly, avoiding eye contact.

"May I see your passport?"

Daresh handed it to her without saying a word. She laid the passport next to the application to make sure the information matched up.

"So you're here from Romania? Bucharest? Have you worked in a kitchen before?"

"Yes, a little. Mostly at home, but I did some kitchen prep while serving in the military. I am very reliable."

"Are you? Well, that is important. We have a group of students here, and this has become a very busy place. How did you cut your chin? Not in the kitchen, I hope?"

"No, a childhood accident." Daresh worked hard at keeping his answers as simple as possible and forced himself to look at her when he spoke, but he was visibly nervous. Mother Ana kept looking over his application that had a work visa folded inside.

"Are you Catholic?"

"I am …since birth."

"Well, that helps. This job is part time and will last no more than six months. You will take your orders from the cook, who is a gentleman but who requires hard work. There are work clothes provided and a dinner jacket is available for special events. I assume you go by Josef?"

"Yes, Mother."

"Okay, Josef. Let's go down to the kitchen and get you started. Your first week will be a trial period, and if it goes well, we will keep you on until our regular prep cook recovers from knee surgery. We are behind in unloading our food deliveries, so there is plenty to do, and you will need instructions on how to use the garbage compactor."

Oldani opened the door for Mother Ana and followed her through the convent to the kitchen. As they walked, she gave him a brief tour and then asked.

"What church did you attend in Bucharest?"

Oldani was caught off guard because he thought the questions were finished. He knew the answer, but coming out of nowhere like that, his internal anxiety created a block on the name. Not hearing an answer, Mother Ana glanced back, looking into his eyes waiting for him to respond.

"Ah…St. Joseph…the church of the husband to our lady."

The delay struck Mother Ana as odd, but with all the activity that was going on, and combined with the constant complaining from the cook, she felt lucky to find someone who was willing to accept the low wage.

16

If working in the mornings and taking classes in the afternoon wasn't enough, the students attended a two-hour seminar after dinner, with an hour break in between. And although the convent was built in the fifteenth century, the Office of the Archbishop had made sure the classes were outfitted with the latest technology. In the chapter room, they had installed a wall screen, a new projector, a laptop, and wired the room for an Internet connection.

The imagery used in the classes came from the Uffizi Collection, the San Marco Collection, and the Vatican Museum. Olivia and Vanessa were sitting next to each other in the classroom talking about the events of the day when Mother Ana Maria came in with Father Paggi. They were assigned to teach this Monday evening seminar on Theology and Florence. Together, they had designed a PowerPoint™ presentation that acted as a framework for discussion. As they set up their presentation, Olivia and Vanessa talked quietly in the back of the room.

"Did you know Finn worked at the Duomo today?" whispered Vanessa with her hand covering part of her mouth.

"No. I wondered why I didn't see him at the convent after breakfast. How did you know that?"

"I saw him walking back from the Santa Maria del Fiore when he crossed the street and entered the convent. He was carrying something, but I couldn't make out what it was. It was easy to tell it was him. You can spot that long hair from a distance."

Olivia felt an attraction to Finn and was careful not to reveal this to Vanessa.

"He must have asked Jeremiah for permission to spend some time there."

Students filed in as Mother Ana Maria finished checking all the equipment. She and Father Paggi had worked together before, and now that Mother Ana Maria ran the convent, their relationship had grown professionally. Father Paggi provided Mass at San Marco, and Mother Ana Maria provided food service for Father and his staff. They both had studied Plato, Aristotle, Rousseau, and others. The room was now nearly full when Finn slid into a seat near the door at the last moment.

Mother Ana Maria looked at him.

"Did you help out in the kitchen tonight, Mr. McNelis?"

"No, Mother. I was trying to see if the Yankees won a wild card berth, but this time zone thing isn't working for me. Sorry I'm late."

The class laughed, as did Father Paggi. He secretly harbored an intense interest in American baseball, which he had confessed to Finn shortly after he arrived, and occasionally they would share and swap information. Mother Ana Maria stepped up to the podium.

"OK, let's start with a question. Does anyone know who said, "For God is thought to be among the causes for all things and to be a kind of principle?""

A hand went up immediately in the third row. It was Kyle, who was sure he had an answer. "Was that Plato?"

"Close. Anyone else?"

Finn raised his hand. "It sounds… more like Aristotle."

"That is correct, Mr. McNelis. Apparently there is more than baseball rolling around in your head. Okay, since we're on the topic of Aristotle, let me ask you another question. Pleasure and happiness, according to Aristotle, are two different ways of looking at the same thing. True or False?"

The class remained quiet for several moments until finally Mother Ana Maria called on a student. James cringed, and then blushed before answering. "I'd say true because they sound like the same thing to me."

Mother Ana Maria's grin could be interpreted a number of ways as she asked, "Does the class agree?"

Olivia raised her hand. "Pleasure is the byproduct of an activity and is neither good nor bad," Olivia said. "Happiness differs in that it comes from rational thinking. So I'd say false."

Father Paggi remarked. "It's a pleasure to hear such an articulate answer, Olivia."

The evening seminars were more casual than the afternoon classes and were intended to be more of a dialogue and discussion based on the readings of Plato, Aristotle, Spinoza, and Rousseau. The point was to illustrate how the Catholic Church based its theology on the work of philosophers, and that decisions were based on the doctrine of faith and reason. Often the discussions were long and heated as the young people presented their views. Near the end of the evening class, Father Paggi made some closing remarks.

"Before we close, I would like to address the church's teaching on the matter of faith and morals. I want you all to understand the role of dogma in the Catholic faith. For anyone who professes to be Catholic, their faith requires them to believe certain teachings with 'divine and Catholic faith.' I'm not sure this needs to be said, but no amount of opinion, conscientious objection, or personal desire can excuse us from acting contrary to the magisterium of the Catholic Church. Are there any questions about this?" When no hands were raised, he continued. "Good. So let me thank Mother Ana Maria for her questions that provoked another interesting session. Good night, and God bless."

17

Students often stayed after class to engage the instructors in more dialogue, but as soon as the class ended that night, Finn quietly slipped out of the chapter room and into the hallway. Kyle noticed and quickly followed. The halls were dark except where small, incandescent lights were located where candles once rested. Kyle had to speed up to catch Finn as he seemed to be in a hurry.

"Hey, wait up Finn," Kyle called out.

The moon lit the square courtyard surrounded by an arched walkway that led to the second floor stairway. Several seminarians sat on benches as debates from the evening seminar carried on. As soon as Finn and Kyle reached their room, Finn located his work clothes and pulled out a small box. Kyle sat on the edge of his single bed.

"Where'd you find that?"

Finn grabbed a cotton sock from the floor and gently removed any remaining dust. He handled the ancient box carefully, making sure he did not damage it in any way.

"It was in the last wheelbarrow of debris, and I saw the edge of the box exposed under some concrete and plaster. David had left early for lunch, so I brought it back with me. I just wanted to see if I could open it. If it was hidden in the wall we took down; it must be old. Could you hold the light closer?"

Once wiped clean, they could see the box was made of rosewood. Its beveled edges were hand tooled, and the clasp was made of copper that had now turned green. Finn removed a small wooden wedge from the clasp and tried to open the box, but it was corroded shut. The small copper hinges were corroded as well and would not move. Both young men looked at the smooth surface of the box and wondered how to get it open. There were five or six symbols carved into the surface of the lid about a quarter of an inch apart. The symbols were filled with a soft metal, most likely lead.

"What are those symbols?" Kyle asked.

Finn shrugged. "They could be a date."

Finn took a safety pin from his bedside table and used the point to clear away the corrosion where the top met the edge of the box. Once he cleaned entirely around the crease; he tried to clean the hinges. Finn did his best not to mark or scratch the surfaces, and eventually the hinges were clean. Kyle held the bottom of the box with both hands, while Finn tried to pry open the top. Suddenly the edge of the top lifted. The inside of the box was clean and well preserved. Finn pulled the light even closer. The contents of the box were a ring and three pieces of parchment that were folded, each sealed with wax. The wax seal on each document was still in place and marked with an insignia that seemed to match the insignia on the ring.

"Wow, do you believe this? This box was in that old wall a long time. It might even go back to when the wall was first built," said Finn, without touching or removing anything.

"It could be worth a lot of money. What are you going to do with it?" asked Kyle.

"Are you kidding?" Finn laughed. "It's an historical antiquity, and it belongs to the church and to Florence."

Finn held the open box in his lap and gazed inside. He recalled a long-ago incident from his work on a newspaper route. He'd been pedaling down the sidewalk when he saw a woman's purse lying in the grass. He'd stopped his bike and looked around before reaching down and picking up the black purse. He pulled out the wallet and unsnapped the clasp to look inside where he could immediately see a lot of cash, mostly twenties and fifties.

As he flipped through the clear plastic windows of identification, he located a driver's license that belonged to one of his customers, Mrs. Ellen Henne at 4900 Eldon, just a few houses up the street. Mrs. Henne was one of Finn's favorite customers because she always gave him a nice tip and would say hello to him in church. Finn put the wallet back in the purse, then shoved the purse deep into his newspaper bag before he turned his bike around and headed for Mrs. Henne's house.

When he rang the doorbell, he knew someone was home because her newspaper that he had just delivered was not there.

Mrs. Henne opened the door, surprised to see him there. Ellen Henne was young and attractive, with short black hair and a smile that everyone noticed. When she saw Finn holding her purse, she was shocked. She pushed open the aluminum screen door and said.

"My purse. Where did you find it?"

Finn was shy around Mrs. Henne because she was so pretty and always nice to him. "I was on my paper route and I saw it in the grass."

Ellen Henne was so happy to see her purse in Finn's hands. She had just cashed her husband's paycheck, and that was all the money they had to live on for a month.

"I had just walked down the street to mail some letters not even fifteen minutes ago, and I stopped to pet Mrs. Marero's new puppy. It must have slipped out of my shopping bag. I thought I misplaced it here in the house when I got home." She opened the door wide.

"Please come in, Finn."

Finn remembered taking his first step into her house and seeing the beautiful décor. He looked around at the wall-to-wall carpet, the living room with soft plush leather furniture, and a beautiful chandelier over the dining room table. Mrs. Henne rummaged through her wallet, then handed Finn a ten-dollar bill.

"Please take it as a reward."

Finn paused and stepped back. "No thank you, ma'am. I don't need a reward. I'm just glad I found it."

Mrs. Henne smiled and looked into Finn's eyes.

"You may not need this, but you deserve it. Someone else could have found it and be long gone by now. I'm lucky you found it, Finn."

She folded the bill in half and forced it into Finn's shirt pocket and then bent down and gave him a kiss on the forehead. Finn blushed and then she said, "I am going to tell your mother about this. She'll be so proud of you."

Finn could still feel that kiss from long ago as he refocused his attention on the rosewood box. By then, Kyle was in his pajamas and under the covers.

Kyle laughed and asked, "So who will you give it to?"

"Brother Jeremiah, I guess, first thing in the morning. He heads up the restoration project. Let's let him tell us what it is."

"Maybe you should wrap it up and keep it protected."

"Yeah, that's a good idea, "Finn said, thinking about how he had almost lost it earlier that day.

18

The chop of helicopter blades cut through the still evening air above Vatican City. It was an Italian police helicopter, equipped with specialty infrared heat sensors to pick up traffic jams in Rome's streets or to closely track a speeding vehicle in the night.

Father Jonathan Fitzpatrick held his hat securely as he walked quickly to the helicopter pad in the Vatican gardens, not far from the back wall of St. Peter's Basilica, at the very heart of the world's smallest state. With the briefcase in hand, he grabbed the hand rail and pulled himself into the helicopter. Within seconds, the chopper lifted off and sped rapidly north towards Florence. The trip would take about an hour, giving him plenty of time to call ahead to Monsignor Delsoni.

"Hello, Monsignor. Father Fitzpatrick. I should be there shortly. Could you have a car for me at the airport?"

"Of course. You'll stay here tonight, no? Have you had dinner?"

"Oh yes. We ate at the briefing. It's much too late for me to eat now. I want to get started early tomorrow morning and go over the itinerary. There are some questions about the tour of San Marco, so maybe we can pay them a visit."

"Of course, Father. Safe flight. See you shortly."

The helicopter landed an hour later and wheeled in a tight circle at the Aeroporto di Firenze as a black limousine pulled up on the tarmac to pick up a passenger. Most helicopters landed in a special area, but not this flight. The darkness of night and remote landing location provided the secrecy the Vatican expected. Father Fitzpatrick walked to the car, where the driver stood holding the door that was embossed with the seal of the Archbishop's office.

"Hello, Jonathan, how was your flight?" asked Monsignor Delsoni as he slid over to make room for Fitzpatrick and his briefcase.

Fr. Fitzpatrick was used to making preliminary visits to any location that was on the Pope's schedule. There were many precautions that needed to be taken, and advance security was critical to a successful visit, but it was the end of a long day and he was tired. "The flight was smooth. It makes traveling here very easy. I need to brief you on some intelligence I received from Interpol before I left."

He opened a small piece of paper from his black coat pocket with an inscription scratched out in pencil: MCDXCII. "Does this mean anything to you?"

Monsignor shook his head. "I don't recognize it."

"It may be nothing, but we should have the intelligence service analyze the date and cross-reference it to the historical record."

The limousine pulled out of the airport and proceeded south towards the center of Florence and the sanctuary of San Lorenzo.

Behind the several sets of walls at San Lorenzo Basilica, Monsignor Franco Delsoni poured himself another half glass of Jameson Irish Whiskey and tipped back in his chair. He and Fitzpatrick had worked together once before when the Archbishop of Florence had visited Rome for a Canonization. They ended up as roommates for a few days and always made time to relax at the end of the day. Jonathan asked, "Franco, did you tell me you were born and raised in Rome?" Franco laughed.

"No, I am from Sicily. I grew up in a small fishing village just outside of Palermo. When I got older, my father sent me to Spain in my mother's hometown of Santiago de Compostela. I lived there with my grandparents and attended the Seminary Façade and became fluent in Spanish. My native language helped me when I was asked to work for the Archdiocese of Santiago as the liaison to the Vatican. Some of my fondest memories are of my grandparents. When my grandmother passed away, I remember feeling like I'd lost my mother. We were that close. Like you, I have never had my own parish and I never wanted that. I pushed paper around until the Pope visited Spain, and I was assigned to help with the logistics. A year later I was working here in

Florence for Cardinal Giuseppe. You know, they move people around like chess pieces, but I must say, I love Florence."

The bottle of Jameson was finished, and the breeze from the open window picked up the sound of motor scooters and chirping crickets. Jonathan and Franco were both high level officers for the Catholic Church, devout in their faith, and loyal in their work. Both men had risen in the church hierarchy to positions of influence and enjoyed the security of their positions. Pope John Paul II would soon be in Florence, and it was their responsibility to secure his safety. But as they left the comfort of their soft leather chairs to retire for the night, they both felt uneasy. The security effort had just begun, and they both knew there were some loose ends.

19

Finn sat at the long breakfast table with several seminarians. He looked for Jeremiah, but he was not in the refectory. He wanted to sit with Olivia, but she was on her way out as he collected his juice, bread, and coffee. After finishing his coffee with his friend James, he got up and returned his tray, but not before folding a white linen napkin and taking it back to his room. Kyle had been up early and left for his assignment as Finn wrapped the rosewood box in the kitchen napkin. He headed down the stairs towards Jeremiah's office only to find that the Brother was in an early meeting with Father Paggi across the street at St. John Fisher. *Perfect,* he thought. *I will be able to explain this to both of them.*

As Finn stepped out of the convent, he stopped and looked toward the city center. Florence was one of the most beautiful and ancient cities in Italy and probably in the world. From his studies, he knew it had seen the birth of many of the men who had profoundly influenced the course of human history in art, literature and philosophy. Most of the world's artistic patrimony was here in Florence, and at one time it was the center of the world. Crowds of visitors attempting to see the city in only a few days were often overwhelmed by the beauty and culture that seemed to permeate the city.

Finn crossed the street, which was crowded with shoppers, street vendors, tourists, and children dressed in uniforms making their way into their school at St. John Fisher. Finn entered the church and walked down the long hallway to Fr. Paggi's conference room. As he approached the open door, he stopped and knocked on the doorjamb. The two men directed their attention to Finn standing in the doorway, waiting to be invited in.

"Good morning, Finn," said Father Paggi. "Are you bringing me some news about the baseball game? Could it be those St. Louis Cardinals are beating your Detroit Tigers?"

Finn stepped forward, holding the wrapped parcel at his side. Jeremiah smiled. "Come sit with us, Finn. we're just going over some renovation plans. How was your day at the Duomo?"

Finn sat down. "Well, that's why I'm here. Yesterday, just as Friar David left for lunch, I found a box in some wall debris. I didn't know where to find him, so I brought it back to the convent."

Finn put the object on the table and unfolded the napkin flat on the oak conference table. Sunlight streaked through the leaded glass windows through which they could hear the sounds of children from the attached school. Finn continued to explain.

"The box was covered in cement and plaster dust, so I brought it back to my room and cleaned it off. The edges were corroded shut, but by using a pin, I was able to get it in working order."

Father Paggi stood up and bent over the box, looking closely as Finn gently opened the Rosewood box. The expression in his eyes was a mixture of surprise and intrigue. Father Paggi walked over and closed his conference room door as Jeremiah asked.

"Did you open the box in your room?"

"I did, but that's as far as I went. I knew it was not my place to go further."

"That may have been risky. These artifacts are incredibly fragile."

Father Paggi carefully removed the contents and laid them out on the white napkin. All three of them stared at the objects until Father Paggi said.

"My sister's husband, Nicholas, works for the Ministry of Cultural Affairs. I'll give him a call. He'll know how to proceed. The cover of the box is hard to make out, but it looks like a date. Would you agree, Jeremiah?"

"If those are Roman Numerals, it would be 1492. I know the balcony was completed in 1501, so the support wall was built before then, probably finished sometime around the turn of the century."

Finally, Father Paggi said, "We'll have to contact the proper authorities and let them examine the contents to determine its authenticity. Until then, I'll put it in the office safe." He turned to Finn. "Thank you for bringing it to our attention. Let's keep this amongst ourselves for now. I'll let you know as soon as I hear something. You probably need to get to your assignment."

"Yes Father." Finn made his exit, closing the door behind him.

Jeremiah and Father Paggi sat looking at the artifact with wonder and amazement.

Jeremiah finally said, "I wonder what's in the documents? The ring appears to be a religious seal, similar to what the bishop would use. What do you think?"

"It's from nobility," Paggi said. "No layperson would produce such a thing nor have access to these kinds of materials. We need to get an expert opinion that will be confidential. The balcony was built by Baccio d'Agnolo. Maybe it was his treasure."

Jeremiah scratched the top of his head and laughed.

"It was someone who was hiding this from the church. I know around that time the church took the extraordinary step to destroy all knowledge of the two second-century Jewish books that it said contained 'the true name of Jesus Christ'…and then later Pope Alexander VI ordered all copies of the Talmud destroyed. Talk about being paranoid."

Father Paggi flipped through his Rolodex.

"Before I share it with my brother-in-law and the authorities, I have a friend who can help us. If it's all right with you, I'll give him a call. Otherwise, let's keep this between us."

20

Finn got back to his room, changed into his work clothes, and made his way to the top of the stairway where a small group of students gathered in front of *The Annunciation* fresco. Friar Gabriel was just getting started with his instructions for the day, when Finn slipped into the back, behind the small group of students.

Friar Gabriel was the youngest monk, and for that reason, one of the favorites. He looked younger than his years and could easily be mistaken as a student. But his training and experience were as good as anyone's on the team. He had worked for his father at the Vatican and started his restoration training at a very early age. Like the other friars, Friar Gabriel wore a light green, muslin coat, but he was the only one who sported a Sony Walkman and ear buds.

"Today we are going to focus on the crystalline accretions of salt that have formed due to moisture, condensation, and a few areas of ceiling leakage. The roof repairs have been made, but as you can see, there are a few areas that are whitened. Let's divide up and work in pairs."

As the group paired off and collected their materials, Finn went up to Gabriel and said. "Friar Gabriel, I noticed a problem with the scaffold on *The Altarpiece* a few days ago. The top braces are missing their cotter pins. It doesn't seem safe. I just wanted you or someone to know and take a look."

Just at that moment, a young female student slipped on the tile floor and went down. Gabriel ran to her and helped her get up. She was embarrassed but seemed fine. Each pair of students worked on a small, defined area of the fresco. They followed the procedures set forth in their training and used small tools, some of which looked like a common toothbrush. Before they started their work, everyone was required to take a picture of the existing problem and then photograph it again when they finished. Friar Gabriel worked alone, repairing cracks and any structural damage that threatened the stability of the plaster.

The Annunciation was one of Fra Angelico's most famous paintings. It greeted all visitors at the top of the staircase leading to the dorm rooms. The intent of the painting was to represent only the bare image of the Archangel Gabriel and the Virgin Mary, giving weight to a movement and spiritual concentration to the figures. As they worked, Olivia joked with Friar Gabriel and asked if he was related to the Archangel.

"You know, it's funny you mention that, as it's a joke with the other Friars and Mother Ana Maria. She wanted me to supervise the work on this fresco because my name was Gabriel. No relation by the way."

A few students laughed through their paper facemasks. At a distance, the students looked like a science exploration project in their muslin lab coats, protective eye gear, latex gloves, and caps. As James used a small cloth and some mineral spirits on the upper left corner section, he remarked, "The architecture in the fresco looks familiar."

Finn pulled down his mask and said, "It should. These arches are the arches in the courtyard here at San Marco. Fra Angelico lived and painted here for almost thirty years, so most of the settings in his frescoes are from various parts of the convent. He wanted to represent the sacredness of Mary in all her glory and simplicity, although he understood the principles of perspective. As we can see here, the rendition of the setting is flat. You probably recognize the iron rods, right?"

James agreed, and seemed embarrassed that he didn't make the connection. James Faugenbaum was a convert to Christianity, and he provided most of the comic relief to the fellowship gatherings. He was on his second set of dental braces in an attempt to straighten a strange arrangement of teeth. His favorite jokes where about deranged orthodontists. He had all kinds of comedy routines he did with his hands and face, usually trying to get a laugh, and once he had you going, he would up the ante with more of his hysterics. His father was born Jewish but married a Catholic woman who baptized her son before he was six months old. Eventually, James' father gave in and converted to Catholicism, but he never thought his son would become a priest. When James entered the Seminary, the father's family became contentious. His grandmother on his father's side considered him to be Jewish and told him he was supposed to become a rabbi, not a priest.

The afternoon went by quickly, and soon everyone was cleaning up. Gabriel collected all the gloves and asked James to wheel the cart of materials to the office. There was only an hour to rest before Mass, followed by dinner, and then the evening seminar.

Olivia had promised her mother a call and noticed the phone in the convent lobby was now available. The phone rang nearly four times before her mother picked up the receiver.

"Mom?"

"Livi! So good to hear your voice. How's it going?"

"It's great, Mom. We've been working on these ancient frescoes. And the City of Florence? It's unbelievable. So much of what I have studied is right here in front of me. I'm rooming with a girl from Madonna, Vanessa. But how are you?"

"I'm fine, Livi. I've been cleaning the house and finally took down the vegetable garden. Have you met interesting people? How are you eating?"

"The food here is good. We all eat together in the same room. It's called the refectory room. The classes are good, especially our evening seminar. I have met lots of cool people. Our art history professor is a woman. I don't have much time as we have to be at Mass before dinner. How's grandma?"

"I had to take her to the doctor yesterday. She forgot to get her flu shot and came down with something. Thanks for calling, Livi. Have fun. Love you."

"Love you too, Mom. Say hi to Grandma."

There had been a huge family celebration when Olivia got news of the scholarship. Olivia owed a great deal to her grandmother and would always go out of her way to send her flowers and attend her university events. At the ceremony of the opening of the new College of Arts & Humanities, Eleanor gave the first speech and praised her granddaughter as her inspiration. After the ceremony, pictures, and a private dinner, Helen talked to Olivia privately.

"It's amazing what my mother has accomplished, and I often feel delinquent in living up to her expectations, but you, Livi, you have done it for me. I am so proud of you. If your father were here, he would be proud as well."

Helen Gianetti was still an attractive woman. She had met her husband at a peace rally in Ann Arbor, where thousands of students had organized against the Vietnam War. Under two administrations, the war had escalated beyond any original expectation. They both worked in a small space at the student union where organizers drafted students from the commons area to help make posters, signs, and leaflets. It was a very unpopular war on all college campuses where young men were being drafted to fight in an undeclared war, and the US body count had just passed forty thousand.

Across the country, colleges had become the hotbeds of society. Berkeley, New York University, and the University of Michigan, often led by Marxists, Socialists, and college professors, all held rallies as often as possible, drawing the media's attention to put pressure on the new presidential candidates.

During the summer before his senior year, John Gianetti had visited his cousin in San Francisco and mailed a certified letter to his draft board, notifying them he was relocating his residence to the west coast. By September, he returned to Ann Arbor and sent a second letter notifying them he was moving back. It was a tactic that could postpone a draft physical for a year as students everywhere were planning an event at the next presidential convention in Miami.

Helen would often recall the first time she sat at a small concrete table on the union patio having coffee with John, where they discussed art, politics, and the new music from England. It was when she first became attracted to the tall young man with striking features, long dark hair, and a smile that was contagious. Helen was confident and knew she was attractive. She could remember intentionally putting her legs up on the concrete bench and leaning back in the sun as she moved her knees back and forth. She loved the way he wrinkled his nose when he laughed. They fell in love, and within a year they were married and expecting a child.

Soon after graduation, John lost his deferment and was drafted. Olivia was born while he was in basic training at Camp Pendleton, and he took his final leave, traveling by train back to Michigan to see his newborn daughter. It was the only time they would meet, and Olivia held closely to the only four photographs that documented his visit. She kept one in her wallet, next to a picture of her mother.

21

Father Paggi ran across the crowded street, dodging people as best as he could. He pulled open the large, heavy doors, entered the convent and rushed directly to Mother Ana Maria's office. Sister Julia sat in the outer office, working at her computer, ordering supplies for the convent, and waiting on visitors to the museum. Part of the convent was a museum, which was not nearly as popular as many of the Florence museums.

"Excuse me, Sister, do you know where I can find Mother Ana Maria?"

"She's in the daily convent meeting, in the church." She looked at her watch. "They should be finished by now."

Father Paggi left without saying a word and quickly made his way around the interior courtyard and down a long hall that connected the convent with the church. As he entered, he could see the meeting was ending, and several nuns were on their way to the kitchen. He waved his hand to get Mother Ana Maria's attention.

"What is it, Father? You look flushed," she said, approaching him in the main aisle.

"I just got a call from Monsignor Delsoni and they are on their way to visit the convent. All he said was that he was bringing Father Fitzpatrick, and they wanted a tour. I think it has something to do with the papal visit. I wanted to give you some warning."

Mother Ana Maria was a solid nun, always dressed in her white starched habit, and ready for duty. She dealt with emergencies every day that varied from illnesses to arguments. Because they had opened part of the convent to the public and had tourists on a regular basis, she was always prepared for the unknown.

"Thank you, Father. We're ready for them. We're always prepared to present the convent and ourselves. No need to for you to worry. But you might want to find your jacket."

The horseshoe drive in front of the convent was made of cobblestones dating back to the twelfth century and provided plenty of room for the Archbishop's limousine to slowly pull in and park. Both Mother Ana Maria and Father Paggi came out to greet the visitors. Although only two men exited the car and walked towards them, there were two more, presumably security, that stayed back at the car. After introductions and pleasantries, the four of them walked through the heavy doors and into the gracious foyer displaying small frescoes and fresh flowers. Standing at the entrance, they could see students working at the top of the stairway on a renovation.

"Let's meet in the chapter room. Can we get you something to drink? Coffee or Tea? Lunch will be served soon. You're welcome to join us if you like," said Mother Ana Maria in her warmest voice. The Monsignor knew Father Paggi and Mother Ana Maria quite well and, before they sat down, he made a more formal introduction to his guest from Rome.

"Father Paggi, Mother Ana Maria, let me introduce my Jesuit friend, Father Jonathan Fitzpatrick. He is the official envoy from the Vatican and will head up the Holy Father's visit to Florence. He works closely with the Guardia di Finanza, the Carabinieri, and the Swiss Guard. He and Domenico Gianni, head of Vatican intelligence, will be planning the Pope's itinerary. Please, everyone, let's sit down."

They gathered around a small conference table, and Sister Julia came in with freshly brewed coffee and sweet bread left over from breakfast. The china was from Murano Island, and the silver-serving tray was rarely used. Father Fitzpatrick kicked off the discussion.

"As you know, we would like to bring the Pope here briefly to see the Art Fellowship underway. He has shown some interest, especially in that these are American students working on the frescoes. Pope John Paul has been instrumental in the beatification of Fra Angelico, and he very much wants the work to be properly preserved. Right now, our schedule is such that we will arrive in Florence on the tenth, and depart on the twelfth. We would like to stop by here for about an hour on our way to the airport before we depart. That would be late morning. The museum should be closed that day, no tourists. We already have a list of everyone here, including the students. Are there any recent hires?"

Mother Ana Maria was taking notes in her planner. "Just a gardener and part time prep cook."

"I'll need their employment papers and photos of everyone. If the Pope is to meet the students, we will need a proper setting, something large enough to accommodate his people, perhaps the Church. Cardinal Guido Marini, the Vatican Secretary of State, is never far from the Pope's side throughout trips and always takes part in many of the private meetings with political and state leaders. All in all, we'll have about twelve people, not including the security detail. We will need floor and electrical plans for the convent and the church ahead of time."

Father Paggi and Mother Ana Maria were visibly nervous. They were never sure this would happen, and to have the Pope come to the convent would be an extraordinary event and honor.

Mother Ana Maria asked, "Could our Sisters attend his visit? And Father Paggi has a few people."

Father Fitzpatrick was in charge and did not wait to hear from the Monsignor on this matter.

"As long as we have copies of their employment papers, and photos. We do in-depth background checks on everyone. The visit should center on the success of the fellowship. I am sure the Pope will say a few words, meet the students, and maybe handle a question or two. If there is time, he will greet your Sisters. Plan on a lot of security. If you will, present a plan of activity to us starting at 11:00 and finishing up by noon. I will be the contact from the Vatican, and your contact here will be Monsignor Delsoni. So, get us any paperwork and photos that we mentioned. The trip is only weeks away, so the sooner, the better. Do you have any questions?"

Father Fitzpatrick stood up abruptly and asked everyone to accompany him on a quick tour of the convent, the church, and the grounds. The students' work continued without notice as the four people toured the halls and rooms of San Marco. Father Fitzpatrick took photos and notes on the floor plan provided by Mother Ana Maria as she tried to answer his questions on the fly. As they returned to the foyer, Monsignor Delsoni pulled Father Paggi aside.

"Stephen, on our way over here, Fitzpatrick asked me about the life of Girolamo Savonarola and his proclamation of 1492. Do you know anything about that?"

Father Paggi looked up. Only that morning when he had met with Jeremiah and Finn had that date seemed to appear on the newly discovered box. He looked at the Monsignor. "I have seen that date somewhere. We just found an artifact at the Duomo, and there may be a connection."

"Let me know if you make something of it. I need to finish up here and get back."

The two men had finished their business. They thanked the Mother Superior and Father for their time and hospitality and instructed the two not to talk about the plans until everything was approved.

All of this occurred before the students took their lunch. Although they saw the visitors taking their tour, no one knew who they were. The Monsignor had made visits before, but it was Father Fitzpatrick in his black fedora that caught people's attention. The limousine left as quietly as it had arrived. The students couldn't help wondering if it had anything to do with the Papal visit. Later that month, their presence on this day would make sense.

22

"Let's go to the market and see some of the back streets of Florence," Olivia said as she and Vanessa finish their lunch. The refectory was especially busy on Saturday, because it was a shortened lunchtime and everyone had to eat there between eleven and noon. Because it was Saturday, the afternoon meant free time for the students of the Art Fellowship.

"We haven't had a chance to see much except the inside of this convent," Olivia said. "I hear they have a wonderful open-air street market that specializes in leather and woolens. It's called the Mercato Nuovo. Nothing like shopping to lift the spirits."

Vanessa finished her soup and responded.

"I told my family I would be calling them this afternoon around two. Plus, I need to finish my paper. I'm still having trouble with the conclusion. I heard this morning that it's supposed to rain, just FYI, but you go ahead and maybe I'll catch up with you later. Can we meet somewhere?"

"If it doesn't rain, meet me at San Lorenzo on the front steps at three. If it's raining, forget it. I'll go to a museum."

Vanessa called home to talk with her two younger sisters who were both on the line at the same time. The older sister played soccer and the younger sister was studying violin. She promised her sisters a very long telephone call midway through her stay at San Marco. She sat in a small booth with a phone glued to her ear and looked into the mirror that hung on the whitewashed wall in the convent lobby. She was self-conscious about the birthmark on her left cheek, but her delicate features and striking blue eyes made her angelical at times. Her sisters had endless questions and insisted on answers in great detail, often beyond her ability to describe. Her family respected Vanessa for her decision to enter the Felician Order. She had always been an excellent student, and after a young man left her in high school for another girl, the trauma pointed her in a direction that surprised everyone. Eventually, after describing Florence, the convent, St. John Fisher, the meals, and the upcoming visit by the Pope, she finally begged off and promised them both a gift from Florence. She left the call a little homesick, but quickly recovered when Mother Ana Maria asked her to run an errand. A breeze made it feel like rain, and it flooded her senses as she headed out to find a calla lily bouquet for the lobby.

The open-air market was constructed of wall-to-wall vendor stalls. Part of the area was surrounded by large Roman columns that provided a canopy for shoppers and vendors. Each vendor had a twenty-foot, wood frame stall that was covered with canvas and a large awning that reached the street. At dusk, the awning could be dropped and tied closed. The streets were made of large stones and formed a diagonal grid as they had been hand built hundreds of years ago.

Olivia wanted to find a gift for her mother. She explored row after row of tent-like displays. The hats, leather goods, jewelry, and wool tapestries surpassed anything she had ever seen, and the prices seemed very reasonable. Street musicians entertained the shoppers with acoustic music. The market was particularly crowded on the weekends. Olivia marveled at the mixture of locals and tourists, children and adults, musicians and jugglers. She found a silk scarf for her mother that she knew she would love and wanted to find her a rosary. She enjoyed being out in casual clothes, jeans, and a simple thin white blouse with her hair loose down her back instead of up for school and work. She was grateful for the diversion from the work at San Marco to freely explore the gifts of Florence.

After work that morning, Finn had decided to skip lunch and visit the Uffizi Museum. Long before he had left for Italy, he knew he wanted to see the collection, particularly the famous work of Sandro Botticelli. In high school, he had written a paper on the life and work of Botticelli, and this was his chance to see the real thing.

The Uffizi Museum was built in 1581 and was one of the many accomplishments of the Medici dynasty. Built on the Arno River overlooking the Ponte Vecchio Bridge, the collection chronicled the early and high Renaissance periods of art with works by Leonardo Da Vinci and Michelangelo. Finn had taken Jeremiah's advice and made reservations ahead of time. He was one of the first in line as the museum opened late that morning to hundreds of people waiting. The fellowship provided an ID card that gave the student entry to all the museums in Florence. The architecture of the exterior was traditional Florentine with a gray sandstone veneer.

Finn marveled at the half-mile exhibit of 17th and 18th century paintings that began with Giotto and ended with Caravaggio. But it was the painter Sandro Botticelli in rooms 10 through14 that Finn had to see. It was not Botticelli's early religious work that drew him, but *Allegory of Spring* and *Birth of Venus* that kept his imagination in suspension. These particular pieces were painted between 1478 and 1486. These paintings were surrounded by traditional religious paintings that dominated art in all parts of Italy and Europe. *Birth of Venus* was a romantic allegory. Botticelli composed these paintings as if they were melodies of a song or verses of a poem. Finn stood ten feet away from the central figure in *Venus* and viewed the goddess born from the sea and blown ashore by breezes as her handmaiden welcomed her, offering her a flowery cloak. As far as Finn was concerned, this image was more erotic than allegorical, but he pushed that thought away.

As Finn finished his tour and passed by the replica of David standing watch, he noticed dark storm clouds moving in from the south. He picked up his pace and hurried across the Uffizi courtyard. It was a good half hour walk back to San Marco. As he made his way across the Piazza del Signoria in the direction of the Duomo, he thought about the box he had found in the plaster debris. The section where he had worked earlier that week was now cordoned off with yellow streams of plastic. As he headed up the Via Calimala and approached the Mercato Nuova, it started to sprinkle. After a succession of thunderclaps, there was a downpour, and hundreds of people scattered to find shelter. Finn looked everywhere to find cover and eventually ran into a closed down vendor tent that was vacant, its front cover drawn shut. As he slipped through the edge of the tarp, he was surprised to see Olivia sitting on a wooden crate, drenched from head to foot.

"Olivia?"

Olivia was happy to see it was someone she knew.

"I was lucky to find this. Obviously, I forgot my umbrella."

Finn grinned. "Me too. I was visiting the Uffizi, and I was on my way back to the convent when the downpour started."

The inside of the vendor tent was dim, the only available light coming from the slits at the end of the long piece of canvas that now rested on the ground. Olivia's thin white blouse was soaked and clung tightly to her chest. Finn took off his jacket and laid it over a crate and shook the rain from his hair. He pulled up a crate and took a seat.

For the next hour as the rain poured hard against the canvas and a steady stream of water flowed across the stones outside their shelter, they talked about their childhoods, their families, early school experiences and shared their tastes in music and fiction. There was an attraction, and it was something they had both sensed upon arriving at San Marco. It was something they had denied, and pushed away. Because of their religious directive, dating was strictly forbidden. They both consciously tried to ignore their feelings and worked to push it aside. But the physical attraction was now complimented by a strong interest in each other's personalities and mannerisms. Within a short time that afternoon, they shared intimate facts about each other's lives.

Finn asked, "In your comments at the first dinner, you mentioned losing your father in the Vietnam War. That must have been horrible."

Olivia's mood immediately changed and she lowered her head. She looked at her feet and then into Finn's eyes.

"They told us he stepped on a land mine. I'll never forget the knock at the front door, and two Army officers standing on our porch in full uniform. They didn't have to say anything. My mother started screaming. I never saw her cry like that before…or since."

The rain finally softened and eventually some sunlight entered the creases at the ends of the canvas cover and cast a beam of light across Olivia's face. Finn resisted his feelings. He wanted to hold her. Olivia did everything she could to stay calm and removed, but it wasn't working. Finn reached out to wipe the tears from her cheek and pushed the hair off the side of her face. She turned to him and without pause he kissed her, and the kiss lingered for a while until they both pulled back. Now, just inches apart, Finn said.

"Hey Livi…"

Olivia looking into his eyes and said, "I know." And then she kissed him softly and then again. As they rose from the crates Finn stepped forward, and their bodies came together. It was forbidden fruit, but what they felt was more powerful than ideas, thoughts, rules, or disciplines. Finn held her close as she rested her head on his shoulder. There would be no turning back. Finally, they kissed and stepped away from each other.

"We need to get back," said Olivia. "And probably not together."

Finn could hardly resist kissing her again, and said instead, "Yeah, that sounds like a good plan. You leave first and I'll wait a while. I'll show up later. But what are we going to do?"

Olivia smiled. "I'm not sorry about this, Finn. Let's give it some time, maybe a prayer or two. All things are meant for a reason."

Olivia pulled herself together the best she could and slipped out through the crease in the canvas and into a crowd of moving shoppers in the market, which had resumed business. The afternoon stayed with her as she walked back in the direction of the convent. Finn sat down on the wooden crate and placed his hands over his face. *What just happened to me? Could this be a new plan?* He then slipped out into the crowd of shoppers and walked back with images of their intimate time together playing over and over in his head.

23

Father Paggi stepped into the Le Fontaine Café nestled off the piazza on Via Nazionale. The very old and established restaurant was bustling with city folk, and not yet discovered by the tourist trade. The popular restaurant had soft mellow lighting and enough noise to provide cover for a private conversation. Father Paggi spotted his old friend Francesco Dacarino sipping coffee.

Francesco was an expert antique dealer, often officially consulted on Italian antiquities. The years had been good to Francesco, who wore decorative gold reading glasses on the bridge of his nose. After thirty years of working for Finarte Roma, where he specialized in rare paintings, jewelry, carpets, and Italian coins, he had left with a good reputation. He had just recently retired to his own private practice with his brother in his home city of Florence. Most importantly, he attended St. John Fisher Church.

They exchanged the traditional greeting of a kiss on each cheek before Father Paggi pulled out a worn chair and sat down. Suspecting the topic of their meeting was unusual, Francesco had chosen a table in the back corner. Francesco looked up over his reading glasses.

"Good to see you, Father. It's been a while. How's your knee?"

Father Paggi laughed. "Much better, thank you, and yes, I would like to get back to playing tennis. But Fran, I have a situation to discuss with you that requires secrecy, something I am not used to."

"I'm comfortable with that. It's pretty much routine in my line of work. What's going on?" he asked.

"A student at the convent was working on a renovation at the Santa Maria del Fiora, where he was taking down a very old wall and found an artifact. It's a wooden rosewood box that must have been placed there during the construction. It's unusual, and I need someone to examine the contents."

Francesco smiled and shook his head slowly. "It's amazing how this city continues to reveal its secrets. Just a week ago, someone brought me a small painting that was undiscovered and signed by Fillipo Lippi. Under infrared light and chemical test, it turned out to be a forgery. A very good forgery, mind you. But something that is found inside a wall, that sounds quite different. Did you bring it with you?"

"I was afraid to, but I did."

Father Paggi pulled the box from his coat pocket, still wrapped in a white napkin, and placed it on the café table. As he folded back the cloth, Francesco's eyes went wide, and his eyebrows rose. The first thing he saw was the crude facsimile of the date, MCDXCII, hand-carved on the top and filled with lead.

"The roman numerals read 1492. That's interesting in itself. Have you opened it?

"We opened it, yes, but we have not examined its contents."

Using both hands, Father Paggi gently opened the box and displayed the contents: Three pieces of tightly folded parchment and a ring.

"Amazingly, the wax seals are still in place. I wonder why these documents are tied with string as well as sealed with wax? Okay, what's next and what can I do for you?"

Father Paggi looked at his old friend and wondered how much he should share with him. The question that came from Monsignor Delsoni floated around in the back of his mind.

"I would like for you to open these documents and translate if necessary. My 15th century Italian is pretty rusty. I'll need to know if they have any historical importance. Finally, I should be with you when you open them."

"Of course. Bring the box to my office. I have a small examining room with tools that may help us, and I'll take some digital, high res photos. How does that sound?"

"Thank you, Francesco. I knew you would help me. This needs to be kept confidential, at least for now. We can talk about the next steps once we know more about the contents."

"Come by the office in two days around this same time. Does that sound good?"

Father Paggi sighed in relief. He would involve his brother-in-law as soon as he knew what he was dealing with. After all, it was church property. It was starting to get dark, and each of the men had ways to walk home. They embraced affectionately and said goodnight.

24

It was the beginning of a new week. After dinner, the students attended a new evening class. Art History: The Art of Fra Angelico. Olivia and Finn sat on opposite sides of the room as the professor began her evening lecture.

Dr. Mariana Morelli was in her early forties, tall and slender with long dark hair worn in a braided bun. Her black-rimmed glasses were classic Italian by design, and she wore a black pantsuit with a Florentine silk scarf. The gold on her fingers, and the Alfa Romeo parked out front were a reflection of her taste and economic class. The rumor was that her husband was an importer of petroleum, and she came from one of the best families in Florence. Her professional credentials were impeccable. Her Ph.D. was in Early Renaissance Art, and she had done her dissertation on the work of Fra Angelico. She now taught full time at the Uffizi Museum and would sometimes teach part time at the University of Arts in Florence.

The Internet connection in the chapter room gave her access to high quality digital images from both the university and the museum. The images were transfers from 4 X 5 negatives and provided the highest of resolution. In previous classes, she had set the historical background for what would now be the main study of the class: Fra Angelico.

Dr. Morelli sat comfortably on the edge of a small table as the class took out their note pads.

"By now you all know who Fra Angelico was: a Dominican Friar, who had no possessions and turned over all of his profits to his order. He and his brother, Benedetto, worked at the Dominican convent, Fiesole. As an apprentice, he came under the influence of Giotto and the work he did at Assisi. He lived and worked here at San Marco and painted frescoes in Rome. But what is it that made Fra Angelico famous?"

The students were reluctant to answer questions for fear of being wrong and embarrassed. There was a minute of silence before Vanessa raised her hand.

"I read that it was his careful arrangements of only a few figures and their expressions of motion and gesture that set the work apart."

Dr. Morelli smiled as she walked slowly in front of the class.

"That's an acceptable answer. Thank you for waking this class up from the digestive state it finds itself in soon after a delicious dinner. Is there any more to say?"

James decided to give it a try and raised his hand.

"I know Pope Paul II conferred beatification on the artist, so he must have done something special."

Dr. Morelli smiled and then laughed lightly. "Well, that's true, but what set him apart?"

The students scoured their notes and textbook to find the exact answer she was looking for. Kyle pulled open his backpack and nervously searched his folders for papers on the artist. All the students in the fellowship had studied the Renaissance and had read extensively about Fra Angelico. The question was simple: What made Fra Angelico's work so famous? Finn had read about the artist, and Olivia had done a research paper on Fra Angelico. Everyone knew he was important. Finn jotted down a few words on his notepad as talking points and then raised his hand.

"Yes…you, the one with the baseball jacket?"

"Fra Angelico was working at a time when the style of painting was in a state of flux and change. We know he demonstrated an understanding of linear perspective and naturalism… sort of what Vanessa referred to…but his work was both conservatively Gothic and progressively Renaissance. His painting moved away from the constraints of wealthy clients, and he painted to express his deep reverence for God. These are private and intimate works of art…he painted noble, holy figures and beautiful angels that expressed the sincerest of religious feeling."

Finn took his eyes off Dr. Morelli momentarily and glanced at Olivia. It was she who had talked at length to Finn about the painter. It was she who expounded on the virtue of Fra Angelico. And Finn looked to her now for approval. Dr. Morelli responded.

"Does everyone understand what he so skillfully articulated? Let the label on his forehead of baseball statistician be lifted and banished forever!"

The class laughed, which gave Olivia the chance to smile. She had held back from raising her hand to see if Finn had been paying attention when they talked. He passed with flying colors. Dr. Morelli continued with a lecture on *The Last Judgment*, the altarpiece *The Virgin Mary and Christ*, and *The Annunciation*. She discussed and went into detail about the attitude and gesture of each, from Reverence, Humility, and Penitence, to Meditation, Compassion, and Recollection. The class was nearly over when she made her closing remarks.

"But it is impossible to bestow too much praise on this holy friar who was humble and modest in all that he did and whose pictures were painted with such piety and facility. All of which put him in the center of artistic activity of the region and brought about the patronage of one of the wealthiest and most powerful members of the city's Signoria, Cosimo de' Medici. Let's also not forget the influence of St. Dominic on these frescoes. They are tangentially connected with biblical events, but because St. Dominic did not witness the events, the narrative content is once removed. Any questions?"

Vanessa raised her hand. "Can you give us some history on San Marco?"

Dr. Morelli smiled and brought up some slides that were not in her lesson plan, but that were beautiful illustrations of the convent. As she talked, she displayed ten different slides that accompanied her remarks.

"Thank you…it's Vanessa? I am sure that since you're all staying here, you're interested in that question. It's one of my favorite subjects. The present convent stands on a site occupied since the 12th century by a Vallombrosan monastery, which later passed to the Silvestrines, who were driven out of San Marco in 1418. In 1438, the convent was given to the Dominican Order. In 1437, Cosimo de' Medici decided to rebuild the entire complex and the church was consecrated in 1443 in the presence of Pope Eugenius IV. Upon the high altar is *The Crucifixion* painted by Fra Angelico between 1425 and 1428. Many of the great figures of 15th-century culture and spirituality lived and worked in the convent. Cosimo de' Medici had his own cell here, where he loved to pray and meditate. From 1436 to1445, the Blessed Fra Angelico painted all these frescoes."

With some hesitation, she went a little deeper.

"Another part of the history here began in 1489, when Girolamo Savonarola, who lived in the convent, fulminated in his sermons against the immorality of the age, views for which he was hanged and burned in Piazza della Signoria. Fra Angelico decorated the cells on the first floor and other spaces in the convent with frescoes charged with profound spiritual and ascetic meaning. The Great Refectory has a collection of works by the School of San Marco, pupils of Fra Bartolommeo. In the Guest House, there are numerous fragments of stone carvings, rescued from the ruins when the Jewish quarter and the old market in Florence were demolished in the mid-19th century. The Museum also includes the former library on the first floor built by Michelozzo where a considerable number of illuminated choir books are displayed. The present convent library specializes in theology and philosophy, and as you can see, I do get carried away. She noticed most of the students' eyes glazed over. "It's getting late, so…to be continued."

25

Daresh Oldani had been given a very clear warning about the concealed weapons law in Florence, but at the same time, he wanted to find a place where he could purchase an extended clip for his 9mm Glock. It would give him a more secure feeling. He asked the older man working in the rooming house office if he knew of any gun shows in the city. The older fellow looked at him with a suspicious eye before scribbling down the address.

"This is an abandoned building that is boarded up, but in the afternoon you will find the rear door open. They sell guns and ammunition, most of which is hot…stolen. The people who run the operation move around. If the door is closed, then they have moved on to a new location. That's the best I can do."

Oldani left the boarding room office with a small piece of paper folded in his hand. He crossed the street and walked south four blocks to a retail store he had seen earlier in the week. Biomedical SRI was a business primarily for pet supplies, but at the rear of the store there was a section for livestock. Oldani entered the store and asked the young girl at the register who directed him towards the end of the aisle. He looked for a small bottle of sodium pentobarbital, potassium chloride, and a couple of disposable plastic syringes. When he set the medical supplies on the counter, a young girl dressed in a white lab coat started talking to him in Italian until she saw the confused look on his face and switched to crude English.

"That enough to kill horse."

Oldani only smiled in response as she rang up the items. He paid her cash as she wrapped up the supplies and put them in a white paper bag.

Oldani left the store and walked ten blocks to the address he held in his hand. The neighborhood changed dramatically when he crossed Via Giambattista. For some reason, the next two blocks had fallen on hard times and For Sale signs littered the old industrial buildings. He walked another block, searching for an address. The building's windows were covered with plywood, and weeds grew up along the foundation.

Oldani walked back along the side of the building where debris had covered the narrow path. As he turned the corner, he saw a door held open by a folding chair with a small piece of paper attached that read ARMA. Inside the building was a cleared out space with makeshift fluorescent lights hanging from what once was a dropped ceiling. Temporary tables put together with saw horses and 4 by 8 sheets of plywood made up the rows that extended the length of the building. Each table had a different weapon, ranging from handguns to automatic machine guns. Near the door, two men collected cash from a line of buyers and wrapped the weapons in cheap plastic bags. There were older men in dark trench coats and young men wearing jeans, T-shirts, and boots, conducting commerce with very little conversation.

Oldani eventually found the table that displayed all kinds of ammunition in a random order. He found a twelve-round clip for the Glock and a homemade silencer that screwed onto the barrel. There was a box of carbon high velocity bullets that had carved out tips providing maximum expansion when they hit the target. While he was in training during his time in the military, Oldani had seen these bullets cause a large watermelon to completely explode.

"Is that it?" asked the heavyset man sitting behind the table. "Twenty Euro…and just so you know, this is our last day at this location. We will be posting a new location on small cards in area laundromats.

Oldani nodded and took the recycled plastic bag that held his new clip and ammo. He knew he was in a dangerous place, and the sooner he left, the better. Once he got back on the street, he tucked both packages under each arm covered by his light jacket, and headed back to the rooming house. The last thing he needed was to be stopped by the local police.

26

Monsignor Delsoni called a stage four briefing at the office of the Archbishop regarding the Papal visit to Florence. Father Paggi got the message just as he finished Mass at St. John Fisher. He grabbed his jacket and left immediately for St. Lorenzo. It was a long four blocks, and he knew he would be late. To make things worse, there was construction on the street that extended onto the sidewalk. As an organized and punctual man, he hated walking into meetings late.

As he walked up to the second floor and displayed is ID, he was handed a packet of papers, presumably for the meeting. The walls were paneled in walnut, the stairs were marble, and the handrail was solid brass. He quietly opened the door and walked into a meeting well under way.

Maps on the wall highlighted the Pope's moves from hour to hour. There was one piece with a list of events, and near the end was the name San Marco. As he looked around the conference table, there was only a handful of clergy. The rest were Carabinieri, Guardia di Finanza, and government officials. Monsignor Delsoni passed out a final, approved itinerary for the Pope's visit. It was decided that he would use the Archbishop's residence for sleeping, as it was one of the most secure locations in Florence. The plan outlined his arrival at the airport, the motorcade to St. Lorenzo and the details of each and every event. Father Paggi was starting to wonder why he'd been invited to the meeting. Perhaps it meant that a visit to San Marco was approved. Then the Monsignor mentioned something that got his attention.

"I want to share with you some information that was given to me by Vatican security. Their intelligence indicates that there is a small cell of individuals called the Piagnoni and they are operating here in Florence. I don't know if Captain Paglia is aware of it, but they are followers of Girolamo Savonarola. For those of you who don't recognize the name, Savonarola was a firebrand preacher and politician who lived in Florence during the late 15th century. Although he was a devout Catholic, he was highly critical of the papacy. As a Dominican friar, he preached and wrote on the sinfulness and apostasy of the time. For his false religious beliefs, his prophecies, and sedition, he was excommunicated by Rome. After the trial, he and three of his Dominican disciples were hanged and burned. Ever since then, and often fueled by radicals in the Dominican Order, there have been conservative Catholics who feel the conclusions reached by Vatican II were blasphemous. This small group operates underground and has gone so far as to demonstrate against the Pope. Their goals are to repress vice, prohibit gambling, and believe only in Gospel law. So, with that as a backdrop, the Vatican has just recently identified a small cell working here in Florence. As we are currently planning on a visit to San Marco, we are aware that Savonarola lived and preached there. We need to locate the Piagnoni and neutralize their efforts. Are there any questions?"

Father Paggi now felt even more worried and nervous. He had heard of Girolamo Savonarola but only in a historical context. He had no idea there were followers that existed today. Only once had he heard the term Piagnoni used, and it was to describe a secret Catholic guild that was formed to preserve Savonarola's memory. Father Paggi was aware of the movement by the Dominican order to begin canonization, but the Jesuits who supported the accomplishments of Vatican II vehemently opposed it.

The small radical group, primarily Dominicans, felt the Vatican II concept of the Church as "People of God" was a false ecumenism, in that it led to the belief that Protestantism is no more than one particular form of the same Christian religion. The Dominicans argued that the Church had arrived at the point of allowing the sacraments of Reconciliation, Eucharist and Extreme Unction to be received from "non-Catholic ministers," and it favored 'ecumenical hospitality' by authorizing Catholic ministers to give the sacrament of the Eucharist to non-Catholics.

Father Paggi stirred in his chair, uneasy. Could it be that San Marco, a heavenly place decorated with divine artwork, was a target for a demonstration? It was unthinkable, but perhaps the Vatican had to prepare for every possibility.

Before the meeting broke up, Monsignor came over to Father Paggi and pulled him aside. He placed his hand on his shoulder and said.

"You needed to hear that. Make sure all the people involved in the visit to San Marco are documented and cleared. We have to take all the necessary precautions. If you see or hear of anything unusual, let me know as soon as possible. I am not sure Father Fitzpatrick is telling me everything he knows. When he asked me about the proclamation of 1492, I was dumbfounded. I still don't know what he is taking about. He asked me to meet with him privately in about ten minutes, so maybe I will learn more."

When Monsignor Delsoni approached the office where he and Fitzpatrick were to meet, Fitzpatrick was on the phone, deep in conversation with the Vatican.

Delsoni discreetly entered the office, and Fr. Fitzpatrick held his hand over the phone and whispered, pointing at the receiver, "Cardinal Barasco Terotone's upset that he's been excluded from the trip and thinks it's my fault. I am up to my knees in alligators here. I'll catch up with you as soon as I am off."

You might say the Catholic Church raised Jonathan Fitzpatrick. He was eventually adopted after being abandoned on an Irish church pew one winter's morning. A sister cleaning the transit before breakfast had discovered the infant. The child had been wrapped in blankets, and no note was found with him.

The nuns kept Jonathan for six weeks while the authorities did a search for the mother, but no one was found. After a year, Father Jerome Fitzpatrick, the priest who ran St. Andrew's Parish in the northeast section of Dublin, legally adopted him. Of course, the church did not formally allow this, but Father Jerome used his contacts to make it work without notice.

In some respects, Jonathan had an extraordinary childhood and learned more than most. By the age of seven, he had learned Latin and worked as an altar boy in three separate local churches. The nuns constantly tutored him while he attended their catholic convent school, and he called Father Jerome his Papa. It was an unusual situation that didn't quite fit the catechism, but no child was more cared for and loved by so many than Jonathan. He completed his grammar school studies in the convent school and attended Trinity Boys High School before being accepted into the School of Divinity at Oxford University.

When he was ordained into the priesthood, Jonathan was sponsored by the Archdiocese to attend the Edinburgh Law School, and for ten years, he worked as the first council to the Archbishop of Dublin. His reputation as a litigator caught the eye of the Vatican and, in time, Father Fitzpatrick was working for Cardinal Sodano of Rome. After winning a major liability case, he joined the legal team representing the Vatican Council and prepared a legal treatise for Pope John Paul II. Jonathan always vacationed in Dublin, where he slept in the convent among the women who raised him. On a rainy afternoon, when the dogwood trees had just bloomed in early April, he gave the homily at Father Jerome's funeral mass. People familiar with the arrangement wept when he referred to him as father.

Tonight, Father Fitzpatrick finished his business and hung up the phone. He'd known from the start of the conversation he would have to get the Cardinal back on the list, and that, because of the size of the jet, he would have to eliminate someone else. He looked over the boarding list and made his decision. Now he had to call Cardinal Kaminski to let him know he was unable to attend the visit to Florence. It was a disappointment, because he and Kaminski were poker partners. He looked over at Delsoni, who sat waiting, and tried to remember the purpose of their meeting. Ah yes... The proclamation of 1492.

27

Leaves tumbled down the narrow stone streets of Florence, and small white clouds drifted against a bright blue sky. During their free time, usually on weekends, Olivia and Finn reunited for a couple of hours in a closed-down vendor tent. Occasionally they brought a lunch of bread, grapes, and cheese that they spread on the wooden crates. They arrived and left separately, only after looking around to make sure there was no one around who would recognize them. They exchanged letters there and read each other sonnets. Olivia kept a brass box with small items she received from Finn: a seashell, a stone, a dried flower, and a small white dove that was hand-carved from a piece of driftwood. Finn now wore a thin gold chain with an antique crucifix around his neck, a gift from Livi. They decided on a code—Good Morning—that meant 'I love you,' and they would say it whenever they saw each other at the convent. And no one had clothes as clean as Olivia and Finn. During the week, late at night, they would meet secretly in the laundry room where they could talk privately, yet always fearful of getting caught.

Their friendship deepened with each story they told, which ran the gamut from family history to dreams to complaints about the food and Olivia's ongoing conflict with one of the nuns who thought she should work more in the kitchen.

If they were sure no one was around, there were kisses and more kisses. Finn had designed a thin string that stretched across the hallway and was attached to a small can. If someone approached the laundry room, the string would be tripped, causing a sound that would warn them that someone was approaching. There was always the chance that others would use the laundry late at night, but most students did their laundry at the weekend, and the Sisters were there early in the mornings, so they could hang their clothes outside in the sprawling backyard. Finn and Olivia picked late evenings because it gave them the privacy they sought.

Finn had just finished drying his clothes while Olivia had completed folding her and Vanessa's clothes. They both dreaded the end of this time together and saved the last five minutes for intimacy. Just after Finn dumped his clothes into the rolling basket, Olivia came close to him and helped fold. Their arms touched and sent sensations through their bodies. Olivia's mouth was so beautiful; he couldn't resist her kiss. As their eyes closed, the tin can rattled ominously. Within seconds, Kyle walked into the laundry room with a handful of dirty underwear.

"Oh, sorry...I was just coming down to wash a load. Ah, are you finished washing?"

Their faces flushed red. Finn put some distance between himself and Olivia and said, "Maybe another time would be better. You know what I mean?"

"Yeah, I am sorry. I didn't mean to barge in like this."

"It's okay, Kyle. Olivia was just leaving. Maybe you could walk her back?"

When Finn got back to the room, Kyle was in bed, but not yet asleep. Finn changed into his pajamas. He was trying to figure out what to say to his roommate in light of what had happened.

"Kyle, are you awake? I washed the rest of your clothes."

Kyle was easy-going and liked Finn. He felt as uncomfortable about what had happened as Finn did. He rolled over, his face barely visible in the dim light from a small window.

"If you and Olivia see each other, that's none of my business. It does seem odd given your career path. What are you going to do?

"I'm not sure. We're giving it a lot of thought. Things may have to change for us, but I don't want this to become common knowledge around here. Do you think you could keep this to yourself? I mean...a secret?"

"No problem. Could I wear your jacket sometime?"

Finn threw his pillow at Kyle, appreciating the humor. "Cut me some slack here, okay? Seriously, if you promise to keep this a secret, when we finish up here, I will give you my baseball jacket. Deal?"

28

The fellowship was now past the halfway point as students moved from fresco to fresco, cleaning, removing candle soot, and conserving surfaces that were in further danger due to bubbling and flaking. Because of the height of some of the frescoes, scaffolding was put into place. The scaffolds were on wheels to make it easy to move them about, but as a safety measure, there were locks on all four wheels that needed to be secured.

Earlier attempts at restoration had left their mark on the frescoes. Close examination revealed the earlier paint bodies were not as stable as what was being used today. Polymer resins provided the base for all the monks' paints and produced a stronger and brighter image. By mixing a range of chemical emulsifiers into the wet plaster, the technical advisers were confident the frescoes would hold up for hundreds of years to come.

Although Jeremiah was the lead Friar, the technical expert on the team was Gabriel. He had worked closely with the restoration of the Sistine Chapel begun in 1994. Gabriel had worked under the direction of Carlo Pietrangeli, the Director of Vatican Laboratory for Research Pictures. As an apprentice on that project, he became familiar with the rules that govern the technical procedures and the latest scientific procedures, which included the use of digital photography to record every stage in the process.

For the San Marco restoration, Gabriel provided all the equipment to produce high-resolution digital imagery. The difference in the San Marco restoration was that the frescoes, for the most part, were in better condition. The cleaning and retouching were mostly due to heat, soot, humidity, and dust.

As a complement to Friar Gabriel, Friar Jeremiah insured the integrity of the artistic imagery. He was an art historian who was familiar with the paintings of the Early Renaissance and understood the history of San Marco. He knew that Fra Angelico's work was devotional and aided by Dominican prayer and meditation. His goal was to match and retain the formed peacefulness and incredible luminescence of the Friar's work.

All the students wore disposable latex gloves, muslin lab coats, protective eyewear, and hair caps. Under the watchful eye of Friar Gabriel, the project maintained a high technical standard that equaled restoration anywhere. Kyle and James were Gabriel's favorites, because they always made him laugh, especially when they did their imitations of Bevis and Butt Head. It was something completely outside the Friar's experience, and the two of them had their routine down to get the most laughs out of any audience.

When the fragrance of fresh baked rolls reached them at their second floor workstations, the restoration work was abandoned in favor of lunch, where Kyle, James, and Finn now sat together discussing the morning's work. They enjoyed the large bowls of minestrone soup and freshly baked bread made early that day. Finn occasionally worked in the kitchen, clearing trays and washing dishes.

"Hey, I worked in the kitchen yesterday and noticed a new prep cook. I haven't seen him before. Has anyone met him?"

James, who had worked in the kitchen recently, said, "He's new. He seems to know what he's doing. I heard he's part-time-temporary."

Finn looked through the window where the food trays were passed and watched the young man cut vegetables into small pieces. His movements were almost mechanical as he kept his eyes focused and lowered. *Weird,* Finn thought.

29

Francesco Dacarino was fastidious and portly, the latter due largely to his addiction to sweets and dark Belgian beer. He took more time than most people to answer the question, and it was questionable as to whether that was due to deliberation or forgetfulness. He loved mussels prepared in a light curry sauce and had visited the Picasso Museum more than most. Trained as a watchmaker, he worked for the auction house, Finarte Rome, for thirty years in the antiquities division, assisting in litigation and doing appraisals of art and antiques. After he retired, he and his brother opened their own small office in a cozy street off Maria Novella Square. His twin brother was an expert in collectable glass, carpets, and dabbled in restoration. They found the market especially lucrative when they appraised art, jewelry, coins, artifacts, and rare prints. They did all their work by appointment, which gave them the flexible schedule they desired. Stephen Paggi had met Francesco through Nicholas, his brother-in-law, at a dinner party when he first moved to Florence and took over the reins at St. John Fisher. When it came to the expert verification of an antiquity and its value, Florence became a very small place.

For Father Paggi, the walk to Francesco's office was a good fifteen minutes to its location just off the square on a small side street. He walked along briskly through the busy street, navigating people coming and going in both directions. He finally reached the address and walked up a flight of stairs to the second floor and knocked on the door next to a brass plate that read: Antiquities. It took a minute, but finally Francesco came to the door and greeted his friend.

"Prego, Father. You're right on time, as always. Come in and let me take your jacket. Would you like some coffee?"

The small room had a nice large bay window filled with plants that faced the street, allowing sunlight to illuminate the front part of the space. Bookshelves occupied most of the walls. It was a good thing that Father Paggi was not a tall man since, except where the large skylight loomed over everything in the center of the room, the ceilings were only six feet high. The floors were made of crosshatched blocks of oak, and there were several tables and a desk covered with piles of papers, books, and unopened mail. Antiques of all kinds rested on the floor, including a Roman chariot wheel, an ancient urn, and coin collections from the first century AD.

"Are these yours?" asked Father Paggi, as he scanned a series of small oil paintings along the west wall.

"No. I am in the process of appraising them. Except for that small daVinci drawing, which was a birthday gift from my wife...very thoughtful of her and probably too expensive. Did you bring the box?"

Father Paggi retrieved the box from his jacket pocket, still wrapped in a white linen napkin.

"Bring it over here Father, where I have more light. That's it. Just set it down and let's have a look."

Francesco put on his latex gloves, applied a couple of drops of precision machine oil to the hinges and pulled down a special light fixture that provided both fluorescent and tungsten light. After slowly opening the box, he gently removed the three pieces of parchment and the ring. He looked closely at the ring and then the wax seals.

"Well, as we thought, this ring was used to produce the seals on the documents, probably belonging to the owner or the author."

Father Paggi sat down next to the table in a wooden chair decorated with English carving. The seat cushion was surprisingly comfortable. He bit down on the bottom part of his lip and could suddenly feel his heart beating hard. As the light reflected from the lead Roman numerals, Francesco took out the three pieces of rolled parchment, much thicker than modern paper. He laid them next to the box and untied the string.

"I'll have to break these wax seals to open the documents."

"Of course," said Father Paggi, as a drop of sweat trickled down the back of his neck. He swiped at it impatiently. With a decorative brass letter opener, Francesco opened the first document that was written in a flourishing hand. He pored over it for some minutes before he began to translate aloud.

> *Dear People of Florence,*
>
> *To all that follow me, let it be clear that we are in the 'Last Days.' With the death of Lorenzo de Medici and Pope Innocent VII, I have had, during my night hours, numerous and mysterious visions. They are of a flaming bent sword that is directed downward towards Earth, and the sky is darkened. As the thunder peals loudly, and the lightning flashes, the world as we know it will be faced with famine, bloodshed, and pestilence. I fear for all of our lives. With the election of Cardinal Borgia to the seat of Pope Alexander VI, my time is now short as moral laxity prevails. He is surely the anti-Christ. We must move to destroy all mirrors, cosmetics, pagan books, and lewd pictures. These transgressions are corrupting our city and our church. The moral corruption of Pope Alexander VI and the Duke of Milan will lead us to the very end of time. To my brother Dominicans, my De Ruina Mundi (The Downfall of the World) is hidden and located in the heel of the crucifix at the church of San Marco. For my survivors, let this document be my expression of devout moral conscience and lead you to correct the transgressions of worldly Popes and those who support their edicts. Let the work of St. Thomas Aquinas and Aristotle prevent the morally corrupt clergy. For my Dominican brothers in the Piagnoni, let the millennialism celebrate our pure and reverent Christian life for now and forever.*
>
>

In God We Trust,
Girolamo Savonarola
>

The two men sat in silence for a while and tried to digest the letter and what it meant. The name was familiar to them both. The Italian religious and political reformer, Girolamo Savonarola, was born of a noble family at Ferrara and in 1474, entered the Dominican order at Bologna.

Francesco walked over to the windows and said of Savonarola.

"What a cheery guy he was. Well, if my memory serves me right, he was excommunicated, hung and burned. Not exactly my idea of retirement. What do you think, Father? Shall we open the other documents?"

Father Paggi was slow to respond. He had information that was not common knowledge. He had just been briefed about a small cell of men who represented the Piagnoni, who had protested against the current Pope and was here somewhere in Florence on the eve of the Papal visit. It was all very unsettling. He thought about disclosing the letter to Monsignor Delsoni, but was not ready to make that decision.

"Let's open the second document and see what we have and go from there."

Francesco opened the parchment and found a hand drawn floor plan of San Marco and the attached church. A small x identified the church crucifix. There was a drawing of the two legs of the crucifix and an indication of where the document was hidden. It did not shed any new light on the findings, but merely gave directions to where the document was hidden. Girolamo Savonarola also signed the drawing. Father Paggi spoke.

"Let's see what else we have."

Francesco opened the third document and his eyes widened. He laid the parchment down and adjusted the light.

"It looks like a drawing…for a large painting, most likely a mural."

Father Paggi moved in for a closer look.

"It seems like a design or preliminary drawing…and quite beautiful I might add. It looks like a depiction of Mother and Child in a field of wheat. And look at the notes."

Francesco scanned them with his magnifying glass, and then straightened up abruptly.

"This is a Leonardo da Vinci drawing and the notes indicate that it's a preliminary sketch for a mural. Amazing…and probably very valuable. The church just hit the jackpot, Stephen. I am very familiar with Leonardo's work. This must be an idea he developed, but never executed."

Both men took a breath and were silent. Finally, Father Paggi spoke.

"Well, now we know what we have. But I don't see this as having said anything new about the preacher. With the exception of the drawing, much of this is well documented. Thank you, Francesco. I'll consult my brother-in-law before I go any further. I'll get back to you."

"Of course, Father. If there is anything more I can do, please let me know."

"I forgot to mention you'll be paid for your services."

"No need Father. You have helped me out so many…Please, it's my pleasure."

30

As Father Paggi walked through the Piazza del Duomo, he looked over at the majestic cathedral dome and Giotto's Campanile. The crowds were everywhere, parents with strollers, tour groups, well dressed women in dark wool suits, and school children chasing flocks of pigeons. He recalled how the flamboyant gothic façade of the Campanile took almost 150 years to complete, and the bell tower rang out just as it did in 1331, part of the essential loveliness of Florence. Father Paggi loved Florence, a busy working city that struggled to balance the needs of its residents with the demands made upon the metropolitan area by millions of visitors. He felt Florence was the birthplace of creativity and that this vitality was everywhere. He was proud of his city, and he was not going to let some radical, right-wing group interfere with his beloved Pope's visit.

A chill wind picked up as he walked, and he pulled up his collar and buttoned his coat. He passed the Pizzeria David, his favorite place to stop for a slice, but he put the idea out of his mind. Today he was in a hurry to get back to San Marco and remove the hidden document in the crucifix. He needed to make sure it could not get into the hands of the Piagnoni. He stopped briefly at the merchant central and picked up some candies for Mother Ana Maria. He chose an assortment of nougat, marzipan, and dark chocolates. It was something not allowed in the convent, but for good deeds, he would sneak her a gift that she would conceal and keep for a special occasion.

He walked up the via Ricasoli towards San Marco as he formed his plan. One of the quietest times in the church was right after dinner. That would be the time to find the concealed documents. He crossed the street to avoid construction work and passed through the Piazza Santissima Annunziata in front of the old church bearing the same name. By now he could smell dinner being prepared at San Marco.

Before he crossed the small narrow street, he paused and waited while several motor scooters sped by, going faster than allowed. He would arrive in time for dinner and then wait for a while before he entered the church.

Weeks earlier, Mother Ana Maria had hired a young man she knew as Josef Dvorsak to help in the kitchen while her prep cook recuperated from knee surgery. There was a lot of lifting and manual labor to the job, and the young man had the physical stature to handle the work. He had responded to an ad in the church bulletin, and his employment papers indicated he had recently moved to Florence on a work visa from Romania. During the interview, he told Mother Ana Maria that he had kitchen experience where he had worked as a prep cook. His references had checked out and because it was temporary, Mother Ana Maria was pleased to find some reliable help. He came in early, did his work, helped clean up, and had very little interaction with the staff. It was not clear to anyone whether or not he was a Christian, but he had said he was.

Dinner had ended, and students dispersed to their rooms to rest before the evening seminar. Father Paggi ate with Mother Ana Maria and provided her with an update based on his meeting with Monsignor Delsoni.

"It's confirmed! The Pope will stop here on his way to the airport. He will have a small entourage and heavy security, so the museum must be closed that day, and we need to finalize the plan they requested while he is here at San Marco. Afterward, he'll continue to Milan, Venice, and then back to Rome. So tell your people the plans are in place."

Mother Ana Maria was beside herself. "I can't believe the Pope is coming to San Marco. It is a message from God."

With the news, Father followed it up with a brown paper bag he pulled from his coat pocket and handed it to Mother Ana Maria. She peeked inside and recognized the wrapper from the Enoteca Alessi confectionary. It was not the first time Father Paggi had brought her candy, but it was their secret. She was ecstatic. She could hardly believe the Pope was visiting San Marco. The art fellowship had brought many gifts to the convent, but the Pope's visit was an answer to her prayers. They sat together and finished their coffee as everyone eventually left the refectory.

Father Paggi excused himself and left for his residence across the street to retrieve some small tools he needed for his investigation. He waited a while before returning to the convent and walked down the long hallway to the church. The general lighting was turned off, leaving the large room in semi-darkness. Small spotlights that lit *The Crucifixion* and the *Stations of the Crosses* cast some light.

Good thing I brought my flashlight, he thought.

Before walking up to the large crucifix that hung center stage behind the altar, he walked down the transit aisle and entered a pew, pulled down the kneeling bar, and prayed.

"Father, I pray that you provide me with the assistance to find what I seek. I need to protect our Pope and San Marco from those who seek to cause us harm. I ask this humbly and graciously in the name of the Father, the Son, and the Holy Spirit. Amen."

He stood up in the dark room, wondering if he had made the right decision to proceed without notifying the police or Monsignor Delsoni. He just wanted to make this go away. He looked at the ancient, primitive crucifix with reverence and crossed himself before moving forward.

He approached the large statue and studied the map with the help of the flashlight, and then moved forward towards the right leg. Using his flashlight again, he examined the heel, noticing nothing unusual. He took his handkerchief from his pocket and wetted a corner of it with saliva. He used the dampened cloth to rub the bottom of the heel, which enabled him to see a two-inch wide indentation. He removed the cover from his pocket knife and scraped at the surface. A little plaster fell away, revealing a small brass cap. Using the knifepoint, he pried off the cap. He could now see a metal tube that extended into the ankle of the statue. Gently this time, he used the knife's tip to coax a roll of parchment into the open.

He sat down in front of the crucifix and unrolled the parchment document while using his flashlight to illuminate the writing. It was the De Ruina Mundi, a one-page treatise that outlined Savonarola's directions to salvation for mankind along with several predictions. That was the last thing he remembered before a blunt object came down on his head. He slumped to the floor while one of the city's many church bells rang in the distance.

When Father Paggi came to beneath the crucifix, he was groggy and confused. When he sat up and tried to orient himself, he realized the document was gone and the flashlight turned off. He stared into the dark depths of the church as he felt the back of his head and winced. His fingers had found a sizable lump that was sensitive to touch. *Who would do this, especially here at San Marco?* He asked himself.

He turned on the flashlight. Whoever hit him must have turned it off and fled with the document. He picked up the brass cap and used the butt of the flashlight to tap it gently back into place. His head hurt now, more than he first realized. He looked around and noticed nothing unusual, except the faint voices coming from the second floor seminar. He gathered his tools and left the church without being noticed. As he crossed the street to his residence, he tried to remember whether or not he had some aspirin. The bell tower rang out eight times. He must have been unconscious for at least a half hour. The local police station was just a block away, and he would have to file an assault report. There was one police officer on duty that took down his information, but with no witnesses, there was little to be done. He was careful. He didn't want the incident in the church to change the decision by the Vatican to visit San Marco. He left the station and stopped at the corner to look up and down the street. Everything seemed quiet and completely normal. But it wasn't.

31

Daresh Oldani's plain nondescript features and average height made him look like any typical man on any street in Florence. He bought a bottle of water before he entered the rundown flophouse from the back door and walked down the hall to his rented room. The hallway was dim, illuminated only by a single bulb that cast a weak spot on the floor directly below it. He unlocked the door and closed it behind him, using the deadbolt to secure his entry.

He placed the stolen document on the bedside table without looking at it. Next to the ashtray lay the Glock with the extra clip attached. The room was small and simple: bed, dresser, and wash sink, above which hung a dirty mirror. His personal possessions were equally sparse: a small suitcase and basic toiletries. He looked at himself in the mirror and fingered the ugly scar on the right side of his chin from a knife fight he'd had in Bucharest.

He was sure no one had seen him in the church, and that included Father Paggi himself. He wasn't sure what the document was for, but it had to be something of importance. That would be for his handlers to decide.

The Piagnoni had hired him to work at San Marco to keep his eyes and ears open. After finishing his cleanup duties earlier, he had walked casually towards the church to give his evening prayer. As he'd stood concealed behind a large supporting column, he'd seen Father Paggi pull something from the heel of the crucifix. His handler had told him they were looking for any documents found at San Marco during the restoration.

The Piagnoni had purchased Oldani an inexpensive cell phone to be used for contact. He got the phone out of the dresser drawer now and made his call.

"It's Oldani. I came across a document. The priest was removing it from the heel of the crucifix at the San Marco Church. It is an old piece of parchment, and I have it here with me. I had to knock him unconscious. No, no one saw me."

Oldani pulled down the faded window shade and sat on the edge of his bed while his contact responded.

"We have learned by way of a listening device planted in the front office at San Marco that when the Pope visits Florence, he may visit San Marco. So, stay calm, quiet, and remain undercover there. Call me in two days for instructions. Keep the document there, and we will have it picked up by a man that goes by the name Nino. He is working for a local food distributor. Any questions?"

"No, but the gardener at the convent has approached me several times. He asked me where I was from and how I got hired, but mostly small talk. I am sure it's nothing."

"We must be careful. We'll check him out. For now, do your best to remain invisible."

Daresh Oldani was born into a Roman Catholic family and raised in Bucharest, Romania. His parents were active followers of Archbishop Marcel Lefebvre, who founded the Society of St. Pius X and took the lead in opposing changes with the church that were associated with the second Vatican Council. They rejected ecumenism in favor of Catholic exclusivism, religious tolerance, instead of religious liberty, and rejected collegiality in favor of Papal supremacy. His father remained true to the use of the Mass of Paul IV and refused to participate in the Tridentine Mass. As a family, they rejected the feminist theory and whispered in Latin while attending mass.

In their neighborhood of Piata Unirii in sector one of Bucharest, his parents were often discriminated against and had trouble finding work. As their beliefs became known, there were times when their lives were threatened. Growing up, Daresh dropped out of school to work in the streets to provide income for the family. When he turned eighteen, he joined the military and was admitted to the Special Operations Regiment headquartered in Bucharest. It was at the Gendarmerie that

Oldani was trained extensively in the use of weapons. After graduation, he returned home and found it difficult to find work. He and his brother had done freelance security work until they were eventually approached and hired by the Piagnoni.

When Daresh Oldani was recruited, he first started working in and around Bucharest. He participated in protests at any appearance by the Archbishop of Romania and worked with efforts to raise funds for the Piagnoni. After working for more than a year, he was selected to work undercover. They spent months severing his ties, changing his appearance, teaching him Italian phrases, selecting a new alias, and now relocating him to Florence, Italy. He worked as a day laborer until they found a temporary position at San Marco. He introduced himself as Josef Dvorsak and presented an elite set of biometric credentials that would survive the most sophisticated background check.

Oldani washed his hands and face, took off his outer clothing and kneeled for his evening prayer. He dreaded going to bed because of a reoccurring dream that came to him, the one that caused him to wake up suddenly in a cold sweat.

32

The evening seminar was livelier than usual as Dr. Morelli compared and contrasted two paintings by the same name. The more famous of the two paintings called *The Annunciation* was by Fra Angelico and located there at San Marco. The other was *The Annunciation* by Leonardo da Vinci and was housed in the Uffizi Museum.

Classmates took sides and argued for the painting they preferred. Finn and Olivia were part of the group that argued for Fra Angelico's work with its informal arrangement of subjects, brilliant transparency of color and intense general atmosphere. Vanessa and Kyle argued that the da Vinci painting was a stronger composition and a more accurate description of detail. They liked how skillfully Leonardo handled the landscape. In the end, Dr. Morelli weighed in, describing Angelico's depiction as more feminine, producing a more reverent Holy Mother, but concluding that the attraction to painting was a very subjective experience.

"How many of *The Annunciation* paintings did Fra Angelico make?" she asked.

Kyle raised his hand. "There are several here at San Marco."

"That's correct Kyle, and it was common for painters during the Early Renaissance to paint their religious scenes more than once, especially as they documented the famous events in the life of Jesus Christ."

Olivia raised her hand. "I think Fra Angelico painted *The Annunciation* six times."

"Very good, Olivia. He repeated the painting six times, most of which are painted in the same setting, but the last one, here at San

Marco, was painted in 1450 and depicts a somewhat different setting. There are other locations where these paintings exist, like the Museum in Cortona, and The Prado in Madrid." Dr. Morelli glanced quickly at her watch. "Ah," she said. "It's well past nine. Let's finish here for tonight."

For some, the discussion carried on, but Finn and Olivia had other plans. Leaving the chapter room at different times to head back to their respective rooms was important. Their relationship had been going on for nearly four weeks, and they had grown stronger and closer in their love for each other. It was after ten when Olivia walked into the laundry room to find Finn reading. Although they brought their laundry to the small room at the end of a long hallway, it was all they could do to stay apart. Finn's wash was already underway as he helped Olivia load her clothes.

"Whose soap is this?" asked Olivia.

Finn shrugged. "It was here when I came in."

They finished loading, dropped in some coins, and Finn put his arms around Olivia. She laid her head against his chest and held him close while she talked.

"Finding you has been a miracle, Finn. I think my plans to become a Felician Sister have changed. I think God has a different plan for me. I have never been so happy. Just being with you is all I want now…and I love you."

Finn kissed her on the cheek and then her eyes, and again softly on the mouth before he whispered, "It's been the same for me, Livi. I have never been so happy and excited about being with someone else. My plans have changed, but I am not sad about that. Meeting you has changed everything. I love you Livi, and I want to marry you. I promise I will always love you."

In his rush to get to the laundry room earlier, Finn had forgotten to set the guard string in place. Sister Julia had left her laundry soap on the washer, and she was in her pajamas when she walked in, wearing slippers that were soft and quiet. What she saw caused her to blush and gasp. Olivia was sitting on the washing machine with her legs around Finn's body as he stood leaning into her, kissing her. They were so engaged they didn't even see her. After what seemed like an eternity, she grabbed her soap and left without saying a word.

Olivia cried out. "Sister Julia!" But the sister continued to hurry away.

"Finn, what's going to happen? I am sure she will talk to Mother Ana Maria first thing in the morning, and then what?" Olivia was flooded with guilt as her mind raced ahead, envisioning the confrontation with Sister Ana Maria.

Finn held her tightly and looked into her eyes.

"It feels like two kids getting caught parking by the neighborhood police. Hey Livi, we haven't taken our vows yet. Not everyone is called to serve the church, and now we both have to address the situation. We have to be honest and pray that people will understand. Let's pray that God will understand. Falling in love is not a crime."

They stayed just long enough to gather their clothes and console each other, wondering what would happen as a result of Julia discovering their relationship. Most importantly, they didn't want this to have a negative effect on the fellowship program. They walked down the long hallway back to the dorm rooms. Finn stopped her in the darkest part of the hall and kissed Olivia goodnight. "I promise Livi, I will always love you. Nothing will change that." As he kissed her with eyes shut, she whispered, "I love you, Finn."

33

The mornings at the convent were always busy, and everyone was in a rush. Preparations were under way for the Pope's visit, and all the sisters had extra duties. His visit to San Marco was just a week away, and the convent had to be presented in its best light.

Finn was finishing his coffee with Kyle and James when Mother Ana Maria came up behind him and tapped him on the shoulder, after having just spoken with Olivia. Her facial expression was sterner than he'd ever seen it.

"Finn, stop by my office when you finish. I need to speak with you."

Kyle and James looked at Finn with their eyebrows raised, but Finn didn't notice. His eyes were on Olivia, who was leaving the room in the direction of Mother Ana Maria's office. He noticed Father Paggi heading for the church. Finn returned his tray and proceeded to Mother Ana Maria's office.

When he opened the door, he saw Olivia sitting quietly, her head down as Mother Ana Maria sat behind her desk talking on the phone. Sister Julia sat off to the side, refused eye contact with Finn, and then got up and made sure the door was shut. They all waited several minutes as Mother Ana Maria finished her conversation. Mother Ana Maria was a large woman in her starched, all-white habit and the heavy wooden cross around her neck. At this moment, she was an imposing presence. She was well organized and always seemed to know exactly what she wanted to say. There was very little empathy in her voice as she turned to Finn and Olivia.

"Well, you both must know what this is about. Sister Julia came to me this morning and told me that she interrupted a meeting last night, that she found you and Olivia embracing in the laundry room. Apparently you're romantically involved. Is that true?"

Almost exactly at the same time, they both responded, "Yes, Sister."

Her face conveyed displeasure. Up to this point, they were expecting some expulsion notice, but then her tone changed.

"So tell me, what is this about?"

Olivia glanced at Finn, who'd decided to speak first.

"At first, we became friends during our work, and then accidentally, you might say; we fell in love. And, if I might add, we are so happy about this."

Mother Ana Maria took her time to contemplate her response. She stood up and walked to the front window that looked over the garden. Sister Julia sat silent and stone-faced. She was waiting for a reprimand that she had seen many times with the Sisters who lived at the convent. The tower bells rang eight times, and school children were walking in the direction of the St. John Fisher School. She turned to Finn and Olivia.

"God works in many ways, and if he has chosen that you two be together, better that he do it now, before your vows. After all, you both know that this is a time for you to decide what your future holds. If this path is your choice, then I wish you all my love and support."

Olivia's fear and anxiety had begun to dissipate in a gush of tears when suddenly Julia stood up, her fists clenched tightly at her sides.

"Mother, what are you saying? They have broken their commitments!"

Mother Ana Maria narrowed her eyes at Sister Julia, then spoke, her voice low and steady.

"Sit down, Julia. If I want your opinion, I will ask."

She let her eyes linger on the Sister a few long seconds before turning back to Finn and Olivia. "I met with Father Paggi this morning, as I wanted his input. His response was very helpful, and reminded me that we all have a calling, and it is God who takes us there. He thought that your attraction, if honest and true, was a blessing. But we both agreed that for the remainder of the fellowship you should conduct yourselves honorably and without further…incident. After all, you are representing your sponsors. We recommend you minimize your personal contact for the duration of the fellowship. If you are planning to spend the rest of your lives together, you should be able to manage to wait two weeks. When you return to Detroit, you will inform your institutional advisors of your intentions. This is not the first time this has happened, and it will not be the last. Finn, Father Paggi, must like you. He seems to think you will be more than happy to accommodate our request."

"Yes, of course, Mother. Olivia and I have already planned to notify our advisors. Your kindness reassures me that it is God's plan for us to be together, and I want to thank you."

Olivia wiped her cheeks dry, and although it was hard to express her gratitude for this understanding, she reached deep into herself and responded.

"Thank you, Mother Ana Maria. Your kindness and understanding are unexpected. I was terrified of being expelled. Instead, your kindness inspires me. You know what I have been going through in my preparation to become a Felician Sister, and my intentions were honest. But now my heart is filled with love for Finn and we want to have a life together serving the Lord and our church in a different way. We meant no disrespect, and we will keep our relationship at a distance and completely confidential. You can trust we will do that."

Finn added, "Absolutely. We mean no disrespect to the convent, or to our fellow students. We will give our full attention to our work and study. I can say that San Marco has been one of the most special experiences in my life and will always be in my heart."

Mother Ana Maria sat down at her desk.

"Then it's settled. The Pope will be visiting us in just a few days, and there is much to do. This conversation will remain completely confidential. Is that understood?"

She looked pointedly at Sister Julia, who nodded. "And now everyone may resume their work and study. God bless you both."

Sister Julia rose abruptly and left the room. Olivia walked over to Mother Ana Maria and gave her a hug. "Thank you, Mother Superior. My life is changing, and you have helped me with that change. I will always be grateful to you."

Finn glanced through the glass paned door and noticed Father Paggi returning from the church. "Thank you again, Mother. This means a great deal to both of us."

When they left the office, the two went in separate directions, Olivia to her room, and Finn in the direction of Father Paggi's office. Mother Ana Maria sat down at her desk, took a deep breath and made herself a note: Future groups might work better if they are divided by gender and time.

The sun cast long streams of light into the marble foyer and illuminated the fresh flowers on the glass table. The arched entrance to the San Marco vestibule made a person feel special, if not holy. Finn had yet another level of appreciation for his experience at San Marco. He finally reached Father Paggi, who greeted him with a smile.

"Good morning Finn. How are you?"

"Good morning, Father. I'm better now that we met with Mother Ana Maria. Before that, I was worried my time here was finished. She mentioned that you and she talked about our situation. I want to thank you for your support. It means a great deal to me."

Father Paggi looked at Finn and could imagine him as his son. Through his experience at the parish, there were many situations that mirrored Finn's. On this matter, it was easy for him to see right from wrong. "Finn, God has a plan for you and all of us. Sometimes it is the priesthood, and sometimes it's not. You'll need to seek advice from your priest at the Seminary and go through the five-stage process that we have been taught to determine our decisions of conscience. But most of all, you need to follow your heart."

They walked a bit further before Finn asked, "Were you able to find out anything more about the documents in the box, Father?"

Father Paggi had anticipated the question. It was Finn, after all, who discovered the box.

"I had the documents translated and it turns out Girolamo Savonarola wrote them. Do you know of him?"

Finn searched his memory. "Wasn't he a radical preacher who opposed the Vatican in the1490's?"

"Exactly. In the letter, he describes the end of times. It may have some historical value, so I am contacting the Cultural Ministry and turning the artifact over to them for safekeeping. I will keep you posted."

Finn needed to get to his work assignment and excused himself. Father Paggi stood in the hallway, looking out the window at St. John Fisher. *I need to meet with Mother Ana Maria* he thought. As Finn left, he immediately reversed his direction and went to the main office where Mother Ana Maria was on the phone. He sat down and waited patiently until she finished her conversation.

"Good Morning, Father. How are you?" Paggi was in a hurry to get to the point, but first said, "Fine...I just talked with Finn. He was relieved. You did the right thing"

She looked at Paggi with a soft smile. "*We* did the right thing father."

Father Paggi went on quickly. "I need to tell you that I was assaulted last night here in the church. Afterwards, I made a police report, but I don't want this to ruin our chances for the papal visit so I would like to keep this between us. Are you good with that?"

She looked at him with surprise. "Are you hurt?"

Paggi rubbed the back of his head. "Just a bump on the head. I'll be fine. But for now, let's keep it between us and let the police do their work."

34

Father Paggi closed the heavy office door behind him and sat down at his desk. Through leaded glass windows, he could see children playing on the school playground. Someone had assaulted him in church and taken the Savonarola document. It troubled him. Surely this meant that people were, in fact, conspiring with the Piagnoni to disrupt the Pope's visit. The fact that he had kept all this information from the Monsignor made it difficult for him to now try and explain the situation. It would only heighten the concern and possibly cancel the Pope's visit to San Marco. He thought long and hard, and then he decided on a compromise. He picked up the phone and called the Monsignor. The phone rang several times before the Monsignor himself answered.

"Hello, this is Delsoni."

"Monsignor, this is Father Paggi. I wanted to brief you on our progress at San Marco. We have finalized a plan for the papal visit. Mother Ana Maria and I finished working on the details this morning. I'll get them to you later today."

The Monsignor was brusque.

"Thank you, leave it with my assistant. I am just on my way to a meeting. It seems several detectives have apprehended a man they think is part of the Piagnoni, so I have to go. Is there anything else?"

Father Paggi hesitated and then said. "One of the students here found an artifact at the restoration of the Duomo. It's an old box that contained documents from Savonarola. It's dated 1492. I thought you might want to share the information with Father Fitzpatrick."

"That would be a good idea if he were still here. He flew back to Rome early this morning to meet with his security team. Look, it is interesting, perhaps important, but not germane to the security of the Pope's visit. Right? Make sure you lock it up and keep it safe. We'll talk later. Ciao!"

Father Paggi hung up the phone and reached for his Rolodex, looking for his brother-in-law's phone number at the Ministry of Cultural Affairs.

Dr. Nicholas Coppola was an attorney turned art historian, who now worked at the Ministry of Cultural Affairs for Florence in a top administrative position. Most of his work involved the appraisal of Italian artifacts and litigation with museums that made alleged illegal purchases of Italian art.

Stephen's sister, Madera, always went out of her way to include her brother in her family events, so he was close to his two nephews. It was at a dinner recently that Nicholas went on and on about a dispute with the J. Paul Getty Museum over the proper paperwork when purchasing an ancient marble bust of Apollo. In addition, Nicholas had just won a lawsuit against the New York Metropolitan Museum after a lengthy court trial that proved the Italian government was the true owner of the Euphronios Krater, an ancient Greek vessel.

Stephen Paggi knew his brother-in-law would provide him with the best advice. After locating the number, he called Nicholas.

"Dr. Coppola's office, how may I help you?" answered a pleasant voice.

"This is Stephen Paggi calling for Nicholas. I'm his brother in law. Is he available?"

"Hello, Father. Let me check."

It was always hard to get through to Nicholas, as he spent most of his time going from meeting to meeting or testifying in court. Madera complained that it was impossible to reach him during the day.

The pleasant voice cut into his thoughts. "I'm sorry, Father. He just left for the courthouse. Can I give you his voice mail?"

"Sure, that will be fine." Father Paggi poured himself a glass of water while he listened to the voice mail prompts. Finally, he heard a beep and made his statement.

"Nicholas, this is Stephen. We found a box dated 1492 during some demolition near the Duomo. It's extraordinary, and you need to see this. I would like you to take a look and offer your advice. Give me a call when you have a moment."

He hung up and looked at his watch. He was due to deliver mass in less than fifteen minutes. He dressed in his ordinary robe thinking; *this incident at San Marco Church is a problem.*

35

Dr. Mariana Morelli stood in front of her office window and watched the Arno swirl slowly under the Ponte Vecchio Bridge. The Uffizi Museum was first opened to visitors by request in the sixteenth century, and in 1765, it was officially opened to the public. Her small office was on the second floor along the administrative wing that faced the river. The Italian architecture provided high vaulted ceilings and large panels of oak that acted as cladding for the thick limestone walls. Located in the oldest part of the Uffizi Museum, her office décor was in stark contrast to the architecture. A long glass table, black leather chairs trimmed in chrome, and a solid black wool throw rug usually caught people by surprise. The contemporary furniture reflected her lifestyle. Juxtaposed to the contemporary furniture was her prize piece of artwork, a small Leonardo da Vinci drawing, The *Study of Arms and Hands* that her husband bought at a private auction in London for her fortieth birthday.

She stared now at the da Vinci drawing and thought about all the media coverage that was swirling around the investigation into a mural supposedly hidden behind a Giorgio Vasari mural that scientists hoped soon to uncover. The newly elected brash young Mayor of Florence, Latteo Frenzi, was a supporter of the research project and had recently signed an agreement with *National Geographic* which would put up $250,000 toward the investigation in exchange for the rights to publish the findings. The fundraising would be used to develop the powerful gamma ray camera that could reveal the hidden mural.

Dr. Morelli knew Dr. Mano Cerisano, who headed up the project, and although they were friends and colleagues, she was not in favor of the exploration. The mural they searched for, described in notes as *The*

Battle of Anghiari, was a violent and bloodthirsty portrayal of the end of times. Most importantly, there were those who were sure it was a mural by Leonardo da Vinci. This would connect Leonardo to Girolamo Savonarola and cast him in an unfavorable light. If located, the largest painting that Leonardo undertook would be exposed to the world. Leonardo da Vinci was given a commission by Piero Soderini, a contract signed by no less than Niccolò Machiavelli himself. A reconstructed blueprint and 16th century document placed the mural on a wall inside the Palazzo Vecchio's Grand Ceremonial Chamber, but it somehow went missing in 1507.

The most recent analysis pointed to the cerca trova clue, translated as "He who seeks, finds," written on a Florentine soldier's flag depicted in the Vasari mural, and advanced radar scanning revealed that a brick wall was erected in front of the existing mural to preserve its existence. Dr. Morelli was at the press conference when Dr. Mano Cerisano revealed that they had detected neutrons bouncing back after colliding with hydrogen atoms, proving the presence of a second wall.

Mariana sat down in her Wassily chrome steel chair and looked at the drawing on her wall. She felt strongly about preserving Leonardo's reputation, and she was not alone. There were two camps among the world's leading art historians: those who supported the finding and those who did not. From all parts of Europe and the United States, art historians weighed in on the topic and disagreed among themselves for various reasons. Some were concerned about preserving the Vasari mural and said that relocating or disturbing the mural would be too risky.

But Mariana was in the small camp of art historians who knew that after the death of Girolamo Savonarola, the Piagnoni had influenced many artists, and this could have included Leonardo da Vinci. They had all written a narrative in many college textbooks that followed the work of the great artist throughout his career, and did not want his reputation tarnished, even if it was true. She had just completed a new work on art history for Taschen Books, a publisher of books on art and architecture. Discovery of a heretofore unknown da Vinci that tarnished his reputation would require massive revisions to the book that would be costly. She wished there was some way to delay the work or to know what lay behind the Vasari mural.

She booted up her computer and prepared her notes on *The Altarpiece* at San Marco while accessing her extensive research on the Dominican Order. After a few commands, her computer displayed her outline: 1) Saint Damian kneels on an inward angle towards the center praising the Virgin and Child. 2) This draws the viewer's eyes towards the painting's vanishing point at the Virgin's chin. 3) The Virgin and Child are featured precisely at the vertical and horizontal axes' intersecting points and are placed above the depiction of the crucifixion.

Fra Angelico was criticized for his imperfect use of scale. While sitting on a pedestal, neither the virgin nor the child seem much larger than the rest of the characters, showing a lack of scale, setting the main subjects apart from other mortals.

36

The students in the fellowship suspended their work for a few days to help prepare the convent for the papal visit. They divided into groups of four to clean floors, wash walls, and dust until the convent was in pristine condition. One team worked under the supervision of the gardener on the small front yard, trimming grass and pruning shrubs, while another team groomed the courtyard. Assisting the monks, they set up scaffolds adorned with restoration tools and materials that would provide talking points for the Pope's tour.

The garden behind the convent stretched back a hundred feet. Rows of hemlock trees defined the border of an intricate stone walkway. The nuns who lived at the convent would walk the gardens in contemplation. Everything at San Marco was simple, neat, and uncluttered, with a sense of elegance that was typical of a humanist sensibility. It was common knowledge that Pope John Paul II had visited San Marco several times prior to his papacy, but this would be the first time that he would visit as Pope.

Mother Ana Maria had a checklist that was ten pages long and conducted meetings each evening after dinner to follow up on tasks and their timing. The preliminary plan was that, upon arrival, the Pope would enter through the front of the convent and proceed to the church for an abbreviated mass conducted by Father Paggi. Mother Ana Maria would make welcoming remarks, and then introduce the fellowship students. The Pope would respond with his comments on the celebration of a Catholic education. Following their time in the large refectory, Jeremiah would head up the Pope's tour of the restoration work. After the tour, they would return to the refectory for refreshments. Father

Fitzpatrick had sent word that the Vatican would have a small gift for each student. The visit would last no more than two hours, which included the mass. By 3:45 p.m. the Pope would exit and head to the airport via motorcade.

Mother Ana Maria had requested extra bouquets of fresh flowers and instructed the cook to prepare lemonade, assorted cut vegetables, including broccoli and cauliflower, and fresh baked sweet rolls with cinnamon and icing. These were some of Pope John Paul's favorite foods that Fitzpatrick had mentioned after Mother Ana Maria questioned him repeatedly. At one of the recent staff meetings, Monsignor Delsoni talked about the Pope's previous visits to San Marco.

"Ever since he was a young seminarian, the Pope has been an avid student of Fra Angelico and his work. When he visited San Marco in 1958, the then Bishop Wojtyla wrote that it is impossible to bestow too much praise on this humble friar whose frescos are painted with such facility and piety. So he has tremendous regard for the importance of this restoration project."

With work, study, and special preparations for the Pope's visit, the students were on overload. It was unspoken, but everyone knew how important this visit was. There were so many meetings, briefings, and security updates it was hard to keep track of all the information. The Florence Carabinieri had already made visits to the convent and conducted several walk-throughs. Each person at the convent, including the students and work staff, would be issued a temporary I.D. All preliminary background checks had been cleared, including that of the man known as Josef Dvorsak.

37

The weekend came quickly, and by Sunday, all the preparations for the visit were in place. Both Father Paggi and Mother Ana Maria wanted to give the students some free time after mass. Once the papal visit was over, they had only one week left in the fellowship, and they had just been notified there was a change in the return flights, which meant that there would be two return flights to Detroit leaving a day apart. The auto booking system had selected the best prices for a return ticket that divided the group in half. Ten students would leave on Friday, and ten students would leave on Saturday.

Olivia and Finn had lived up to their promise and refrained from spending time together. They both went out of their way to avoid any behavior that looked like they were anything but friends. Instead, they immersed themselves in work and study. But when they got word there would be some free time on Sunday, Finn mentioned the market place to Olivia, and without speaking, she agreed. Finn left right after mass and Olivia first went to her room to change her clothes. Vanessa was in the room when she entered.

"Hey, what are you going to do this afternoon? Do you want to visit the Uffizi?"

Olivia had never found the right time to confide in Vanessa. She wanted to, but she knew it would mean a very long conversation about leaving the order. The only person outside the convent who knew was her mother. In a long conversation, Olivia explained to her what had happened, and although her mother was shocked momentarily, she came around to understanding and finally supporting her daughter's decision. It came after a detailed description of what had occurred and especially the discussion with Mother Ana Maria. In the end, after seeing some pictures attached to an email, her mother was overjoyed, but now dreaded having to tell Olivia's grandmother.

But Olivia didn't have time to think of that now. She had to think of some way to put off Vanessa. She and Finn hadn't so much as talked to each other since the laundry room incident. The only communication they had were a couple of letters secreted in the pages of an art history book they passed to each other in the hallway.

"Thanks Vanessa, but I promised the first grade teacher at St. John Fisher that I would help her with her classroom first chance I got. If I get finished early, maybe I can catch up with you."

It wasn't exactly a lie, as she had promised Sister Lynn, but the time was set for later that day or evening. All Olivia could think about was Finn waiting for her, and by now, he might already be there. She quickly changed her clothes, grabbed a sweater, and glanced into the mirror. She gazed at her face and wanted to put on a touch of lipstick, but she would wait and do that on the way to the market.

Finn got to the market and sighed in relief to find the vendor stall still unoccupied with a small sign tacked to the side support. It was an advertisement for the rental of the space with a phone number written at the bottom. He grabbed the sign and gently loosened it from its nail, and slipped inside, noticing the crates were still in the same position as before. No one had been there since their time together weeks ago. He looked around and arranged everything so it would be comfortable. His mind was filled with Olivia, and now he recalled images of their first meeting, along with their passionate discussion. He recalled her mouth on his. It was all he could do to stay calm.

Olivia made her way into the crowded Sunday street and noticed the police stationed in front of the convent. They're already here, she thought. Crossing the street, she encountered tour groups spilling from the narrow sidewalk into the cobblestone street, as children played kick-ball. A street musician played a lute opposite a popular gelato store where families and their children lined up all the way down the block.

As Olivia walked quickly down the via dei Martelli, she passed San Lorenzo and noticed the driveway was crowded with white police cars. She wondered if it had anything to do with the preparations for the Pope. She took out her only tube of lipstick and placed a small amount on her finger and covered her lips lightly. As she approached the market, a three-year-old boy chased a large group of pigeons, causing them finally to lift in flight. She knew Finn was there, as he'd left a good ten minutes before her, but when she slipped into the vendor stall, the space was empty. Her heart sank, until from behind, his arms encircled her waist.

"Good morning, good morning, good morning!"

Olivia turned to him. They placed their foreheads together and held each other in silence. The sounds from the street did not affect their concentration. They stayed together some time without speaking, until Finn kissed her gently. Her body vibrated and her heart beat so fast it almost frightened her. She was a changed person, open to a new world of feelings and emotion that she had never experienced. She'd had a few boyfriends in high school that she liked, but she'd never felt like this. Finn kissed her and then spoke. "Tell me more about yourself, Livi. Like what were your favorite things as a child?"

Olivia paused. "I studied violin for four years. I collected buffalo head nickels and two dollar bills, and in middle school I started collecting bird feathers, all kinds."

"I missed you Livi. I miss holding you close like this. I want us to be together. Do you know what I mean?"

She nodded. "I want the same. I talked to my mother and told her everything. She was surprised but very happy."

"Wow, I told my mother as well, just last night on the phone, and she was happy. She said that she knew just how to tell my father. All of this surprised me, as I thought she had her mind made up that I was going to be a priest. And now, she might be a grandmother some day. I love you so much, Livi."

Olivia looked into Finn's eyes, and she could see his passion and his open sincerity. In her mind, she jumped far ahead and envisioned a life with Finn. She could see their children playing at the beach. Everything had changed. God had given her a new purpose.

"I love you so much, Finn."

Their time together was limited, as they both had to be back before dinner and to a special meeting regarding the Pope's visit. They held each other close and kissed and talked.

"I promise, Livi."

"I know, Finn. I promise, too."

Finn kissed her one last time and left the vendor stall, quickly stepping into the crowd.

Across the street, Sister Julia was also on her way back to the convent, using a shortcut through the market she often took. As she scanned the busy crowd, she noticed the tall, dark-haired boy slip out of the closed vender stall. She paused to make sure it was Finn, and then she observed Olivia leave the stall headed in the opposite direction. Julia turned away so as not to be noticed and thought...*they broke their promise.*

Olivia walked quickly. She still had time to stop by St. John Fisher and help Sister Lynn for a little while at least. The street in the market was crowded, and it was several blocks before the mass of shoppers thinned out. As she walked, Olivia kept flashing back to Finn's smile and the feel of his body against her. She could hear his laugh and the tenor of his voice. Walking along at a brisk rate, she dodged children and tourists. She kept bringing back the details of their intimate time together. It kept her in a place she loved, in Finn's arms, holding him close. In the crowd, Sister Julia stood still and pensive, contemplating her next move.

38

Daresh Oldani kept his profile as low as possible. He entered the convent each day through the back gate and worked quietly, executing his duties without drawing attention to himself. He avoided talking to anyone, took his lunch separately, and did not interact with the other kitchen staff. It was only the gardener who often approached him for conversation. On the first day back after a call from his contact, he brought the Glock into the rear part of the kitchen and entered the stock room. Making sure it was loaded properly, he wrapped the carbon fiber handgun in a towel and buried it in a large burlap bag of red beans. He was told that security would be at the convent in advance and to be sure to stash the weapon before they arrived. It was early in the evening when he received another call from the Piagnoni. The voice was soft but harsh, and the directive minced few words.

"On the second day of the Pope's visit to Florence, he will stop by San Marco. This has just been confirmed. It is not on the public schedule of events, but we have learned that he will make a short visit to the convent on his way to the airport. We will not be protesting publicly as planned. Rather, we are putting all of our efforts into your presence at San Marco. This is what we have been waiting for many years, and the time has now come. We would like you to wait until you get as close to him as possible and take one shot to the head. We will have a car waiting for you down the side street if you are able to escape, but in all likelihood, you will be apprehended. Do not resist. We will start planning a way to break you out of Italian custody."

"What about my family?"

"Your parents have been moved already and will be taken care of generously as we agreed. Your brother is already working with us, so he will be safe. They will have a hard time establishing your identity as we have destroyed as much of the original documentation as possible. Your fingerprints are not on file with Interpol, and you have a completely new identity. You must focus entirely on your mission and take out this deranged Pope. On the day of his visit, remove all your possessions from your room and place them in a nearby dumpster. Destroy your phone and dispose of the parts. This will be the last time we speak. Do you have any questions?"

Oldani listened intently and then said.

"I would like verification that my family has received the money."

"We could issue a bank statement, but contacting your family at this time is out of the question, and would be unsafe. By now, you should just trust us. Anything else? Do you have any concerns?"

"Just one. As I mentioned, there is a gardener who keeps asking me questions. He has asked me about my family and how long I've been in Firenze. It's not good."

"Your cover there is critical to our efforts. We have found out he is no one. Here is what you do. At the end of the workday, when the time is right, take him out. Make it neat and clean. Do you understand?"

"I understand."

Oldani pressed the button to disconnect. Daresh knew that his parents would receive a good amount of money for his assignment, but he was also motivated by his devout faith. He removed a small Bible from his dresser and began his regimen of ultra conservative prayer. Under the threat of excommunication, Daresh prayed against freedom of conscience, personal rights, and the belief in pluralism. With his head bowed, he repeated his father's mantra. "Church in the person of Peter's successor has not yet substituted the traditional Magisterium with this new one and... neither has the Church of Rome."

39

The phone rang on Father Paggi's desk, and the secretary told him it was from Nicholas, his brother-in-law. "Hello Nicholas, how are you? Thank you for returning my call."

"I'm sorry it took so long. I have been swamped lately with court testimony. Tell me about this box you've found."

"There was a very old wall that became unstable, and to replace it meant some demolition. The monk in charge was being assisted by one of our fellowship students, and he found a box in the debris. It must have been there for more than five hundred years. Along with some parchment scrolls, the box contained a handwritten letter by Girolamo Savonarola."

"That's incredible! What does it say?"

"It is the end of times rant. He points to a small group to carry on his work."

"The Ministry has a collection of his writings, and this could be made part of that. Most of it is stored at the San Marco Library. Is that what you had in mind?"

"Exactly. It belongs to Florence and should be part of the antiquities collection. I will bring it by the office when you have time."

"Let's do it in a couple of weeks. There is a lengthy verification and registration process. Protocol. It drives me crazy. Madera told me you have the Pope coming, is that right?"

"We do, and we are very busy. We are a little worried about an underground group called the Piagnoni. They are Catholic right-wing zealots who want to radicalize the church. Apparently they are here in Florence for the Pope's visit. I hope they don't make a scene, you know? Cast Florence in a bad light."

"I know what you mean. Okay. I have to go. I'll have my secretary set up a time. And don't worry about a small group of dissidents. The police can control these things. Thanks, Stephen. Ciao."

Father Paggi sat at his desk and looked at the beautifully framed photograph of his sister Madera, Nicholas, and their children. They were all the family he had in Florence, and he knew he could trust Nicholas to do the right thing with the contents of the box. He was worried about the incident at the church and the De Ruina Mundi document he had found in the crucifix heel. He was embarrassed by his failed attempt to recover the document. It was a reflection on his own Achilles heel, his competence. He now faced a dilemma. What did the De Ruina Mundi mean to the Piagnoni, and how could it be used against the church?

40

Father Fitzpatrick watched St. Peter's Basilica grow smaller and smaller as the Vatican helicopter headed north away from Rome. He was taking three of his top security people to Florence in advance of the Pope's visit. The trip gave him some time to read over his most recent intelligence notes and plot an updated plan of action once he arrived at the airport. When the helicopter touched down, Monsignor Delsoni and the Florence Chief of Police immediately met them. With the exception of a few traffic controllers, the incident went without notice. A black limousine and a white police car were parked fifty feet from the yellow circle that marked the dark green tarmac. As he walked down the steps from the chopper, Fitzpatrick had to hold onto his hat while the blades of the helicopter continued to rotate. He joined the Monsignor in the limo while his men loaded into a police car. It was a fifteen-minute drive to San Lorenzo where other security officials stood waiting for a briefing. The Monsignor turned to Fitzpatrick.

"Did you get anything from those who were apprehended?"

"We did. We know that the Piagnoni is here in Florence and operating a small, covert cell. We found out they have moles in place, possibly in law enforcement or in places where the Pope is scheduled to visit. We have just broken their encryption codes and are now analyzing the intelligence. From these confirmed sources, we know there has been recruitment activity in Bucharest. One of the men captured was a common street criminal who was seen demonstrating in Rome. The Piagnoni are using outside people as hired assassins to protect their own people from being exposed. These men are mercenaries who can infiltrate and work quietly until they are called upon. We will know much more this evening."

Traffic was at its rush hour peak, and a local funeral procession made it more congested. Monsignor Delsoni could sense the intense pressure placed on Fitzpatrick. The Piagnoni had been plaguing the Pope for several years, mostly taking the form of public protests, but in recent years, there was intelligence chatter that indicated they could go so far as to hire an assassin to make an attempt on his life.

After finally reaching San Lorenzo and passing through several security procedures, they entered a part of the building that very few people even knew about. Below the basement level, there was yet another level identified as C Level. As they proceeded down in the elevator, Fitzpatrick asked where they were going.

"There is a secure lower level where only those with top secret clearance are allowed. It has the most recent technology and networks that connect to the five major intelligence services around the world. It is owned and operated by the Interpol NATO Alliance, and it runs its networks on high-speed encrypted fiber and satellite technology that is connected to Global Command and Control Systems.

The Monsignor placed his hand on a stainless steel wall device that photo matched his hand print while extracting a small drop of blood from his middle finger. Within seconds, the analysis triggered a release and opened the large steel door. Behind it, people sat at computer workstations watching a wall of glass where data and imagery were displayed. They stopped at what seemed like a command desk, and the Monsignor introduced Fitzpatrick to an Indian-born man with short, gray hair wearing a dark suit.

"This is Dr. Gremki Lechnari, retired CIA, and working for Interpol's NATO Intelligence Service. Their organization sublets this space from the Archdiocese of Florence and uses our facility as a cover. I appealed to their agency to allow us to work with them for the papal visit, and they have provided us with some results. Let's see what you have."

The large, translucent wall produced seven male faces with a flood of data below each profile. One of the images was an older photo of Daresh

Oldani under yet a different alias, with longer hair and a shortly cropped beard. Dr. Lechnari went carefully through each person and their attached information. Multitudes of surveillance cameras identified each assailant on the streets of Florence.

"This is how we know they are here. The photos were captured over a period beginning ten days ago. We have yet to determine exactly where they are living or what they are planning to do. Previous to this event, there were some demonstrations, but we have reason to believe these men are different. They are not the anti-Pope zealots we have seen at rallies. They are hired assassins. We can produce these images along with the information and distribute it electronically to all the phones on the police force."

Monsignor Delsoni spent more time going over Dr. Lechnari's bio with Fitzpatrick as they walked through the facility.

"He now heads up the Interpol NATO operation and is the principal technology intelligence consultant who covers a wide range of interfaces: virtualization, server operations, and on-line analytical processing. The large screens were imported from Palo Alto, and they use high definition, forensic bit stream imaging capability. His group does all the data surveying, staging, and parameterized reporting to the field in real time."

The two men with the most responsibility for protecting the Pope were worried. As they stood there, a call came in that one of the men was spotted and apprehended. The police were in route with the suspect in custody. It was not Daresh Oldani.

41

It was the end of the workday. Through the small kitchen window, Oldani could see into the courtyard where the gardener was putting away his work tools. Oldani walked out into the area that surrounded the courtyard and leaned on the wall nearest the gardener.

"How's it going?"

The gardener moved his thick torso and now noticed the man called Josef standing there in his apron. He rested his weight on his rake and wiped his brow before responding.

"Not much left to do on the grounds before the season changes. I've done all the work for the Pope's visit."

Oldani looked around. Leaves had been raked and placed in large paper lawn bags. There was no one in the courtyard. The small rows of boxwood shrubs were neatly wrapped in burlap. Oldani said, "Could you give me a hand? I've got a pallet in the storeroom that I need to move, and the cook just left for the day. I don't think I can move it by myself."

"No problem. Just let me store the rest of my tools in the shed."

Oldani led the gardener to the back of the kitchen and opened the extra large doors that led into the damp, chilly storeroom. An odor filled the air from a mousetrap that had just caught its prey. Closing the door behind him securely, Oldani stood behind the gardener pointing to the pallet of rice and beans.

"I need to move this pallet to the back so we can get in here with a hand truck."

As Oldani walked around the man, he pulled a syringe from his apron pocket and injected the gardener in the side of his neck. The man turned reflexively from the pain of the needle, but the fast-acting sodium pentobarbital brought him to his knees within seconds. He fell on the concrete floor, paralyzed. Oldani stepped back and watched. The gardener was conscious, eyes open, but unable to talk or move. Oldani pulled a second syringe from the apron pocket and injected 100 milligrams of potassium chloride into his arm. His eyes briefly widened with in fear before slowly closing. Oldani again made sure the storeroom door was closed and locked. He waited about ten minutes and then folded the man's body in half and pushed it into the waste compactor. When he hit the switch, the large hydraulic arms forced the mass into the waste chamber and within minutes produced a block of compacted waste. He wrapped the block of human remains in heavy opaque plastic and, using the hand truck, wheeled it out to the dumpster. As he stood in front of the dumpster, he glanced around and saw no one. Only when he returned to the kitchen did he start to see students climbing the stairs to their evening seminar.

42

With only two days left before the papal visit, Mother Ana Maria and Father Paggi insisted that the fellowship stay on schedule. Dr. Morelli called the convent to confirm that the seminar was meeting that night. She had given the students an assignment to be prepared to discuss the San Marco *Altarpiece, Virgin Mary and Christ*, which depicted the Holy Mother and Jesus surrounded by a variety of saints. It was common knowledge that in 1493, Fra Angelico had completed this most famous of his paintings. Dr. Morelli appealed to the students to attend the lecture prepared to discuss the significance of the large fresco.

As Dr. Morelli prepared her digital images for projection, the fellowship students wandered in and took their usual seats out of habit. Finn came wearing his signature baseball jacket. He took his seat next to the door. Olivia and Vanessa were together near the back corner of the room talking about the restoration work earlier in the day. Kyle and James sat near the front of the room and reviewed their notes.

By seven o'clock sharp, all eyes were on Dr. Morelli. Standing in front of the room with a small remote in her hand, she was a fashion show all by herself. Her unusually thin figure was always clad in an Italian designer suit, accented by subtle but expensive jewelry. Her long, dark hair was always rolled up and held in place with a hairpin that was probably a valuable antiquity, and she always wore the same black-rimmed glasses. She could have stepped off a movie set. As beautiful and attractive as she was, it was her knowledge and her command of the language that set her apart. The announcement had just filtered through the convent that she had recently published an article in Art News about the controversial Degas sculptures.

"Good evening," she said. "As always, it is good to see you all. I know everyone has been very busy because of the upcoming Papal visit. If you recall our last meeting, I mentioned *The Altarpiece* here at San Marco. Who would like to start with some opening remarks and observations of this work?"

As usual, most students were reluctant to lead with opening comments, but as the class had matured, there were a few who were eager to start a discussion. James raised his hand, and Dr. Morelli acknowledged him with a nod.

"I have always noticed that St. Dominic is looking toward the heavens," James said. Did Friar Angelico hold St. Dominic in higher esteem than others?"

"We begin with an intelligent question. Thank you for that, James. Would anyone like to respond?"

Olivia had done her homework and spent time in the San Marco archive reading about *The Altarpiece*. She raised her hand and was recognized.

"In the fresco, he makes reference to the idiosyncrasies of the Dominican mass, like kneeling. Some of the saints are kneeling at the altar, while the saints who surround the Virgin and Child represent the Dominican congregation."

By now, the students could tell by Dr. Morelli's expression when she was pleased with students who expressed ideas that were not commonplace.

"Is there anything that sets *The Altarpiece* apart from other paintings done during the same period?"

Vanessa responded to her question. "There is a devotion to this Monastery….well at the time it was a Monastery… and through the choices he made, he created a mirror of the real world here at that time. He allowed the viewer a window into this heavenly world at San Marco."

Finn raised his hand and followed up on Vanessa's train of thought.

"I am always aware that these frescoes were not painted for clients, but as devotions. The rich colors, particularly the reds and greens, portray God's indescribable majesty. Although their faith was tangible, there still was a higher power to retain. And his figures are always thin and delicate. Their gently curving draperies echo the curves in the vaulted ceilings, and the halos, rather than being foreshortened, are flat circles placed on the far side of the head. The friar was using light to convey a sense of spirituality and the presence of Christ."

Dr. Morelli was reminded of why she entered the field of art history and made the decision to teach. These fellowship students were far more sensitive than normal graduate students who majored in art history. The combination of living, working, and studying at the convent had provided them with insight that might only come when working with primary sources. Their comments inspired her to elaborate.

"We need to remember that Fra Angelico received his training as an illuminator, possibly working with his older brother, Benedetto, who was also a Dominican Friar. We think Lorenzo Monaco was one of his first teachers. Here at San Marco, with the support of the Medici family, he retreated from the world. These are devotional frescoes that depict the life of Christ. Images of the Madonna and Child were commonplace, but here in this famous painting, the saints stand squarely within the space, grouped naturally. We see how his work was transitional, from early to later influences on the Renaissance."

It was at times like this that the Fellowship students felt special and honored to be in Florence and at San Marco. The work, the classes, and the evening seminars were executed with the highest level of professionalism.

Finn's position allowed him to see out the door and through the stairway where he saw a person walking to and from the kitchen to the refectory. It seemed late for someone to be there.

The informality of the evening seminar allowed people to step out if they needed to use the restroom, and although it was rare to do so, Finn decided to walk down the stairway and have a look. The downstairs first floor area was dark, and only a small light from the kitchen illuminated the hallway to the refectory. Before he reached the bottom of the stairs, he stopped to observe the man he knew as Josef Dvorsak, still in his kitchen working clothes, walking to and from the two rooms as if he were rehearsing. Finn watched the man repeat the route several times, his arms outstretched as if carrying a tray. Finn decided to check it out.

"Hey. You work in the kitchen, don't you? Is everything all right?"

Oldani was visibly startled. He froze in place and lowered his arms, avoiding eye contact. He spoke in a small, hushed voice.

"Everything is fine."

Finn moved closer, noticing a small scar on the young man's chin and a light sheen of perspiration on his forehead.

"Isn't it a little late to be here? Does Mother Ana Maria know you're here?"

"I am rehearsing my duties. I don't want to make any mistakes," said Oldani slowly with a flat affect.

"Good idea." Finn hesitated but pushed back the uneasiness he felt. This was none of his business, and he didn't want to be a jerk to this poor guy who was trying hard to please. "Well," he said finally, "don't forget to turn off the light. The sisters are pretty intense about energy conservation."

Oldani did not respond, except with a slight bow of his head, affirming Finn's point. Finn walked slowly up the stair, the uneasiness still with him. He remembered having a conversation with him weeks ago. Finn's strong intuition told him there was something weird about the guy, and he wondered if he should mention it to somebody. But who?

43

Monsignor Delsoni arranged for a small private dinner with the Archbishop to brief him on security matters for the papal visit. Many other high ranking officials had worked on the visit that included arrangements for a large mass at the Mother Cathedral of Florence, Santa Maria del Fiore, a special meeting with religious leaders, and a youth rally at the Piazza del Duomo. In addition, there were lunches, formal dinners, and a brief visit to the Uffizi Museum. The small private dinner at the Archbishop's residence would only include Archbishop Guiseppe Gellini, Monsignor Delsoni, and Father Fitzpatrick. It would be a delicate matter discussing the Piagnoni and describing their presence in Florence.

As part of the San Lorenzo religious compound that included the Medici Chapels and the Laurentian Library, the residence of the Archbishop was inside and just off the courtyard. When the two men arrived, Father Bianco, who was the personal assistant and aide to the Archbishop, met them at the door. The large reception foyer was rich with tapestry and the floor was decorated with inlaid tile that formed an intricate relief.

They walked down the hallway and entered a formal dining room that could easily seat twenty, but for tonight's dinner, only three seats were set with fine china. Father Bianco seated the two men on each side of a decorated chair at the head of the table. Behind the seat was a large marble fireplace, and on the north side of the room were very large, leaded glass windows that cast a soft northern light and looked out into the garden courtyard. Father Bianco asked.

"May I get you a glass of wine? The Archbishop will be with you shortly."

Both men agreed to a glass of red wine, as the Archbishop had a reputation for an exquisite collection of Chianti Classico Reserva. Father Bianco brought the wine, left the bottle, and lit the three candles on the table, and then left the room, presumably to return with the Archbishop.

Delsoni and Fitzpatrick had decided they would keep their report factual and simple and would certainly exclude anything that would upset the Archbishop, who depended upon the Monsignor to represent him without difficulty. It was Delsoni's responsibility to make sure the Pope's visit was safe and secure. It had been a few years since Florence had hosted a papal visit, and Gellini expected that no issues or items would remain unresolved.

The Archbishop Guiseppe Gellini was an elderly Cardinal with orthodox leanings. He was considered to be one of the most conservative Cardinals in Italy and a favorite of Pope John Paul II, as they had shared time together as seminary students in Rome. The two guests, dressed in black suits with white collars, grew silent as the Archbishop entered the room wearing a black suit trimmed in red with a cape that was open in the front. On the back of his head, he wore a red mitre. He proceeded slowly, followed by Father Bianco. The two guests stood up.

"Good evening, gentleman. It's nice to see you both on the eve of such a joyous occasion. Father Fitzpatrick, so good to see you again. Please sit."

But the two men waited for his grace to be seated before returning to their seats.

Monsignor Delsoni said, "Your Grace, good evening and thank you for this private dinner."

"You'll repay the favor by telling me about the progress of our fellowship students. Are they cleaning our beloved frescoes?"

Father Bianco poured the Archbishop a glass of wine and refilled the glasses of the visitors. Monsignor Delsoni responded.

"The students are doing a fine job, and the project has been a great success. They are nearly complete, and the frescoes look like new!"

The Archbishop held up his glass and made a toast.

"To a wonderful and successful papal visit, let us pray…Dear Lord our Father, protect us from harm and make our Holy Father safe during his visit to Florence, our beloved city of the Renaissance. For it is by grace you have been saved, through faith… and it is not from yourselves, it is the gift of God… Amen."

As the soup was served, all three men settled comfortably into their meal. The Monsignor decided to present his simple outline.

"We would like to brief you on the events of the next couple of days. As you know, we will begin with a large mass, then meetings with the clergy, and finally, a student youth rally…everything is all set. On his way to the airport, he will stop at San Marco and meet with the fellowship students?"

The Archbishop clapped his hands together once in delight. "Marvelous! And that's as it should be. It was his doing, after all, that made it happen."

They spoke through the main course about the restoration work and other issues that beset the church of late. Over dessert, Father Delsoni decided to mention the potential bump in the preparation for the papal visit.

"Your Grace," Delsoni said, hesitating a moment longer before continuing, "I feel we must make you aware that we have discovered a small group of dissenters who we think intend to disrupt the papal visit."

The Archbishop frowned and gestured at Delsoni to continue.

"Your Grace, these are Catholic zealots who have been following the Pope in recent years. We have discovered they are now here in Florence. They call themselves the Piagnoni."

The Archbishop looked up in dismay. "Now there is a name from the past. I thought we were long past those days. It reminded me of my religious history classes when I was in the seminary studying the fifteenth century. The last time I checked it is now the twenty-first century?"

Father Fitzpatrick responded now.

"Your Grace, we have been following this group for some time. Until recently, they were active in and around Rome. They are mostly radical Dominican friars who criticize the working decisions of the church since Vatican II. We are doing everything in our power to make sure they do not embarrass Florence."

Although the Archbishop was elderly, he was nonetheless lucid and sharp.

"I would be worried about something happening at San Marco. That's where that preacher Girolamo Savonarola lived back when it was a monastery controlled by the Dominican order. Perhaps some extra precautions there would be a good idea."

"We have already arranged for that, your Grace," Father Fitzpatrick said. "We have closed the museum for the duration of the visit and have executed background checks on the people there, including all the students. We should be good."

The Archbishop responded sharply, "Should be good isn't good enough. I want this visit airtight. Do you both understand?"

Delsoni and Fitzpatrick nodded simultaneously, as they looked at each other. The tone of the Archbishop was clear.

The meal concluded; there was now time for the men to enjoy each other's company. The Archbishop held his wine glass gently in one hand, making the slight tremor more obvious. Although they tried to relax and enjoy this rare time with the Archbishop, they could not take their minds entirely off the day after tomorrow when the Pope was due to arrive. They were, after all, ultimately responsible for his well-being.

44

After dinner, Olivia stepped into the evening light, intending to take a walk in the convent gardens. The double brick wall that extended around the entire perimeter of the compound was eight feet high and topped with a decorative cement cap. There were rows of mature olive trees, trellised grape vines, and large vegetable and flower gardens.

This was not the first time Olivia had walked the cobblestone path to meditate and contemplate. As she walked slowly along the walkway, she noticed someone sitting on a bench in the far corner of the garden with her back to the convent. From a distance, it was hard to see who it was, but as she got closer, she recognized Julia's long hair, streaked with grey, flowing down her back.

As Olivia approached the bench, she called out from a distance so as not to startle the Sister. "Hello, Julia. May I join you?"

In spite of Olivia's attempt to be careful, Julia was caught off guard and turned abruptly, her eyes wide.

"Oh, hello Olivia," she gestured to the bench beside her. "You're welcome to join me, of course. I often come here to think and meditate after a long day. We have been working so hard to prepare for the visit."

Olivia knew Julia was not her friend. From the very first days at the convent, she treated the students brusquely and made sure she enforced the convent rules to their fullest. Because she had been the one to discover Olivia and Finn in the laundry room, there was no telling what was going through her head now. But Olivia was a warm and open person and someone who was able to forgive. She always saw the glass as being half full.

So when Julia slid over and gave Olivia plenty of room to sit down next to her on the stone bench, Olivia was pleasantly surprised and sat. It seemed like ten minutes before Olivia dared to break the silence.

"Julia, how long have you been a nun?"

Julia did not respond at first and then finally said.

"It will be almost fifteen years now. I have been here at San Marco for ten years after having been transferred from a convent in Sienna. The Order of the Immaculate Conception. Do you know of it?"

Olivia sensed the tension ease and replied.

"No, but there are so many orders it's easy to get confused. Is it better for you here?"

"Oh, so much better, I can't tell you. My introduction to becoming a nun was a while ago, and there were many misconceptions back then."

"Really?" asked Olivia, "Like what?"

"I came into the order right after graduating from high school, and the convent system had not changed much in hundreds of years. What they told my family and me was in stark contrast to the reality. Sisters were forbidden to have friendships and were forced to use scourges to dampen their sexual desire. We had little to say about our clothing, our food, and our accommodations. My first cell was very small, and I was forced to sleep on wooden planks. What I sought was to develop self-discipline, to love and serve Jesus Christ, and master my religious skills. But after four years, I had lost any sense of my individuality. I was exhausted from guilt, frustration, abusive behavior, and I was very lonely. I gradually slid into a state of mild depression and then experienced a mental and physical collapse. Finally, at the request of my family, I was transferred here, and that's when things improved. I thank God for that."

Olivia waited a while before responding.

"That's a horror story. My experience with the Felician order has been much different. We are taught to embrace the charisma of the Blessed Mother Angela. Eventually, the call challenges us to live a vowed life of poverty, chastity and obedience, in the spirit of the beatitudes. I have heard that many things in our religious orders have evolved and changed."

Julia looked off as the sun began to set just above the brick wall and seemed to relax slightly, as if she had been waiting a lifetime to tell her story.

"I am sorry about the way I reacted to you and Finn. It was selfish. You represent something I wanted, something we all romanticize about. But misery loves company, as they say, and when Mother Ana Maria embraced your situation, it shocked me. I was jealous and resentful. I realize now that I was not angry with you, but at myself."

Sister Julia took a deep breath before she went on.

"I saw you and Finn leave from the vendor stall the other day at the market. I couldn't help wondering what that would be like, to be in love and enjoy the physical pleasures of a man. I didn't say a word to anyone, and I am not going to. I want the best for you."

Olivia touched Julia's hand tentatively. She empathized with the nun and wondered what she could say that could help. As dusk deepened, a small flock of evening grosbeaks landed in an olive tree nearby. These were robust birds, lightly colored, and more commonly known as finches. Their heavy, conical bills were pale greenish yellow. Julia observed them hopping from limb to limb, searching for fruit. Their song made for a pleasant distraction.

"Love is powerful, and it makes people do certain things. Thank you for keeping this to yourself. We both appreciate that."

Olivia waited a beat before continuing.

"Julia, I have seen you sitting with Sister Mary at dinner. You should nurture that relationship. Friendship can be powerful, and she is lovely. Let me tell you that being here at San Marco is very special. Perhaps you're so close to it, you don't appreciate what kind of life you have here."

Julia turned to Olivia, her eyes silvered with tears.

"Perhaps you're right. I want to be happy here. I wish you the best, Olivia. I admire your courage. It takes a lot of bravery to do what you are doing. I'm proud of you."

As Olivia and Julia walked slowly back towards the convent courtyard, Olivia noticed two men having a conversation at the rear of the kitchen doors. She recognized the new prep cook Josef, talking with Nino, the food deliveryman. They exchanged an envelope. She wondered what that was about? Unbeknownst to anyone, Nino had seen and made a copy of the seating arrangement that would be used to serve the Pope and his people. Josef would now study the document and become intimately familiar with where the Pope would be placed.

45

The Aerodrome Tower at the airport was staffed with veteran controllers, and everyone was briefed on the special aircraft that would be arriving at six hundred hours. The area controllers had eyes on the Falcon 900 Charter jet, just a hundred kilometers out, before handing off the route-landing phase to the Tracon approach controllers. The private jet had been given UEA Class A airspace prior to radio contact.

"Falcon, this is the Florence Airport tower making contact for clearance to land on runway four. You have just entered our airspace, and we have you on radar. We read your altitude at ten thousand feet."

The Falcon had had a smooth trip from Rome and banked east before starting its decent. A large storm had just moved north prior to the jet entering the Florence airspace. The pilot responded.

"Roger that. This is Falcon 610RST47, radio contact confirmed. At vector 233, we are 7.2 kilometers out southeast of Sienna, VOR reducing airspeed."

Everyone in the control room watched the screens as the small jet followed the proper landing procedure.

"Flight 610RST47, your airspace has been cleared for landing on runway four. Welcome to Florence."

The Falcon 900 charter jet touched down on the tarmac at the Amerigo Vespucci airport during the early morning hours before the fog had a chance to lift completely. The passengers hardly felt the touchdown. The exact time of arrival was not published. Only Monsignor Delsoni had the exact information, which he had received only the day before. The jet taxied to a secure location where half circles of black limousines were parked along with six police cars.

Emerging from the jet door and walking slowly down the stairway was a mini Vatican entourage just small enough to fit on the jet, but diverse enough to respond to any unforeseen challenges: a diplomatic crisis, a security breach, and reporter questions. As part of the larger entourage, the Pope's physician accompanied the group in case of any medical emergencies. Father Fitzpatrick and his men, dressed in elegant black suits, surrounded the Pope. Many of the key players on the Vatican traveling team were veterans with decades of experience. The most visible was Cardinal Federico Lombardi, the Vatican spokesman. The sixty-eight year-old Jesuit had years of public relations experience. Cardinal Guido Marini, the Vatican Secretary of State, was never far from the Pope's side.

Father Jonathan Fitzpatrick and his men were aggressive, insisting on procedures that often irritated others. Pope John Paul II was slow-moving as he made his way to the vehicles where his old friend Archbishop Guiseppe Gellini greeted him warmly. The two exchanged kisses on both cheeks and embraced. The entourage looked on as Pope John Paul II knelt down and kissed the red carpet tarmac as an expression of his appreciation for a safe trip and to celebrate his beloved Florence. Cardinal Marini reached down and assisted the Pope up from his kneeling position. The last person to leave the plane was Dr. Benito Guastella, the Pope's personal physician. Dressed in a very expensive dark blue Italian business suit, he was on call 24/7 for the duration of the trip.

Everyone gradually boarded the limousines, which were then surrounded by white police cars of the Carabinieri with their blue lights flashing. The caravan began to move slowly toward the highway. Families, children, business travelers, and airport workers stood watching, their faces pressed to glass windows, hoping to catch a glimpse of the Pope. There had been extensive publicity leading up to the papal visit, and these people felt privileged to experience the arrival. There was no contact with the airport officials, as all the arrangements were treated with state security procedures.

The caravan made its way toward the heart of Florence and the large conclave of San Lorenzo. Although the path through the city had been predetermined, cleared for security, and analyzed by the police, a storm had just blown through the night before and there were fallen trees in a variety of city locations. A large field maple tree and several limbs had fallen on Via MGuattia at the cross section of Via Martelli. As the four-car motorcade came up on what now seemed like a construction site, a large forklift tractor pulled out and brought the motorcade to a halt. In seconds, the agents in Father Fitzpatrick's car were out and surrounding the Pope's limousine, weapons drawn.

The street suddenly became unusually quiet, and the air was tense, as mothers on the sidewalk pulled their children close to their bodies. Fitzpatrick quickly knelt down and looked under the limo as its dark black windows automatically snapped shut. There was nothing unusual under the car. All eyes were on the operator of a large yellow tractor as it scooped up a twenty-foot limb and slowly pulled backwards into a side alley.

He flashed back to an incident in Brazil just two years earlier, when a large passenger bus pulled innocently in front of Archbishop Antonio Castro's car. The bus had been full of gunmen. The archbishop had lost his life in the gunfire. Jonathan Fitzpatrick had been called in to investigate for the Vatican and could now remember the gruesome black and white police photographs. The images were the first thing that registered as he saw the tractor come to a stop in the middle of the street.

While children watched with their faces up against a large glass window from the inside of a small grocery store, it seemed as though people were now scarce. And then a traffic policeman emerged wearing a fluorescent vest and held up a sign with a red circle on top, waving the motorcade through. The debris was cleared, and the cars were free to proceed. As the security detail returned to their car, Fitzpatrick waved to the workers and sighed with relief. As he entered his car, he turned his head towards his men in the back seat and said, "Not exactly the way I wanted this to start."

46

The city of Florence was a place of great celebration, and it was evident everywhere. There were banners and signs throughout the city welcoming Pope John Paul II to Florence. Signs were especially evident at all the events held in his honor. At San Marco, last minute preparations were underway. Every part of the complex had been thoroughly cleaned, including the stained glass windows that sometimes reached several scaffolds high. The nuns had washed, starched, and pressed their habits and each one had been given a photograph of the Pope to be signed at the time of his visit. No one at San Marco, including Father Paggi, had ever dreamed they would meet and spend time in the presence of the Pope. If it weren't for the Art Restoration Fellowship, the visit would not have happened.

Outside the convent, at the front and rear entrances, the Florence Police moved metal detectors into place. In addition, small digital cameras were mounted on telephone poles around the perimeter of the complex to monitor people coming and going to San Marco. The Interpol NATO Intelligence Service had satellite surveillance up and running on the city of Florence with the ability to cross-reference their intelligence. The Archbishop had struck a chord with Father Fitzpatrick when he mentioned San Marco as a possible site for some disturbance, and he had immediately ordered an electronic sweep of the convent as a precaution. Although redundant measures were in place, each person responsible for the Pope's security was concerned about the visit to San Marco in spite of the fact that nothing concrete had been detected.

As Father Paggi exited Mother Ana Maria's office after a brief meeting where they were finalizing all the details, he saw Finn working on a scaffold. He remembered that he had asked about the details regarding the ancient box, so he walked over and greeted Finn.

"Good morning, Finn. Do you have a minute?"

Finn carefully came down from the scaffold and shook hands with Father Paggi.

"Good morning, Father. As you can see, we were just doing some last minute arranging of materials for possible cleaning demonstration during the Pope's tour. Father, what happened to the side of your head?"

Paggi reached up and touched the small bandage. "A mishap in the church. I think the ceiling beams were made for smaller people back then. So, I have heard from the Ministry of Cultural Affairs, and they are very interested in adding the box and its contents to the collection of materials from that period. They have an entire exhibit on Girolamo Savonarola and would like to include it as part of his writings. I asked that they give you formal credit for discovering the antiquity, and they agreed. Congratulations."

Finn smiled. "Wow, thank you Father, but you didn't need to do that. It was just my work here as part of the fellowship. I was just curious whether or not it had any value."

Father Paggi looked around at the interior hallway and thought that the convent had never looked so good. When his eyes returned to Finn, he said, "Don't be silly, you found it and deserve some credit for being so observant. Otherwise, it would have been thrown in the dumpster with the debris. It does have additional historical value, and they were delighted to have it for their collection."

Finn was pleased, and then his facial expression changed.

"Father, there is something else I would like to mention, a prep cook who seemed a bit odd. I saw him rehearsing his movements the other evening after dinner. He made very little eye contact with me when I asked him a few questions. Earlier, I had observed him as he kept repeating his movements. It was like a ritual. I wanted to tell someone. I don't know if it's worth mentioning, but you be the judge."

"Thank you Finn. I will look into it. We cannot be too cautious. I mean, tomorrow, the Holy Father will be standing in this hallway. Listen, I had better let you get back to your work. I will see you tomorrow."

Father Paggi left Finn and headed towards Mother Ana Maria, who was in the foyer giving last minute directions on a flower arrangement.

Father Paggi pulled her aside. "Excuse me, Mother Ana Maria, do you have a moment? Is there someone new working in the kitchen?"

Mother Ana Maria looked puzzled.

"I hired a part time prep cook about a month ago. His name is Josef Dvorsak. He's not here today, but he will be working tomorrow. Is something wrong?"

Father Paggi thought back to the episode in the church the night he'd been assaulted. He had told no one.

"Thank you. I just wanted to know. We can't be too careful. I will let you know if there is a problem."

With the name scribbled on a small piece of paper, Father left the convent and crossed the street to his office. The Via Cavour was crowded as usual with shoppers and children from the St. John Fisher School playing on their recess. When he finally got to his desk, he made a call to the Monsignor whose assistant answered.

"Monsignor Delsoni's office."

"Sergio, it's Stephen Paggi. Can I talk with Monsignor Delsoni?"

"I'm sorry Father. He's with the Archbishop at a luncheon for the Pope. Can I take a message?"

"Please have him call me as soon as he has a chance. It regards a new prep cook hired at San Marco. His name is Josef Dvorsak. Okay? Thank you Sergio."

"Got it. Thank you, Father."

Sergio added the message to a pile on the Monsignor's desk, not aware of its importance. The breeze from the open doorway picked up the messages and scattered them across the floor. Later that afternoon, Sergio picked up the messages and placed them neatly back on the desk, now using a glass paperweight. Unfortunately, the order of the messages had changed.

47

Daresh Oldani had paid for his room through the end of the week, but tonight would be the last night he would sleep at the sleazy accommodation. Nino had picked up the document retrieved from the church crucifix days earlier. Daresh had completed the task of destroying everything in his possession by filling a large garbage bag and disposing of it in a dumpster down the street. He no longer had a wallet, a wristwatch, or a cell phone. He was completely separated from any personal evidence and on his own.

The convent had provided the kitchen staff with a white cotton shirt and black trousers to wear while serving. He kept his underwear, shoes, and black cotton socks. Although he had registered his room under a false name, if it was searched, the authorities would find nothing. He sat down on the floor, crossed his legs and began a routine of breathing exercises before his nine o'clock prayer ritual. He needed to stay calm and focused. Once he confirmed where the Pope was seated, he would retrieve his weapon, cover it with a white dishtowel draped over his arm, and keep it next to his body. When he got close enough, he would take one single shot to the head. He had already decided he would not flee, but drop to his knees and surrender.

He was confident that his presence at San Marco had gone undetected. If he were going to be exposed, it would have happened by now. The high carbon weapon had been planted long before the police arrived on the scene, and because he had buried it deep in a large 50-pound bag of red beans, he was sure it would go undetected. It was only this week he had observed the Florence police at San Marco with a mobile metal detector sweeping the rooms for weapons. The kitchen was the most difficult challenge for the police because everything was made from stainless steel, including the counters, stoves, and refrigeration units. The stock room stored large steel pots for special applications and next to the beans was a box of rolls of aluminum foil. As they did their inspection, he stuck close by pretending to be busy, waiting to see if they discovered the weapon. When they finished, they found the area clean and acceptable. Daresh was relieved. It was another step forward in the plan.

Back in his room he focused on his breathing and eventually entered into meditation. Afterwards, he made his confession of faith prayer, then lay down on the single bed and closed his eyes. As he drifted off to sleep, he could hear the distant sounds of motor scooters racing through the Florence nightlife and he wondered if he would ever own a motor scooter. Later in the night, the reoccurring dream set in.

There were several versions of the dream in which he was ten years old, and his father was ranting about the changes in his Catholic religion. This version of the dream was set in St. Joseph Cathedral, where his family had worshipped as far back as he could remember. His father was standing in the middle of the third row, a place they always sat after getting to the church early. He was standing, and his hands were waving in the air as he pointed his finger at the priest, complaining about the changes to the church since Vatican II. In the dream, everyone around his father was angry at his radical comments and outrageous behavior, but he refused to sit down. He continued to shout at the top of his voice at the priest standing behind the altar, who listened far beyond what would be usually tolerated, and then the priest began to scold his father. The young Daresh saw himself just several seats away from his father, looking to his brother, his mother, and then himself, noticing the three of them had no clothing. The bells of the cathedral began to ring, and large black birds flew high inside the church above the Sacristy. Daresh could now see his father, along with his family, ushered out of the church by large, muscular men, while parishioners' screams of anger trailed after him. As they exited the church in humiliation, they were led to the cart where four elderly men in white robes stood waiting for them. They were all loaded into the cart. The driver, a man who looked identical to the gardener at San Marco, took the family to a landfill on the outskirts of town, dumped them in the garbage and warned them not to return.

48

On the eve of the papal visit to San Marco, dinner was joyous. Everyone was excited and expectant. After nearly everyone had finished their meal, Mother Ana Maria stood up and tapped her spoon against her glass.

"We've made it, and I think we are well prepared. The convent and the church have never looked so good. I want to thank everyone for all their hard work. When the Art Restoration Fellowship was in the early planning stages, we had no idea there would be a papal visit to Florence, but as time moved along, everything fell into place. When I say I want to thank everyone, I mean just that: the nuns who live here, the students who have been studying here, and our staff who work here. If there is anyone who I would like to give special thanks to, it would be Father Paggi. He has been my partner in all the planning and has acted as our liaison to the Archdiocese. Thank you Father. So I hope you all get a good night's sleep and prepare yourself for tomorrow."

Everyone stood up and filled the refectory with applause. All the petty disagreements and personality conflicts vanished, and a feeling of unity filled the room. The nuns were jubilant about meeting Pope John Paul II, and the students felt very privileged to be present during the visit. After returning their dishes, everyone dispersed to take care of their own private matters, and Olivia noticed that Finn walked off in the direction of the church. She couldn't help wondering where he was going. In the evening, the church was mostly dark except for a few small spotlights that illuminated the crucifix and *The Altarpiece* fresco. Finn walked down the middle aisle to the front of the church and lit some candles. He entered the first pew, knelt down, bowed his head, and began to pray.

There was so much to be grateful for. He had a sense that this experience over the past month would be with him for a lifetime. He had studied hard, worked hard, and met wonderful people. Father Paggi had become his friend, and Mother Ana Maria had shown such compassion and understanding. And then, there was Olivia, who had changed his life.

As he had journeyed through his first year at the seminary, he had a vision of his future life. He imagined being placed in a small struggling parish on the southwest side of Detroit and working with a pastor who was elderly and conservative. He could see himself delivering Sunday mass and working hard on his homily. All of that had changed, and he now pictured himself getting married and having a family. He had rehearsed his remarks to the seminary elders, and both feared and rejoiced in their response. He could predict who would be supportive and who would be disappointed, but at the heart of decision was his love and respect for Olivia.

But that day, while working on a fresco, she had noticed Finn talking privately to Vanessa, and their laughter had made Olivia jealous. She said something to Finn afterward and for the first time they exchanged words that sent them walking in different directions. At dinner that evening, they sat at opposite ends of the refectory, out of each other's line of sight. As he prayed now, he could visualize her so clearly, standing just a few feet away.

"Finn? Is everything all right?"

She stood in the doorway, backlit from the hallway. He gestured her to come sit by him, but she chose the pew one behind him and kept about 15 feet of distance between them, even then. Finn sighed.

"I have been praying. I wanted to come here to get away from the tension. Everyone's so nervous. I just felt like praying."

Finn looked up at *The Altarpiece* fresco and said.

"*The Altarpiece* is beautiful, don't you think?"

Olivia crossed herself and nodded her agreement.

"I loved Dr. Morelli's lecture on this fresco. She's brilliant. I didn't know it was also called Madonna and Saints, or about the intertwining of the Dominican religious themes. I'm not sure I understood everything she was talking about, but I guess you did."

Finn knew this was her way of breaking down the barriers between them, so thought carefully before responding.

"*The Altarpiece* is a portrait of the Virgin and Child, seated on the throne and surrounded by angels and saints. Scholars talk about its misuse of perspective, but I think that misses the point. I like the symmetry and formal, balanced use of space. It allows the viewer better to see the painting from a distance, and I think he intentionally makes the Virgin and Child larger in size. That's where the criticism comes from, because if it were accurate in terms of perspective, they would be smaller as the space recedes. I think it is an early example of where the Virgin and Child are together with others, as opposed to being set apart."

"In class you mentioned metaphors," Olivia said. "What did you mean?"

"The two metaphors of perspective utilized in the fresco are the open window and the mirror. The open window metaphor of perspective implies continuity between real space and the space of the image. The mirror metaphor divides the real and the imaginary."

Finn smiled and although they sat far apart, he was confident they were alone. "I'm sorry about this afternoon."

Olivia looked at him helplessly.

"Finn, it was stupid. I…"

Suddenly, Sister Mary appeared at the church entrance. Though they were 15 feet apart and sitting in separate rows, they both jumped as guiltily as they had the night Sister Julia walked in on them in the laundry room.

"Olivia, there is a call for you. It's your grandmother."

Olivia looked at Finn. "Later."

Olivia hurried after Sister Mary to the glass-paneled phone booth not far from Mother Ana Maria's office. She stepped in and closed the door.

"Hello, Grandma."

Eleanor's voice came to her deep as ever, seasoned by years of smoking. "Olivia, how are you? I got the number from your mother, so I thought I'd give you a call. I haven't so much as heard your voice in so long…I miss you. How's the fellowship?"

Olivia swallowed hard, knowing her mother had probably told her about Olivia's plans to leave the order.

"The fellowship had been wonderful. I have learned so much, and now the Pope is visiting Florence, and we may get a chance to meet him. Can you believe it, Nana?"

It was a name she used from her early childhood, and now found her falling back in time with her response. Olivia's grandmother was not a diplomat and often got straight to the point. "How wonderful. But Olivia, your mother mentioned that you have a friend…a young man, and that you're considering leaving the order…is that right?"

Olivia paused and tried to gather her thoughts.

"Olivia?"

"I'm here, Nana. And yes, it's true that I've become close friends with one of the seminarians. I'm not sure where all of this is going."

Having plenty of experience at being a disciplinarian, Eleanor Grandville could easily slip into her role as a principal.

"Olivia, you realize we've spent years and worked very hard to get you to where you are today. I don't want to see you throw all of that away over some infatuation. The Felician Order has put you on a pedestal. Leaving would be a huge disappointment to the order and to me. Do you understand?"

"The last thing I want to do is disappoint you and the order, but God may have a different plan for me."

"Remember what happened to your mother, Olivia. She got picked up by that hippie radical boyfriend at college, and that was the end of her career. I wanted a better life for you. If you pray on this, I am sure you will make the right decision." There was a long pause. "Take a lot of pictures and we can talk more when you return. I love you."

Finn walked slowly by the phone booth and waved, and then headed up to his room.

"I love you Nana. Take care." Olivia cradled the receiver and sat in the booth resting her forehead against the glass. She closed her eyes and took a deep breath. She'd known this time would come. She had just hoped it would wait until she returned to Detroit.

49

The arrival of the Holy Father marked his first visit to Florence as Pope. He had previously visited the city in 1967 when he was serving as Archbishop of Krakow, Poland, and could easily recall the art and architecture of the city described as the birthplace of the High Renaissance. The city and its people were full of energy as Pope John Paul II gathered in the heart of Florence at the Piazza della Signoria with thousands of young people. It was one of many youth rallies designed by the Vatican to provide the Holy Father with an opportunity to speak directly to the young people. The lengthy program included dynamic, well known speakers, and many young people gave testimonies to their faith. Throughout the afternoon, the youth of Florence and surrounding areas had the opportunity to celebrate their love of Christ.

Later in the afternoon, Pope John Paul II held a symposium on the life of prayer and the special relationship with the Blessed Mother. The event brought thousands from parishes within a fifty-mile radius as various local and city officials jammed together to celebrate the Sacrament of Reconciliation. In the evening, the Holy Father addressed the youth for a special prayer service. Catholics joined together in the heart of Tuscany to build a spiritual life, whose shared vision calls all people to action. Within the proximity of the Palazzo Vecchio lay dozens of historic structures, among them the Franciscan Church, San Croce, the Giotto frescoes, the Santa Maria Novella, and at its center, the Duomo surmounting Brunelleschi's triumphant dome.

It was easy to see how art became an instrument of knowledge and research into the city's reality: it was a real science, based on rational theoretical foundations, like the rules of perspective. The key-concept of the "imitation of nature" was based on the contrast between classical and Byzantine traditions but would also be understood as the geometrical organization of the object of the painting within a given space or a panel or wall to be frescoed.

On this picturesque evening, it seemed as though, within the immense gathering of youth, there could have been a young Leonardo da Vinci, Raphael, or Michelangelo in the crowd. It was as if their spirits lived on quietly through the spirits of Florence's inhabitants.

Hundreds of candles reflected off the panels of bulletproof glass that surrounded the Pope's podium, and the crowd quieted as the Holy Father delivered his remarks.

"Dear young people of Florence. As my visit to your city draws to an end, I have come to this place as a pilgrim pastor and servant of Jesus Christ. I have come to proclaim Christ's Gospel of peace and reconciliation. I have come to celebrate his saving action in the Sacraments of the Church, and most of all, I have come to call you to Christ. To all of you here tonight, I say it is in prayer that the Holy Spirit transforms our lives. It is through prayer we come to know God."

Large video screens displayed close-ups of the Pope as he continued to deliver his remarks, and what was once a loud and vivacious crowded, now listened in near silence. His formal remarks would last for a while, followed by a procession from the central square back to San Lorenzo. Throughout the evening, thousands of people would continue to celebrate with over forty youth performances, all of which were designed and carefully planned by the city's Cultural Ministry of Affairs. The evening and its events went on without disturbance or signs of protest or dissent. Co-mingled in the crowd were hundreds of plain-clothes policemen as a security precaution, and the Vatican security around the Pope and his entourage was tight. Thousands of images were captured using remote cameras and scanned through the highly sophisticated identification system two floors beneath San Lorenzo. So far, the visit to Florence had been without incident.

Back at San Marco, Mother Ana Maria had asked Vanessa to help Sister Mary in the kitchen with extra preparations for the Pope's visit. That evening, after they finished their work and over a cup of camellia tea, Vanessa asked Sister Mary about her order at San Marco. "Sister Mary, can you tell me about your order here?"

Sister Mary was shy and always dressed in the same neatly pressed habit. She was often seen with Sister Julia, but with everything going on, Vanessa had never had time to find out about their order. Sister Mary sipped her tea and spoke softly.

"We are Dominicans, called by God to serve Jesus and pray for mankind. Our order was founded in 1206 here in Italy, and we have all gone through a process where we respond to God's calling, consecrating ourselves to Him by public vows of chastity, poverty, and obedience. You might be surprised to know that two of the Sisters here at San Marco choose to be cloistered and contemplative nuns: Sister Julia, and Sister Navara. If you notice, you only see them at our meals. The rest of us are daughters of the church who are faithful to the Magisterium. Our life here at San Marco is one that is regulated by the liturgical cycle and the rule of St. Dominic. The rules of the Papal enclosure oblige us to live within the confines of the convent. We go out for medical purposes only, as volunteers do all the shopping. Our families can visit twice a year and write once a month…friends less often."

Vanessa asked if nuns ever left the order.

Sister Mary was silent for so long Vanessa thought she had offended the nun. Finally, Sister Mary said, "It's rare…but it does happen. There is confusion in the general society about what is a nun and what is a Sister. Sisters often do not live in cloisters, but are out in the world working as teachers, nurses, or missionaries. Nuns are Sisters, but Sisters are not nuns. They both profess their vows, but a Sister's vows are "simple" and a nun's vows are "solemn." It's a technical distinction. When you hear of someone being an ex-nun, it's usually a Sister. Does that help?"

Vanessa looked at Sister Mary's beautiful features and clear complexion. At 5'2" she could not have weighed more than one hundred and ten pounds. Vanessa had heard her play the piano and organ during Mass and envied her talent. All of this made her think back to how much she marveled at her active-contemplative order. It was just recently that she had dreams of her Chapel at Madonna, where she saw herself at the final profession of faith receiving the Felician wooden crucifix suspended on a simple cord around her neck.

50

The Archbishop of Florence, Cardinal Gellini, sat with Monsignor Delsoni over morning coffee while the Pope continued to recover from the previous long day of activity. The Archbishop's staff had created accommodations for the Holy Father and his senior staff at the Basilica of San Lorenzo while the rest of the Vatican team was housed at the Basilica of Santa Maria Novella just a couple of blocks away. Everyone was exhausted after the two-day whirlwind of meetings, presentations, and masses, culminating in a large youth rally. His next scheduled visit was to Milan, followed by a day in Venice and then back to Rome.

The Basilica of San Lorenzo had a large presence in Florence. Dating back to 393 AD, it was the oldest church in the city. The New Sacristy that had been designed by Michelangelo and housed the Medici family tombs flanked the church. One of the largest complexes in the city, it was situated in the center of all activity. Michelangelo magnificently designed the Laurentian Library, and many of the Pope's staff spent their free time enjoying the New Sacristy based on the artist's designs. During the stay, the Pope held a small mass in the Medici Chapel for the priests of Florence. It was something Father Paggi would never forget. He savored the moments where the small intimate mass brought all of his close colleagues together for such a unique spiritual experience. In one of the south transepts, there was a famous painting by Rosso Fiorentino, *The Marriage of the Virgin*, and a favorite of the Vatican staff.

The Archbishop's residence had an outdoor patio on the second floor that overlooked the formal cloistered garden. The morning sunlight lit the west side of the gardens of hedges and pomegranates while the two men chatted and waited for the sounds of the waking city. The

Monsignor sipped a small cup of espresso and managed to apply some cream cheese to his small cracker.

"This has been a perfect visit for the Holy Father. I think he is very comfortable here. I mean look at this setting; it is so elegant."

The Archbishop smiled, paused, and then replied.

"Well, it's not over yet. We need to get him safely on the plane and then I will breathe a sigh of relief. I am always worried about his safety, and this San Marco visit has me nervous. If the Piagnoni is going to raise its head, it makes perfect sense to do it there. It would be symbolic, don't you think?"

The Monsignor did not want to go there, but he knew the Archbishop was right.

"You mean the fact that Savonarola lived and preached from there? I suppose, yes. But we have doubled up on the security there, and I personally made sure the entire area is cordoned off. The perimeter is two blocks in all directions. If there is a protest, the Pope will not see it."

As the two men discussed their concerns, they saw the Holy Father proceeding in their direction. He was making his way towards the patio to join them for breakfast, and although he was inside the interior of the Basilica courtyard, he was still flanked by two Vatican security guards. They watched as the Holy Father walked slowly with his arm around his Secretary of State, Cardinal Guido Marini. The two men would join them shortly, and then the Archbishop turned to Monsignor Delsoni and said. "He is in good health for his age. You know, many Cardinals thought he was too young to be Pope, but he has proved everyone wrong. He played such an important role in ending Communism in Eastern Europe. I think he will go down in history as one of the greatest Popes of the century."

The security people were the first to arrive and quickly surveyed the entrances and exits to the patio. The Archbishop and the Monsignor stood up as the Pope entered, smiled, and greeted his friends.

51

The motorcade pulled out of San Lorenzo through large, black iron gates and moved very slowly up via Cavour. People saw the Pope was seated high in the black limousine behind extra-large windows. Parents, children, shop owners, and tourists lined the famous boulevard, waving affectionately. Children sat on their fathers' shoulders, smiling as the Pope moved his hand slowly in response. The driver was instructed to move slowly to give the bystanders as much time as possible to see the Pope. Four plain-clothes policemen walked briskly at each corner of the long black car, wearing dark sunglasses.

It was a bright afternoon, and the crowds were jubilant, often extending six to seven people deep along the sidewalks. Small girls and boys stood between their parents' legs, waving Vatican flags. The bells at San Lorenzo rang loudly. Up ahead, barricades lined with uniformed policemen demarcated where the crowd ended as seven cars came to a stop. The official yellow barricades were moved aside, allowing the motorcade to pass, and just ahead, the motorcade rolled into the horseshoe driveway at San Marco.

Although the blocks surrounding the convent were cordoned off, people were hanging from second and third story windows to try and get a glimpse of the Pope. Across the street at the St. John Fisher School, the bell tower rang, and the entire school was moved to the second story to watch the caravan pull into the driveway. Gradually the Pope emerged from the middle limousine wearing his all-white traveling clothes, including a white cap on the back of his head. Across the street, he could see children waving frantically, and he responded by waving back and making the sign of the cross.

Father Paggi and Mother Ana Maria waited at the entrance with four nuns at their side. Mother Ana Maria was dressed in all-white habit, and the nuns were wearing their formal all-black habits. The limousines emptied slowly, and then everyone walked towards the entrance led by Pope John Paul II. Monsignor Delsoni got out of his car quickly and accompanied the Holy Father down the walkway to make introductions. There was a lot of handshaking as the Vatican officials walked slowly behind the Pope and his Secretary of State, Cardinal Guido Marini. Inside, beyond the foyer, the young religious students were standing in a group, wearing the uniforms that represented their respective orders, and at their side were four monks wearing their traditional brown robes. They were introduced as a group, knowing there would be a time later for individual introductions.

In the kitchen, the head cook had prepared the sweet bread for baking and was now preparing a special tropical punch with ice. Oldani was busy cutting vegetables: broccoli, cauliflower, mushrooms, and carrots. In the large refectory room, small glass plates and cups surrounded a punch bowl. White linen napkins were set in a long row next to the very old sterling silverware. The entire convent was decorated with flower arrangements. A large bouquet of white calla lilies graced the center of the long refectory table. The papal procession proceeded to the welcoming area and shook hands with all the students before making their way into the church. Mother Ana Maria led her Sisters into the church, and after everyone was seated, Father Paggi led everyone in prayer.

Stationed at the back of the church and throughout the convent, plain-clothes police kept vigilance, and the Vatican security team stayed within four feet of the Pope at all times. Father Fitzpatrick was seated behind the Pope as his entourage all sat together on the south side of the middle aisle of the church. On the other side were the religious students, Mother Ana Maria, the convent nuns, and a place for Father Paggi, who now stood at the altar. He was nervous.

"Good afternoon. We would like to welcome your Holiness and your guests to San Marco. We thank God for your presence here today.

San Marco Convent is a special place located here in the magnificent city of Florence. San Marco, once home to Dominican Friars, is the resting place of forty-two frescoes by Fra Angelico. We thank the Holy Father for his support of the Art Restoration Fellowship that now draws near completion. Without the support from the Vatican, the new restoration work would not have been possible. We believe that it is through the work of the Holy Spirit that these monks and religious students have brought new life to the artwork. *The Altarpiece* behind me is a good example of this accomplishment. Before we embark on the tours, let us pray."

After a short prayer, the students immediately dispersed to their locations at the various frescoes throughout the convent. The monks had designed and orchestrated the tour, which was led by Mother Ana Maria, Father Paggi, and Friar Jeremiah. It was decided early on that Father Paggi would individually introduce the students at each of the seven stations. There were three students at each station to explain that part of the restoration and answer any questions. The seven stations selected for scrutiny were the frescoes: *Annunciation, Transfiguration of Christ, Baptism of Christ, Coronation of the Virgin, Christ Carrying the Cross, Martyrdom of St. Lawrence,* and the *Ordination of St. Peter.* At each station, there was a scaffold, materials, and lights. Before the Pope moved on, a photo was taken of the three students with Pope John Paul II in front of the fresco. Unbeknownst to them, it would be a gift from San Marco to the students on their last day of the Fellowship.

The tours moved along at a snail's pace. Everyone in the entourage had questions. The nuns helped prepare the refectory room where everyone was scheduled to gather at the end of the tours. Finn, Olivia, and Vanessa were assigned to be at the *Annunciation* fresco at the top of the staircase. The students were prepared to answer questions, but they were nervous.

James, Kyle and Deloris were standing at the *Baptism of Christ* when the tour approached their station. They were all wearing white lab coats, protective eye gear, and latex gloves. Jeremiah gave the overview of each fresco restoration, outlining the condition, the problems, and the remedies. Afterward, he invited questions. The Secretary of State Cardinal Barasco Terotone asked a question.

"What restoration work was done to this fresco?"

Kyle took the question. "Your Eminence, most of the work was done to the lighter, more pastel parts of this fresco. That included the Christ figure, the sky and the river. Most of what was removed was candle smoke comprised of soot and wax. After completing the photo examination, we used a sequencing of Rotec and Arte Mundit® to remove the discoloring elements. The monks followed up by replacing the pigmentation that provided a new fresh layer of appropriate acrylic, polymer-based color. You can see the results in the before and after photos."

Kyle handed the photos to the Secretary, who then passed them around to the members of his tour group. Pope John Paul II examined the photos intently. Everyone on the tour was impressed with Kyle's explanation as the photos clearly demonstrated the value of the restoration work. Many walked up close and tried to see where there had been an area of renovation. They could see, after careful consideration, that the monks had taken a tremendous amount of deliberation in making the choice of color pigment to best match the existing work.

The guests were divided into four groups and toured the convent simultaneously, allowing all of them to finish up at the same time. The Pope and four others were accompanied by Friar Jeremiah, ending up at the last station, *The Annunciation* fresco on the second level at the top of the stairway. It was Finn, Olivia, and Vanessa who stood by nervously as the Pope and his group approached. When they came to a stop, Jeremiah began with an introduction.

"Well, here we are at our final stop. This is *The Annunciation*, but not just any, as there are six Annunciations here at San Marco. This one is the most famous. Completed in 1445, the fresco was linked to Luke 1:28, in which Mary is greeted devoutly by the Arch Angel Gabriel, who announces that she will give birth to a son from God.

'Greetings, you who are highly favored! The Lord is with you.'

Of all his frescoes of this scene, none is more popular. These two beings, one human and the other angelic, are inclined towards each other as if engaged in a private conversation. They are looking into each others' eyes with an intensity that makes us feel that something important has happened. The lack of depth delivers a sense of simplicity and quiet understatement. These three talented students skillfully performed the cleaning and removal of candle soot, and I would now like for them to introduce themselves."

This was the protocol used at each station, providing the students a formal opportunity to meet and address the Pope. Vanessa bowed and spoke first, remembering their instructions to keep their introductions brief.

"Your Holiness. I am Vanessa LoDuca from the Order of the Felician Sisters. We live and study at Madonna University in Livonia, Michigan."

"Your Holiness, I am Olivia Gianetti, and I am also a Felician Sister in training from Madonna University, and it has been an honor to be part of this fellowship."

The Pope smiled at the beautiful young girl and nodded before turning his attention to Finn.

"Your Holiness. I am Finn McNelis, and I am here representing the Major Sacred Heart Seminary in Detroit, Michigan. I feel privileged to be part of the Art Restoration Fellowship and enjoyed working on this fresco."

Up until this point, the Pope had said very little during his tour, instead allowing others to ask questions, but this was the last station and he asked.

"Finn, that's an Irish name, is it not?"

"Yes, your Holiness. I am Irish-American on both sides. My Mother is from Donegal, and my father is from Limerick…and I love baseball."

Pope John Paul II laughed and glanced at Cardinal Terotone and then said, "St. Patrick is your patron saint. Perhaps he can help you with your baseball team."

Monsignor Delsoni stayed behind while the tours moved through the convent. He walked around and checked each security location to make sure everything was secure before sitting down at a small table off the courtyard. From there, he could see the groups moving from fresco to fresco. It was a beautiful and peaceful afternoon in Florence, and it was hard to find a cloud in the sky. He took a deep breath and pulled a sheaf of messages from his pocket. He flipped through the papers and stopped at the third message. It was from Father Paggi, dated yesterday, something about a prep cook at the convent by the name Josef Dvorsak. He had seen Father Paggi today, but had not had a chance to speak to him. Monsignor Delsoni returned to the refectory where preparations were still underway, and approached a man who was setting the table with glass plates. The man was in his mid-thirties with dark, short hair, light skin and was dressed in a white serving jacket. The man kept his eyes on his work until the Monsignor spoke.

"Excuse me, could you tell me where I can find Josef Dvorsak?"

Oldani, worked hard to maintain composure. He was shocked at the question. His mind spun in search of the right response. He clenched his teeth, paused, took a breath, swallowed, and then replied.

"He wasn't scheduled to work today, but he will be here tomorrow. Can I help you, Father?"

The first tour group had just entered the room and started to take their seats at the long table.

Delsoni felt some relief. "No, thank you. I'll let you get back to your work." He took the man's response at face value and shifted his attention to the table. Daresh Oldani quickly slipped back into the kitchen to keep himself out of sight.

All this time, Father Fitzpatrick was monitoring his security men via a proprietary walkie-talkie system in coordination with the Florence police force. There were no signs of demonstrations outside the convent, and everything was proceeding as planned. As Fitzpatrick walked the hallway in the direction of the refectory room, one of his men approached him. "Father, one of our scanners just picked this up. A listening device was discovered behind a picture frame in the main office." The man held out a thin device smaller than a dime. Fitzpatrick looked up. The Pope and his entourage were entering the refectory room. His mind raced and his stomach tightened in anxiety that was all too familiar. He raised his walkie-talkie. "Stage four alert. All eyes on the refectory room. I'm on my way."

Three nuns had set up in the corner and were tuning their string instruments while looking over the sheet music. They had rehearsed for many weeks. A string bass, cello, and violin created soft acoustic background of sacred music as each tour came into the room and found their seats. Bach's Agnus Dei in B Minor floated softly through the refectory as the Holy Father entered the room. Still flanked by security, Pope John Paul II was deeply engaged in a conversation with Father Paggi about the life of Fra Angelico. Monsignor Delsoni could tell it was not a good time to approach Father Paggi with questions about his message.

Clearly the Pope had really enjoyed the tour of the restored frescoes. His face radiated enjoyment, and this pleased his hosts and hostesses immensely. Mother Ana Maria's idea for the tour of the restorations was a great success. Even though they were running late, the Pope was led to his seat at the center of the long table as the last tour entered the room. The classical music of Bach and the carefully placed flower arrangements gave the refectory room a lush, sensual feeling that put everyone at ease. As drinks were served, vegetables arranged on long wooden boards were placed in front of the guests, followed by bowls of fresh baked sweet breads decorated with pecans and a dark maple sugar coating. Mother Ana Maria tapped her glass and made the opening remarks.

"Your Holiness, would you grace us with your blessing?"

Pope John Paul II smiled, flattered by the request. He then reached out to those sitting on each side of him, extending his hands, and everyone followed his lead.

"Let us pray. Father, bless our food and the people who gather with me today at the convent of San Marco. It has been such a sacred experience to be here with such kind, devoted people…"

The table conversation was full of what everyone had experienced on the tour and of the holy work of Fra Angelico. Fifteen two-foot candles set at two-foot intervals softly lit the long table as the nuns continued to perform. A casual observer entering the room suddenly would have seen thirty people at a table surrounded by six security men as the nuns played on and the group conversed while enjoying the refreshments. Father Fitzpatrick stood near the doorway and looked out the leaded glass windows for any unusual movement.

The white-coated work staff looked after the guests, refilling their glasses and taking away dishes as they finished. After the food was consumed and the dishes were cleared, a small mint was placed in front of each of the diners. Two workers brought coffee served in ancient china that had been rarely used.

Oldani emerged from the kitchen with a white towel draped over his arm. Finn recognized the man from their meeting a few nights ago. For some reason, Finn continued to watch the man walking slowly in the direction of the Pope. As he turned, Finn caught a glimpse of a gun barrel under the towel. Adrenaline surged through his body as Oldani continued towards the Pope, who was engrossed in a conversation with Monsignor Delsoni. Sitting across the table from Finn, Olivia caught his expression and immediately knew something was wrong.

Finn stood up, scaled his bench seat and placed his other foot on the table. Immediately, the security guards began to move. Oldani now saw Finn on the table and picked up his pace. As he approached the Pope there were reactions around the table, mostly from Finn's erratic movement. People first assumed he was jumping in the direction of the Pope. Some of the guests screamed as Finn lunged at Oldani. Now only fifteen feet away, Oldani had brought his weapon to bear at the Pope's head. The shot rang out, but not before Finn's body hit the assassin with full force. The shot missed its target as the impact of Finn's body knocked Oldani's arm astray. Finn was a much larger person, and his body thrust the assailant to the tile floor as the bullet lodged itself in the refectory wall.

The Pope ducked and placed his hands over his head as a precautionary reaction. Monsignor Delsoni forced his body over that of the Holy Father. People at the table ducked down or backed away. The whole event lasted no more than ten seconds but seemed to play out in slow motion as all the security guards converged on Oldani's body. Finn lay partially over Oldani's small frame, and with his hand, he forcibly pushed the weapon away and kept his body in place. Within seconds, handcuffs were applied to the now docile Oldani, who made no attempt to resist. Immediately, several close aides moved the Pope from the room in the direction of the front door and into his waiting limousine. The entourage quickly gathered themselves and followed, leaving the students, nuns, and security men to take care of the chaos.

Outside, the crowd was thrilled when they saw the pope emerge slowly from the convent as if nothing had happened. The crowd cheered. The Holy Father waved, entered the limousine and the motorcade slowly moved out the driveway and in the direction of the airport. But what had started out as a beautiful event had ended up as an assassination attempt on the life of Pope John Paul II.

Inside the refectory, guards and police carried Oldani out the back door and into a police car. Only Cardinal Federico Lombardi, the Vatican spokesman, stayed behind and ordered Mother Ana Maria, Father Paggi, and Monsignor Delsoni into the front office and closed the doors. Everyone leaving the refectory room was in a state of shock and ordered to wait in the church for instructions. The Cardinal sat behind Mother Ana Maria's desk.

"Okay, this is how this is going to work. I know you are all very upset. It is understandable. Many advised against a stop at San Marco, but the Pope would not be persuaded. He is constantly under attack by his critics, zealots, and terrorists. In this case, it was right-wing revolutionary Catholics. We had been briefed on the presence of the Piagnoni here in Florence, and I would not be surprised if this man were hired by them to assassinate the Pope. The first thing you need to do is forget this ever happened. Let me put it this way…this never happened. There will be no statement or police report. You will need to meet with everyone here today and make them understand that by acknowledging this, it will give credence to their efforts. Even an attempted assassination that failed would be a success for the Piagnoni. Everyone here will have to sign a document pledging to absolute secrecy.

We will be in touch with the Archbishop and he will coordinate with the Florence Police. We cannot give the perpetrators the satisfaction of a news report or any publicity for even a failed attempt on the Holy Father's life. This is not the first time this has happened, and it will not be the last. As you witnessed, our first concern was to move the Pope into a secure environment. By now, he is on his way to the airport. We will give no notice or acknowledgement of this happening, and no one here should do so either. Your job now is to make sure no one, absolutely no one, talks to anyone about this. Do you understand? Of course, there will be a thorough investigation, but that will not take place for some time. Also, what happened today is not your fault. Let everyone here know that this is the nature of our existence, and I am only sorry we could not have discovered the man's presence earlier. Apparently, there were no accomplices, and the Pope is nearly at the airport by now. There is a police car waiting for me, and I need to join him. The Archbishop of Florence will be in charge, and I assume that you, Monsignor, will be the liaison to people here. Do you have any questions?"

Mother Ana Maria wiped a constant flow of tears from her cheeks. Father Paggi, also in shock, wrapped his arm around her shoulders. The Cardinal stood up and walked towards the door and then said, "One last thing. I want the name of that student…the one who jumped the assailant from across the table. Can you email his name and his biographical information?"

52

Finn sat on the tile floor with his back to the wall. He watched the police conduct their work after having removed the assailant from the room. He was exhausted, and although he was scratched up and psychologically shaken, he seemed to be all right. Olivia and Vanessa waited until the police finished and then rushed over to him.

Olivia kneeled beside him. "Are you OK?"

Finn managed a smile. "A little banged up, but I'm okay."

Vanessa kneeled beside Olivia. "How did you know he was armed?"

"I saw a gun barrel underneath the towel over his arm. He was the person I saw rehearsing the other night. I thought there was something weird about that guy. I mentioned it to Father Paggi."

Olivia touched his arm lightly. "You saved the Holy Father's life, Finn. Do you realize that?"

Finn paused, his eyes on Olivia.

"Is the Pope all right? I heard a shot. I assume it missed him."

"He's fine. He's on his way to the airport. All of us have been instructed to go to the church for a meeting. Here, let me help you up."

Everyone in the refectory gathered in the church and sat in the pews near the front. The nuns huddled together, kneeling and praying the rosary. The students sat together, still trying to process what had happened. The monks stood in a circle near the altar, hands linked and heads bowed as they prayed in silence. Two police guards stood just outside the entrance to the church where the large vaulted walkway connected the church to the convent. Streams of colored light washed down the main aisle of the church as it did each late afternoon. Monsignor Delsoni entered the church and sat with the nuns. When

Mother Ana Maria and Father Paggi arrived, they closed the doors behind them. With their heads bowed, they walked slowly to the altar. They kneeled, prayed, and crossed themselves before standing up and facing their friends. Mother Ana Maria walked over and joined her nuns as everyone gave Father Paggi their full attention.

"We have just come from a meeting with Cardinal Lombardi, and I need to brief all of you regarding what has taken place this afternoon, at San Marco. We know you are horribly upset, as are we. We all worked so hard to make this papal visit perfect, and now this. But I want you to know that this is not our fault. Some of us were aware of a clandestine group, the Piagnoni, who often seek to attack the Pope and Vatican policies. We now think this man was hired by the Piagnoni to infiltrate San Marco in advance of the Pope's visit. They were highly sophisticated in their ability to produce false documents that cleared him of all the background checks. But here is the message we have been directed to give to you: this event needs to be completely forgotten. You are not to mention this to anyone. There will be no media reports or acknowledgements to the press. The Cardinal made it clear to us that news of this would only serve the perpetrators' purpose. So all of you can help immensely by keeping what you just experienced secret. Let me just say, this is a formal request from the Vatican spokesman, Cardinal Lombardi. Monsignor Delsoni, who is here with us, has an agreement of confidentiality that we ask everyone here in this room to sign. In addition, you all can be proud of your work in preparing a wonderful reception for Pope John Paul II, and I would be remiss if I did not mention Finn's courageous act. Finn, your actions saved the Holy Father's life."

At first there was a single clap, and then everyone in the church broke into applause that lasted quite a while.

"For now, I would like to hold a brief mass to help us process what has taken place in our lives. It will act as a vehicle in giving us a way to thank God for the health, welfare, and security of our Holy Father, Pope John Paul II. When we finish mass, you can all return to your rooms or places of rest. Remember to see the Monsignor and sign the agreement and not a word of this to anyone. May God bless you all."

53

As soon as he left the convent, Monsignor Franco Delsoni walked briskly in the direction of San Lorenzo. Upon arrival, he passed through the huge Renaissance interior. It was cool, airy and lined with chapels. He crossed the north transept, the oldest part of the present church, which contained the tombs of several members of the Medici family. Monsignor Delsoni walked down the long marble hallway towards the office of the Archbishop of Florence. He had been there many times, but this time was different. He reached the reception desk and looked into the face of a young priest from Sienna. Delsoni was obviously nervous.

"Take a seat Monsignor. He shouldn't be much longer."

Delsoni looked at the clock and realized it had only been an hour since the incident at San Marco, but he knew that the sooner he spoke with the Archbishop, the better. He watched the small color monitor behind the reception desk that was tuned to a twenty-four hour news program, checking to see if anything had leaked. So far, media reports focused only on the Pope's various appearances and ran footage of the Holy Father walking up the steps to his private jet and waving. *Let's keep it that way*, Delsoni thought.

"You can go in now, Monsignor. The Archbishop is ready to see you."

Delsoni slowly pushed open the large, oak door. Archbishop Gellini sat behind his desk, but the chair was swiveled away so that Delsoni could only see the man's back. Gellini appeared to be staring out the windows into the courtyard. Finally the chair rotated slowly to face the room. The Archbishop folded his hands and placed them on the desk.

"I told you I was worried about the visit to San Marco. It was the obvious place for an attack."

No pleasantries, Delsoni noted. A bad sign.

The Monsignor stepped closer.

"Your Grace. I must accept blame for this incident. It was just yesterday we had a tip on this man, and I missed it. Father Paggi left a message at my office, and it fell through the cracks. Once I read it, I pursued the lead while at San Marco, but I ran out of time. To make things worse, I spoke to the assassin without knowing who he was. How stupid of me."

Archbishop Giuseppe Gellini of Florence was an extremely intelligent man who would analyze the situation and follow logic to a conclusion. He had to work at being sensitive and forgiving, but he would not be where he was today if he could not be decisive.

"John Paul is safe and on his way to Milan. That is the bottom line. I just spoke to him while you were waiting. He insisted that this was not an isolated incident and is something they deal with all the time. He told me he loved his visit to Florence and especially enjoyed his visit to San Marco. Can you imagine? Someone tried to kill him, and he enjoyed the visit? He insisted that I do not blame anyone here and that we now put our energy into keeping this from the media. No exposure. Not one word about this to anyone. In fact, the assailant is being transported out of Florence as we speak. He will be detained in Perugia for the time being."

The Monsignor sat down on one of the overstuffed chairs, and he could feel his heartbeat slowing down. He and the Archbishop were friends and had worked together on many things, but this was different. The attempt on the Pope's life, if successful, would have cast Florence and the Archdiocese as reckless with the Pope's life. It would have been a black mark. He wanted to reassure the Archbishop that there would be no leaking of the information.

"The people of San Marco have been briefed and signed a confidentiality document. They are our people, and they will not say a word. I am sure of it."

The Archbishop closed his eyes and moved his head from side to side and then said. "Let's hope so. They want the name and information we have on the student. What's that about?"

"As the assailant approached the Holy Father disguised as a prep-cook working for the convent, one of the male students in the restoration project spotted the man's weapon, leaped upon the table, and knocked him to the floor. If it weren't for his action, the assailant would have been successful. I still don't understand it. We screened those people thoroughly, up and down. We need to review our procedures on that. A highly professional organization obviously placed him."

The Archbishop rubbed his eyes. "Just make sure this doesn't get out. We haven't heard a word as of yet. Let's keep it that way. The Vatican wants no word of this. Are we clear?"

"Yes, your Grace. Again, I personally witnessed everyone sign the agreements."

54

Finn's wrist was swollen, and he had some cuts over his eye. Father Paggi held the boy's arm. When he flexed it slightly at the wrist, Finn winced. He decided it was best to take Finn to the clinic that San Marco residents normally used, largely because he knew the people who worked there, and as it was now evening, most of the clinics would be closing. St. Vincent DePaul Clinic in Florence was only four blocks from the convent, but Father asked Mother Ana Maria to call a car and Finn reluctantly agreed to go. Most of the clinic staff had attended St. John Fisher.

As they entered the clinic, Celeste Bologna, the registered nurse who worked the triage station, greeted them.

Father Paggi greeted her and said, "I've got a young man here in the waiting room that needs some attention. Can you help us?"

"Hello Father, sure. What seems to be the problem?"

"Finn is one of the students working at San Marco. He took a fall this afternoon, and I thought it would be a good idea if we had him checked out."

"Sure thing. Just fill out this form, and we'll take a look. I heard you had a visitor this afternoon."

Father Paggi used his communication skills to respond to a question that was to be expected. Everyone in the neighborhood knew the Pope was in Florence and scheduled to visit San Marco.

"We did. The Holy Father stopped by to see the restoration work. In fact, Finn has been working on restoring the frescoes. It was a great honor to have His Holiness in our presence."

Celeste came out into the waiting room and could see Finn sitting in a chair holding his hand on his wrist. She recognized him as the boy who had asked her to hold onto his box.

She sat in the chair next to him. "Well, hello, Finn. Do you remember me?"

Finn focused on the woman's face, and although she was missing her scarf, he recognized her from their first meeting.

"You held the box for me. I remember your lapel pin, a red cross. You must be a nurse. It's a small world."

Celeste smiled. "Yeah…It seems like every time we meet, you're in a scrape. Come on back with me, and let's see if we can get you feeling a little better."

Celeste took Finn into one of the examination rooms where she checked his vital signs, and then took a small vial of blood. After taking an X-ray of his wrist, she cleaned the abrasion over his eye with hydrogen peroxide and applied Neosporin, and then covered it with a band aide.

When she walked him out to meet with Father Paggi, she said, "The wrist is not broken, just a mild sprain. I applied a small air splint. He'll need to wear it for a few days. I bandaged the scratch over his eye. He's good to go."

"Can you send the bill to San Marco? Thank you Celeste, we just wanted to make sure he's okay before he heads back to the U.S."

"No problem, Father. See you in church."

The sun was now close to setting, and the streets were darkening. As they walked along La Pira Avenue, a chill wind like a tiny twister picked up leaves and debris and swirled them around their legs. Father buttoned up his coat, and Finn zipped up his jacket and slipped his hands in his pant pockets. Marble shop fronts gleamed dully, but restaurant and store lights now illuminated the narrow sidewalk as people scurried along, jackets and sweaters gathered tightly against their bodies.

Finn felt better, but he had something else on his mind.

"Thank you for looking after me, Father. My wrist is a little sore, but I think I'll be Okay. There's something I would like to ask you if you don't mind."

Father Paggi smiled. "Of course. What is it?"

"You know I have decided to discontinue my studies in the priesthood, and I was wondering if I could talk with you about how I have been feeling."

"I know about your fondness for Olivia, if that's what you mean. My office is just up here. Let's get off the street so we can have some privacy."

Father Paggi opened the gate to the playground area of the St. John Fisher School, and the two of them walked to the entrance of Father Paggi's office. The hallway was lit with decorative lamps mounted along the sidewalls that were painted a light rose color. He took out his keys and unlocked the door, then hit the light switch.

"That's better. Sit down, Finn. So how can I help?"

"When I was finishing high school, I would read or hear that Jesus was the truth, the way, and the light. I heard it from my counselors and our parish priest. I wondered from time to time if the priesthood would be my vocation. I decided, after much deliberation, to let the Holy Spirit guide me. So I signed up to attend the program at the Sacred Heart Seminary to prepare for the priesthood. When I met Olivia, I fell in love with her. No question. I've never felt like this before in my whole life and, everything's changed because of it. We will be leaving our orders and getting married sometime in the near future."

Finn paused and frowned. "I feel guilty, like I have misled someone. I don't know how to handle that."

Father Paggi listened to Finn and thought about his own journey. When he was a young man studying to become a priest, his good friend met a girl and got married shortly after their first year together at the seminary. He wanted to help Finn in the best way possible, so he chose his words carefully.

"I can only speak for myself and relate to you what I have learned over the years. First, let me say, that over the past fifty years, over twenty thousand priests have left the priesthood for one reason or another. It is more common than you might think. Some of these men fell in love with a woman after they were ordained and spent much of their time praying and feeling imprisoned as they watched others celebrate their love openly. The good news is that you have not yet been ordained, so in essence, the Holy Spirit has moved you in a new direction. You need not feel guilt about this. You are not yet part of the ecclesiastical institution that requires celibacy. You need to be sure about your decision and then proceed to celebrate your discovery and go on to live a holy Roman Catholic life. Finn, this does not take anything away from who you are as a person."

Finn sat quietly and listened. It was as if all the energy had drained out of his body. A lot had transpired in the past four hours and he needed to rest, relax, and exhale. The excitement was unbelievably high when he'd met the Pope and talked about the restoration of the Fra Angelico fresco, along with the preparations for hosting the visit. And then, his involvement in the assassination attempt on the Pope's life, and now he was sitting across from Father Paggi talking about his decision to leave his training to become a priest.

"Thank you Father. You've been very helpful. When I get back to the Seminary, I will discuss this with my counselor, my advisor, and my priest. I think I'll head back to the convent and get some sleep."

55

It was quite amazing. The next day everything at San Marco was seemingly back to normal. It was as if nothing unusual had happened, and everyone was playing his or her usual role. If there was any mention of what took place, it happened behind closed doors. Everyone knew it was his or her job completely to forget the assassination attempt.

The phone rang in Mother Ana Maria's office just before lunch.

"San Marco, can I help you?"

"Hello, Sister, this is Father Fitzpatrick from the Vatican security team. It's been nearly twenty-four hours, and we have not heard or seen a thing in the media, so that's good. I am calling to remind you that any inquiries should be directed to me here. Are we clear on that?"

Mother Ana Maria had been operating on cruise control since the incident, but she was still very unsettled. Right then she had to work at coming up with a civil response.

"No one has called Father, and I have your number right here."

"Good. Also, we want you to know that everyone did a great job. What happened had nothing to do with your work or your duties, or anyone else at the San Marco Convent, and the Pope had a lovely time."

"Thank you. I understand, Father."

"Okay. I will check in with you in a couple of days. God bless you, Sister."

Mother Ana Maria hung up the phone and asked Sister Julia to step into her office.

"We need to monitor all incoming calls, and especially make sure we do not respond to any inquiries about the events of the Pope's visit. If someone wants information regarding the Pope, give them this number."

Sister Julia nodded, and then asked, "Sister, are you all right? Is there anything I can do to help? I mean, I have never seen you like this."

Mother Ana Maria closed the office door, placed her hands over her mouth and started to cry. It was something that she would never imagine doing, but Sister Julia stepped forward and held Mother Ana Maria in her arms and whispered softly.

"It was horrendous. I know. We will hold ourselves together and thank God that our Holy Father is fine. It was not our fault."

Mother Ana Maria, still in Julia's arms, whispered back. "But I hired him. I put him here."

Julia continued to hold Mother Ana Maria.

"He was professional and cleverly placed, just like Father Fitzpatrick explained. You did nothing wrong. None of us knew. Thank God Finn sensed something and stopped him. We will all support each other and stay strong. Okay?"

Mother Ana Maria stepped back, wiped her face. "Thank you, Julia. I needed to say that to someone, and I am glad it was you. Thank you. All we can do is pray, remain strong and get on with God's work."

56

It was the last evening seminar and Dr. Morelli's final presentation. Just as she walked into the room carrying a large box, Olivia passed Vanessa a note asking if they could talk tonight after the Seminar. It was unusual, because they always talked after class, so Vanessa knew this must be something more personal.

Dr. Morelli set a box on a small table next to the podium, opened the top and passed out copies of her new book, *Art During the Renaissance: An Inside Look*, to all the students. The art history text was just released by her London publisher, Taschen, less than a month ago to rave reviews, and Dr. Mariana Morelli was flying high.

"This is a small gift for each of you. It's something you can take back with you as a reminder of our time together. I can't tell you how much I have enjoyed this seminar. It has been an honor to spend this time with students who are so close to the work of Fra Angelico."

Dr. Morelli brought up the first slide, an illustration of Florence around the year fifteen hundred. It showed the early perimeter of the city and some of the main streets, and the then fortified wall that surrounded the city. She put on her glasses and glanced at her notes.

"During these Renaissance periods, of which we have spent most of our time discussing the life and work of Fra Angelico, I think it is important to place the work in context. The papacy employed most of these artists, and the two major artistic centers were Florence and Rome. To talk about Florence during this period without mentioning Sandro Botticelli, would be a mistake. Not to mention that I am very fond of his work, especially the non-religious paintings, like *Primavera* and *The Birth of Venus*."

The images of each came up on a large screen behind her.

"These were painted for the Medici families and do not rely on a biblical text, but on a more universal theme, a linear rhyme that exemplifies a romantic grace. And let us not forget: Botticelli was influenced by Savonarola, who governed Florence for a brief time."

Finn perked up when he heard the name Savonarola because of the document he had found in a box buried in the Duomo debris. He raised his hand. "Wasn't he the outrageous radical preacher who railed against the Vatican?"

"Exactly, Finn. After the Medici family was run out of town, there was a very short time that Florence was under his influence. In fact, after he had burned much of the art in the Bonfire of the Vanities, he was excommunicated by Pope Alexander VI, tortured along with his two closest supports, and then executed. We cannot be certain how long or how much Sandro Botticelli supported the zealot. But we should not forget the other major artistic influences of the period. Leonardo da Vinci was a master of atmospheric perspective. He is famous for his psychological insight in his depictions of *The Last Supper* and a contemporary personality, the *Mona Lisa*. He was the first to do anatomical drawings that were the first modern scientific illustrations. Raphael followed later and was known for the tonality of his figures, along with near perfect perspective. And then, Michelangelo's talent turned to sculpture in *The Pieta* and the fresco work of the Sistine Chapel."

Finn asked. "I have read about a mural by Leonardo that is hidden behind a fresco in the Palazzo Vecchio here in Florence. Is there any truth to that?"

"For decades scholars have labored to find the lost masterpiece by Leonardo da Vinci. It is believed to be behind a fresco by Giorgio Vasari that was created in the late 1500s. There is an art historian here in Florence, Dr. Mano Cerisano, who is leading the work to find the *The Battle of Anghiari*, hailed by some to be Leonardo's finest work. As we speak, they are bombarding the wall with gamma rays to determine whether or not there is a fresco behind a fresco. Over the years, he has used everything from ultrasound to thermal imaging to radar scanning in an effort to determine the likely location of the Leonardo painting, and has come to believe that a piece of it is directly behind the cerca trova sign in the existing fresco. I think we should know something soon, and hopefully, for better or worse, it will put the question to rest."

Finn raised his hand again.

"What kinds of things do art historians ask when they study a famous piece of art?"

Dr. Morelli looked at Finn and realized he had asked a question that could take an entire evening to answer. Synthesizing an answer was quite a challenge.

"Sometimes they first need to determine how old it is. They are often interested in the chronology, and there are many ways to determine that. By using physical evidence, documentation and stylistic evidence, they try to place it in time. There are many styles, both in the period and in the region, and then there may be personal style. Usually they then shift to subject. That takes them to who made it and lastly, who paid for it. It may have been commissioned by a king, a pope, a museum, a collector, or by a government. And then they may ask, who bought it? They then move on to the analysis of form, composition, materials, and techniques. It can differ slightly when they are considering different art forms, like sculpture versus painting. Some art historians rely on criteria built around a matrix; others rely heavily on the techniques of science. It can vary."

Mariana Morelli could talk about the Renaissance and Florence for days, and the students were spellbound by her depth of knowledge and waited patiently after class for her to sign their books. Although he got there late, Father Paggi attended the last seminar, wanting to learn as much as possible. The in-depth seminars had been so interesting to attend and at times revealed information that would never be discussed. It was through the fellowship that he had met and gotten to know Dr. Morelli. He sensed from her remarks that she was not supportive of the investigative work of Dr. Cerisano, so as the class ended, he approached her privately.

"Mariana, once again, I enjoyed your lecture tonight. These lectures have been so important to the fellowship. You've done such a great job!"

Dr. Morelli watched the students file out of the classroom, distracted by sadness that the fellowship was ending. The students waved and said goodbye as they passed by and thanked her for her work. Eventually, she regained her focus as Fr. Paggi stood waiting for a reply.

"Thank you Stephen. You must know how incredible it has been for me. I rarely have such well-prepared and motivated students. I think this whole fellowship has been an important project, and you and Mother Ana Maria should be congratulated."

Stephen blushed and fumbled with his next question.

"Can I ask you about the lost mural project that came up in tonight's lecture? I got the impression that you're not supportive of the investigation headed up by Dr. Cerisano."

She was not prepared for his question, nor was she comfortable expressing her personal view about the research project. She didn't want to appear as someone who was opposed to discovery. She gave herself a moment to think, and then realizing she could trust Stephen and that he was a friend, she carefully gave her response.

"Stephen, this is my life's work. I have studied da Vinci since I was an undergraduate, and I have a great deal of admiration for his body of work. He was an Italian Renaissance polymath: painter, sculptor, scientist, and even writer, whose genius, perhaps more than that of any other figure, epitomized the Renaissance humanist ideal. I think you know he is widely considered to be one of the greatest painters of all time and perhaps the most diversely talented person ever to have lived. In addition, I have lectured on his work and written extensively about his life. If the discovery of this new mural connects him to the work of Girolamo Savonarola, it will be a huge blemish on his life and his reputation. So, I guess I feel like we should leave well enough alone."

Stephen was surprised at her response. He had not revealed the contents of the box to anyone except Francesco, who'd helped him open and translate the documents. He recalled the drawing and decided to share the discovery with her.

"Mariana, let me tell you something that is not known to anyone at this point, so I ask you to keep it secret. A very old rosewood box was found during demolition at the Duomo. Among its contents was a drawing. The notes describe it as a preliminary sketch for a mural to be executed by da Vinci. It is a pastoral scene that includes Mother and Child. It is not an end of times depiction that many believe to be *The Battle of Anghiari*. They may be successful in finding the lost mural, but it's not going to be the violent mural everyone is expecting."

"How do you know this, and how sure are you that this drawing was intended to be the mural?"

"I have had it examined by an expert, and he authenticated the da Vinci drawing. There were documents in the box that were sealed with a wax stamp that dated back to the 1500s. We will have it carbon-dated, of course, and you will be welcome to see the documents, but the note detailed the proposed mural and the location, which is right in the place they are looking now. So, this might help you with your dilemma."

"That's incredible! Thank you, Stephen, and I would like to see the results, but it does put my mind at rest. Thank you for sharing this."

57

Vanessa and Olivia sat quietly on a bench in the moonlit courtyard. The finches gathered in the olive trees to gather fruit and a train could be heard in the distance. Olivia finally spoke softly.

"I am leaving the Felician Order."

Vanessa's eyes and mouth opened wide.

"No. You're kidding."

"I am not kidding. I am going to meet with my advisor as soon as I get back. I wanted to tell you sooner, but I was waiting for the right time, and. ...time got away from me."

"Why? And why now, after this incredible experience here at San Marco? I would think if anything, this would strengthen your commitment to your faith."

"My commitment to my faith has not changed. It's probably stronger than ever, but I have decided on a different life, because...I have fallen in love."

"With who?"

"Finn."

Vanessa was an extremely intelligent young woman, but she lacked intuition. Although she knew Olivia and Finn were friends, she did not know about their involvement.

"Finn and I have spent a lot of time together, mostly during our free time, and we have fallen in love. I have wanted to tell you, but I was afraid, and I wanted to make sure. Now I'm sure. I love him, Vanessa. I've never felt this way before."

"You've done a good job keeping it secret. Does anyone else know?"

"A couple of weeks ago, Sister Julia walked in on us in the laundry room. She immediately told Mother Ana Maria and Father Paggi. She called us into her office, but instead of being angry, or shipping us home, she was very supportive. I think Father has been counseling Finn. We are both leaving our studies, and we want to get married. I am so happy. Does it shock you?"

"Oh my God, yes, but I'm happy for you. I mean the Holy Spirit can move in mysterious ways. If this is right for you, then God bless you both."

Olivia started to cry and Vanessa put an arm over her friend's shoulder.

"I will always be a devout Catholic," Olivia said, sniffling, "but I will work to serve God in a different way, and I would like for you to help me. Advise me on how I should tell my school teammates about my decision."

"Have you told your mother?"

Olivia nodded. "It was one of the hardest things I've ever done, and she had to tell my grandmother, but in the end and after much explanation, she wants what is best for me."

They talked non-stop late into the night, as Vanessa wanted to hear all the details. It was a tremendous relief to tell Vanessa about her relationship with Finn and how this would now impact her life back at Madonna. As the moonlit courtyard finally became dark, Vanessa and Olivia made their way to the dorms, hand in hand.

58

The office at San Marco was busy dispensing plane tickets and passports and making arrangements for ground transportation to the Florence Airport. Mother Ana Maria was making preparations for the final day of the Art Restoration Fellowship. She had made plans for a send-off dinner followed by a graduation ceremony. She was going over her checklist when the phone rang.

"Hello, San Marco."

"Hello, Mother Ana Maria, this is Monsignor Delsoni. How are you? I trust you haven't had any inquiries regarding the Papal visit?

"No, Monsignor. It has been quiet here, but busy. We are preparing for the graduation ceremony for the students. How can I help you?"

"Could you send Finn over to San Lorenzo tomorrow morning around 11:00 a.m.? The Archbishop wants to have a few words with him. In fact, if you and Father Paggi are available, we would like to have you come along."

"I can't speak for Father Paggi, but I can surely come."

"Good. Make sure the boy's presentable. I'll call Father as soon as I get off the phone. See you tomorrow. God Bless."

Monsignor Delsoni called St. John Fisher and asked the secretary to locate Father and bring him to the phone. Delsoni held on while they tracked down Father Paggi, who was out on the playground with the upper school students.

"Hello, Franco. What's going on?"

"Stephen, the Vatican has sent a letter of recognition for the student who stopped the assassin, Finn. We would like to give it to him personally tomorrow, and we're hoping you can join us. Mother Ana Maria has already agreed."

"Sure, I can do that."

"Great. Eleven o'clock. Just come to the front gate. They'll have your name. See you then."

Non-clergy was rarely invited to the Archbishop's office, so Father Paggi and Mother Ana Maria were a little nervous. The gate guards asked their names and immediately found them on the morning memo. The three of them proceeded up the stairs and down the long marble hallway until they came to the office that displayed the Cardinal's seal juxtaposed over the flag of Florence. The young priest at the desk knew Father Paggi and opened the door as the Archbishop and several members of his staff, along with Monsignor Delsoni, sat waiting. Monsignor Delsoni stood to greet the three of them as they stood on the long, intricately woven red carpet ten yards away from the Archbishop.

"Your Eminence, may I introduce Father Paggi, Mother Ana Maria, and Mr. Finn McNelis, the student from the Art Restoration Fellowship.."

Because of the secrecy around the event, the audience was very small, just the Archbishop and Father Bianco, his personal aide. The Archbishop spoke up. "Of course, we met at the San Marco dinner. Enough with the pageantry. Come closer, please. Let's not make this too formal." All three walked forward and stopped just five feet short of the Archbishop.

"Thank you, Father Paggi and Mother Ana Maria, for coming along with this young man. Mr. McNelis, you must know what this is about?"

Finn looked sheepish. "Not exactly, your Eminence."

"Well then, let me explain. Our Holy Father, Pope John Paul II, would like to recognize you for your act of bravery. So he has drafted a personal letter thanking you. To show his appreciation, he wants you to know that you and your family will be invited to visit the Vatican at your convenience. Your round-trip expenses and accommodations will be provided. Congratulations, Mr. McNelis. In the name of the Father, the Son, and the Holy Spirit. God Bless you, my son."

Finn smiled and felt incredibly humbled as he stood and shook hands with all those in the room. Mother Ana Maria gave Finn a huge hug, which came as a surprise. He wasn't sure whether or not he was supposed to say anything until there came a moment when it quieted down and he could tell everyone was expecting him to respond.

"Thank you, your Eminence. This comes as a shock, and such recognition humbles me. What I did was instinctive, or perhaps the Holy Spirit guided me. I want to thank you and the Pope. I am grateful for this honor and will cherish this forever."

"What you did was extraordinary, and you should be proud. Finn, you saved the Holy Father's life."

No one but the Archbishop had known in advance about the particulars of the meeting, so everyone was as surprised and shocked as Finn. They all knew this was a generous gift.

The small group mingled and congratulated Finn on his award as Father Bianco brought in refreshments on a rolling cart. The Archbishop managed to separate Finn and Father Paggi from the others for a minute and spoke quietly.

"Finn, I am also instructed to say that there is a position available to you if you're interested, working at the Vatican. Cardinal Lombardi, spokesman for the Vatican and His Holiness, is in need of an assistant. You would be housed at the Vatican, continue on with your studies, and be liaison to the Vatican newspaper, L'Osservatore Romano. Give it some thought and let me know what you decide. It would be an extraordinary opportunity. Just let us know your decision before you return to the U.S.."

Archbishop Gellini moved on, leaving them both speechless. Finn looked at Father Paggi.

"Did you hear what I heard?" Finn asked.

"I sure did. They offered you a position at the Vatican. Not an internship or a work-study program, but an actual assistant position to Cardinal Federico Lombardi. He handles all the media relations for the Vatican. I can't think of a more desirable appointment. I think you should give it some serious consideration. How's your Italian?"

Finn shook his head from side to side. "Not that good."

The ceremony came to an end as the Archbishop exited the elegant green room. Father Paggi, Mother Ana Maria and Finn didn't say much as they navigated the labyrinth of medieval streets that encircled San Lorenzo. Mother Ana Maria left in another direction to visit a friend, but not before congratulating Finn again and making Father Paggi promise to pick up a bag of organic onions at the market. While Father shopped, Finn watched people gather fruit, vegetables, and clothes as the market slowly merged with vendors selling antiques, and local artisan goods. All of this would normally be interesting, but Finn was distracted. He had a deep sense of appreciation for what had been bestowed upon him, and he was now faced with a decision. He knew there would be support from his family and his fellow seminarians, but what about Olivia? *Should I accept the offer?* he thought.

He would have to have a serious discussion with Olivia as soon as possible.

The cool breeze gave Finn and Stephen a reason to walk quickly north in the direction of San Marco. As they walked up Via Martelli, past the Palazzo Medici Ricardi, and museums and monuments, they were forced to weave their way through groups of art students studying at the Academia. They approached San Marco Square and stopped to let traffic pass. Finn looked over at the two ornate rams heads that adorned the gates to the Medici Gardens. Finn flashed back to the times when he and Olivia found sanctuary in the park from the busy streets. It was Olivia who reminded him that this was once a place where the young Michelangelo studied drawing. The large herbaceous borders and upright conifers that surrounded the 16th century garden were pruned to form an enclave that provided fleeting intimacy. *And now this,* he thought.

59

With the exception of large multiple scaffolds set up in the church to clean and restore *The Altarpiece* fresco, all the equipment and materials were packed up and ready to be returned to the suppliers. Mother Ana Maria and the convent nuns had worked hard preparing for the final dinner on the last night before the first group of students left for the states. For the flight back to the U.S., the students were divided into two groups. Ten students, including Olivia and Vanessa, would leave on Friday, and the other ten, including Finn and Kyle, would leave on Saturday. The nuns who had performed for the Pope's visit set up in the refectory and the long tables were decorated with candles. As everyone got their meal and sat in their normal spot at the table, Father Paggi stood to give the blessing.

"Dear Father, we ask that you bless this food for our final supper together. These young students from the United States have enriched our lives and brought a dimension to San Marco that we will cherish for some time to come. May they all have a safe journey back home, and remember to keep in touch with us here at San Marco. In the name of the Father, the Son, and the Holy Spirit, Amen."

The evening supper lasted much longer than usual. There was no pending evening seminar to attend, just some final packing. After everyone had finished his or her meal, Mother Ana Maria tapped on her glass.

"Well, to describe these past eight weeks as uneventful would be misleading. I know I could never thank you enough for being here and restoring the frescoes to a condition people have not seen for hundreds of years. As a result, we are now planning to expand the museum area to include the rest of the convent. This will provide the public with the opportunity to see more of Fra Angelico's work. None of this would be possible without your hard work. From all of us at San Marco, thank you. We have a small gift we would like to give each of you, so when I call your name, please come forward."

Mother Ana Maria, as part of the project budget, had created a photo of each student, standing by his or her fresco with Pope John Paul II. The photo was mounted on a small piece of walnut with a brass plate inscribed San Marco Art Restoration Fellowship. For each student who came forward, Mother Ana Maria had prepared a few remarks.

"Kyle Larson, you've been such a pleasure, and we will miss your humor, but I must say, our food costs will diminish considerably. Vanessa LoDuca, thank you for help that went far beyond the call of duty. We wish you well as you return to your Felician Order at Madonna University. Olivia Gianetti, you have graced us with your kindness and your help with the children at St. John Fisher. I know the Sisters will miss your support and friendship."

The evening proceeded as, one by one, Mother Ana Maria fashioned remarks that made each student feel incredibly special. She saved Finn for last.

"Mr. Finn McNelis, last but not least. None of us knew we were in the presence of a super hero! From the very first day when your suitcase opened by mistake, and you walked in sporting a baseball jacket, I knew you were special. If it weren't for you, Finn, this project, these people here tonight, and this entire convent, might be in a different place. So I have saved this moment to announce that just yesterday, Father Paggi and I had the pleasure of accompanying Finn to San Lorenzo where he received special recognition from the Vatican. We owe Finn our thanks and our gratitude for what he did. We will miss you Finn and in addition to your photo, we have a special gift for you."

Mother Ana Maria sat down, and Father Paggi stood up and handed Finn a baseball that was signed by everyone in the room.

"Let this be our gift to you and remind you of your time spent here with friends."

There was an extra amount of applause saved for Finn as he stood, blushing, holding the signed baseball. Olivia looked at Finn with love, respect, and admiration. She knew they needed to talk before they left for home.

Later that evening, people were talking in groups throughout the convent, saying their goodbyes and exchanging information. Earlier, Finn whispered to Olivia to meet him later in the courtyard. They both wanted to talk and spend some time together before their flights back home, and each of them was anxious about what lay ahead, like notifying their schools about their decision to leave the program. They had both been given advice and knew to notify their advisors respectively, but after being selected for the fellowship, they knew there would be some disappointment.

Finn walked into the courtyard where Olivia sat at the end of the marble bench at the back of a long corridor. The moonlight lit her face in profile, and Finn marveled at her beauty. She was dressed in a simple black skirt and an off-white blouse. A tiny gold necklace bore a small cross. Olivia's high cheekbones caught the light as she turned to him, smiling.

"Hey, good morning."

"Good morning. Did you get enough accolades tonight, my now famous super hero?"

Finn laughed. "It's ironic. People were congratulating me on this and what it meant to my vocation, while all along I was thinking how short-lived this career might be."

Olivia caught the end of his sentence and said. "Might be?"

"The Archbishop took me aside and offered me a position in Rome at the Vatican in the office of Cardinal Lombardi. He heads up the media relations. I have to make a decision before I leave for home."

Olivia went silent and turned away slightly to hide her emotion. Everything she envisioned for her future began to melt. She tried not to cry, but as Finn gently pulled her shoulder around so that she faced him, tears rolled down both cheeks.

"I haven't made my decision yet. I wanted to talk with you first. I want you to know how much I have been thinking about you, and I want to start a new life with you, and now this."

"This is a once in a lifetime opportunity. You need to take this, Finn."

"I am going to call home, hopefully tonight, and talk with my family."

"So...what does this mean for us?" she asked.

Suddenly they were interrupted by Father Paggi who stood at the edge of the courtyard, gesturing at Finn to join him and a few others. "Finn, hey Finn. Can you come here for a moment?" Father Paggi motioned again.

Finn waved at Father Paggi, then turned quickly back to Olivia. "We need to talk more, but I'd better go." said Finn, disappointed, and in a hushed voice he added, "No matter what, I love you Livi."

Olivia watched him jog gracefully to the waiting group. Fifteen minutes ago the sight of him would have made her glow. Now she was terrified. She walked back to the main building found the nearest restroom and threw up in the toilet. Fortunately, she was alone. She looked in the mirror and wiped her eyes. Things were changing.

60

Father Paggi was at the convent right after completing morning mass at St. John Fisher helping load the bus and making sure the first group got off smoothly. Vanessa brought her luggage down early and visited the church while the others finished last-minute packing. Olivia spent some of her time with Julia, exchanging phone numbers and addresses. Finn walked up and helped her with her luggage.

"I tried to call home, but no luck. I told Father Paggi to let the Archbishop know that I would be interested in the position, so let's see how that goes. I will see you for sure as soon as I get home and hopefully meet your mom."

Olivia had a blank stare as if she knew that was coming. Right now she was on autopilot and going through the motions of leaving, which seemed to help her contain her emotions. Everyone began loading onto a small bus and Olivia got a last word with Sister Julia.

"If you ever have a chance to visit the United States, please come to Michigan and stay with us. I'll show you around and introduce you to the Felician Sisters. And if I am not mistaken, there may be a Dominican Order nearby. I will check. God Bless you, Julia, and thanks for everything."

Olivia gave Julia and Mother Ana Maria a big hug and wiped away her tears. Finn stood back and watched, wishing he were leaving on the first flight. He helped load the last suitcases onto the bus and gave Olivia a hug.

"Good morning and have a safe flight. I'll see you soon."

The wind that morning had a cool chill, and Finn had his baseball jacket zipped up. The bus was loaded and ready to leave when Vanessa came running out of the convent, the last to get on the bus. Everyone waved, and Mother Ana Maria placed her arm around Julia. The students and the people who lived at San Marco had formed a bond that would stay with them for years to come. As the bus pulled slowly out the driveway, Jeremiah called out to the remaining young male students.

"Okay, I need some help getting the scaffolding down in the church. Could you guys give us a hand? It shouldn't take us more than a couple of hours."

The large truck from the supplier pulled up and parked close to the back door, making the job a little easier. To clean and restore *The Altarpiece* fresco in the church required twenty-six scaffold frames that extended five units high. They started at the top, Kyle and Finn removing the side bracing and then lowering the main frames down. Once the braces and frames were lowered, they then removed the planking that supported the standing platform.

The bus ride to the train station was unusually quiet, as everyone seemed to focus on the quaint urban landscape of Florence. They passed the large basilica, Santa Maria Novella, and recalled a luncheon they'd attended in their honor. Across the street was the cemetery, and just down the street, they passed a small church, San Barnoba on Via Guelfa. The pigeons, the street vendors, school children, and tourists mingled along the small ancient streets. Each student, in their own particular way, felt a profound effect as a result of their experience at San Marco, and as the bus pulled up and stopped at the Station Centrale, the sound of trains coming and going made them realize the fellowship was ending. Vanessa reached into her purse and searched for her rosary.

"I can't find my rosary." She said to Olivia. "I think I left it in the church pew this morning."

"You can call the convent from a pay phone at the airport and have someone check. I have some change."

The short train ride was smooth, and the process of checking in and proceeding through security moved along without difficulty. Their wait for boarding the United 747 jet was about forty-five minutes, so Vanessa searched the area near her boarding gate for a pay phone. As she unfolded the small piece of paper, she tried to remember where she sat in the church that morning. I must have set it down next to me, or maybe it fell, she thought. The phone rang and rang, much longer that she expected, and she started to get worried until finally someone answered in a small, faint voice.

"Hola, San Marco."

"Hola, this is Vanessa calling. Whom am I speaking to?"

With a heavy Italian accent, the woman responded. "Hola, Vanessa, this…is Sister Rosario. How can I help you?"

"Rosario, I think I left my rosary in a church pew this morning, and I am calling to see if someone could look around for me. I think it is in the second row off the center aisle, on the east side of the church."

Rosario was having difficulty understanding. Of all the nuns in the convent, her understanding and use of English was the most elementary.

"Rosario, can I speak with Mother Ana Maria or Julia?"

"They are not here. Everyone ran down to the church. There is a big problem."

Vanessa frowned and wondered if she understood the question.

"Problem? What kind of problem?"

"One young man is very hurt."

"Which one?"

"I am far from him. He is facing down and wearing a sport coat. They call for medical."

Vanessa completely disregarded her issue with the rosary and tried her best to get more details.

"Can you tell me anything else about his condition?"

"No, he was unconscious. There is some blood. Father Paggi with the boy. The medical to come. You call again?"

"Okay, thank you, Rosario."

Vanessa hung up the phone and suddenly felt nauseous. All she could think of was one of the seminarians lying face down on the church floor. She realized that she would have to tell Olivia as she heard the boarding call for her flight come over the public address system. She rushed back to her gate and could see half of her group had already boarded while Olivia waited, searching the crowd for her. She cut into the line next to Olivia where she stood holding her boarding pass.

"There you are. I was worried about you. Did they find your rosary?"

"There are going to look for it."

The stewardess took Olivia's boarding pass and tore off a portion. Vanessa looked frantically in her purse and finally pulled out her pass and handed it to the woman. She was upset. *When should I tell her?* she thought.

61

The jumbo jet lifted off the runway right on time, quickly gained altitude, and gently banked west. Olivia and Vanessa sat next to each other, and both felt less anxious after the captain removed the 'fasten your seat belt' indicator. Vanessa had to work at acting normal while all along she was thinking about the conversation with Rosario. She finally realized that the sooner she talked to Olivia the better.

"Olivia, you know that call I made to the convent…it rang forever and eventually Rosario picked it up."

Olivia pushed back in her seat and pulled a paperback book from her purse.

"That's odd. I don't ever remember her working the desk. She doesn't know a lot of English."

"Exactly. She said there was an accident in the church and everyone rushed down there. She told me someone fell from the top of the scaffold, someone wearing a sport coat, and they had called for an ambulance. She said the young man was unconscious."

Olivia felt faint, as if all the blood had left her head.

"It couldn't be Finn. He doesn't even own a sport coat. Is there some way to make a call so we can find out who it was? What about these phones in the seat backs? Can you call the stewardess?"

The stewardess came quickly.

Vanessa asked, "Is there any way we can use this phone? It's an emergency."

"You'll need a credit card."

Olivia didn't have one, but Vanessa had one that her parents gave her in case of an emergency.

"How does it work? Can you help us?"

The stewardess swiped the card, entered the flight number, and then the convent number. The call connected as Vanessa listened to the ring, but there was no answer.

"No answer. We'll try again later."

Olivia laid her head back and closed her eyes.

"How could that have happened? Those scaffolds were secured, and the monks made sure they were safe. I wonder who fell? And who would be wearing a sport coat while they were working?"

Vanessa placed her hand on Olivia's shoulder. "We're going to have to wait until we can talk with someone who has more information… and better English. Try to rest. We have a long flight."

An hour later as Olivia napped, Vanessa tried to use the phone again and this time, as the large jet flew 30,000 miles above the Atlantic Ocean, there was an odd busy signal. The Airphone system worked well over a populated landmass, but had trouble connecting over oceans. They both knew that the communication at the convent was difficult after having tried to contact their families during the fellowship. The only phone in Mother Ana Maria's office was often left unattended, and the Italian telephone service was, on a good day, average to poor. They both realized the connection to the convent would have to wait until they reached Detroit, which just made the situation direr.

62

The flight landed at Detroit Metro early in the morning. Olivia's mother was waiting in the luggage area as passengers disembarked from a long flight from Florence, Italy. Helen had not seen her daughter for more than eight weeks, and she'd missed her more than ever before. When Olivia had left, her plan was to become a Felician Sister. Now that had changed. Helen could not wait to see her and talk with her face to face about what exactly had happened. Finally, she saw Olivia with Vanessa coming down on the escalator.

Olivia's stomach was in knots. She was exhausted and worried about the possibility that it was Finn who'd fallen. As the escalator moved slowly downward, she could see her mother rushing to the place where she would step off. Once she was in her mother's arms, Olivia started to cry.

"Honey, what's the matter?"

"Something happened to a seminarian after we left. Vanessa called the convent from the Florence airport, and one of the nuns said someone had fallen from the top of a scaffold. I don't know who it was, but it could have been Finn."

Helen clung to her daughter as she cried against her shoulder, something she had not experienced since Olivia was a young girl. Olivia and her mother were as close as a mother and daughter could be. As Helen held her daughter in her arms now, she soothed her as best as she could.

"You don't know the details, right? Please, don't think the worst. Let's get your luggage, and when we get home, you can call the convent. Okay?"

As they waited for the luggage, the girls and their families mingled together and listened to stories about San Marco. Vanessa's parents were happy to see their daughter back and in good health. She'd decided at the last minute to travel in her distinctive Felician garment, making it all the more noticeable that Olivia was dressed in street clothes. Olivia could see from the expressions on their faces that they had questions and remembered that Vanessa said she had mentioned to her mother Olivia's plans to leave the order. She spoke to Vanessa's mother.

"In case you're wondering or have heard something, I have decided to leave the order. I should say it was a hard decision, but things had changed in my life, fortunately before I took my vows."

Vanessa's family were conservative Catholics and respected her enough to not ask her more than was offered. There would be plenty of time for that when they saw her privately. The luggage finally appeared, and everyone headed off in the direction of their families' cars. Olivia gave Vanessa a hug and said to her in a whisper, "Thank you for everything. I'll call you."

Vanessa looked into Olivia's eyes with sadness and apprehension. The long flight had given her time to think about what Rosario had said about the sport coat.

"Olivia…please don't overreact to this, but you know how I told you Rosario described the seminarian as wearing a sport coat. No one would have been working in a sport coat. Maybe she means a sports jacket, like…"

Olivia's eyes widened, and she flashed on Finn wearing his baseball jacket just before they left for the airport. She covered her face with her hands and started crying.

"Oh, God, Vanessa, am I being punished? Is God punishing me for what I did?"

Vanessa placed her hands on Olivia's shoulders and pulled her close.

"No one is punishing you and we don't know if it's serious. It might be nothing. Wait until you get home, call the convent, and get a hold of someone who can explain what happened. And call me as soon as you know something. Okay?"

Olivia walked slowly back to her mother who was waiting near the exit to the garage. Her mother could see that her conversation with Vanessa had affected her.

"What happened, Livi?"

Olivia shook her head.

On the drive home, Olivia told her mother stories about her time in the fellowship, starting with her first encounter with Finn when his suitcase had accidentally opened, and she'd helped him get his clothes back into it.

"There I was, folding his underwear and placing each garment back into his suitcase while all the nuns watched. You should have seen him blush. So we gradually got to know one another because we were in classes together. Then, about two weeks into the fellowship, there was a night when we were alone in the laundry room."

Olivia's mother was glued to the conversation, experiencing the romance vicariously. As they entered the subdivision, Olivia could see their house.

The Gianetti's house was a small, two-bedroom brick ranch that was tucked away in a subdivision built in the 1960's on the outskirts of Detroit. Over the years, her mother had worked hard to make the mortgage payments and keep up with the expenses of owning a home. It was the only investment she had, and after her husband's unexpected death, she relied heavily on her family for support. Olivia always had a part-time job, and together they managed to get along on a tight budget. They depended on each other for financial and emotional support. When Olivia received financial aid from Madonna University to attend the Felician Order and complete her undergraduate studies, it was as if a gift came down from God. With only one semester left to complete her BA, she wondered if she would be allowed to finish school, even though she was leaving the order.

They pulled up the driveway and unpacked their very old station wagon and brought Olivia's luggage into the house. Olivia was happy to be home. She noticed slight changes in the way the furniture was arranged before entering her bedroom and threw herself onto her bed. It was so much more comfortable than her cot at the convent. She opened her suitcase and pulled out the bag of gifts for her mother and went to the kitchen where Helen was making lunch, a cheese omelet with onion and bacon, Olivia's favorite.

"I brought you some things from Florence."

She handed her mother the bag containing the gifts. Inside were three items: a rosary from St. Lorenzo, an Elizabetta silk scarf and a plaque with a photo of her standing next to Pope John Paul II and the fresco she worked on.

"That's Finn standing next to me. Isn't he handsome? Everyone had his or her picture taken when the Pope came around to each fresco. Do you believe I met the Pope? What an experience. I can hardly describe what it was like when all these people from the Vatican came to San Marco to see the work we did. We were so proud."

Helen looked at the photo for a long time, holding the rosary and scarf in her other hand before she said. "It's incredible. And thank you. These are beautiful gifts. I love everything. Let's put the picture in the living room so everyone can see it. I am so proud of you, Livi."

"Oh, that's another thing, Mom. He calls me Livi."

The leaves from a large oak tree in the front yard had fallen, and there were three pumpkins on the porch that had already seen their first frost. She loved the fall season in Michigan, and in some ways she had a new appreciation for their home and its amenities. She opened her purse and found her small address book, looking for the information she wrote down about San Marco. She found the convent phone number and dialed. It would be seven p.m. in Florence. The phone rang and rang, until finally someone picked up.

"San Marco, how can I help you?"

"Hello, Rosario? This is Olivia calling from the U.S. I am home in Michigan."

"Hola, Olivia. You okay?"

"Yes, everything is fine. I just got home, and I heard there was an accident. What happened? Was it Finn McNelis?"

"I do not know. He is with hospital."

"Rosario, can you call me at my house as soon as you know something? It's very important. Here is my phone number."

Olivia slowly gave the phone number to Rosario and asked her to repeat it back. She again asked her to call her as soon as she knew something. Helen had stood close by during the conversation.

Olivia looked tearfully at her mother. "She didn't know who had fallen, but I asked her to have someone call me. I'm so worried, Mom."

"I'm sure he is getting the best of care and they are doing everything they can. Try not to think the worst."

63

Finn finished packing his suitcase after returning from the hospital, knowing now that Kyle was in recovery and his condition was upgraded to good. Finn had kept his promise and given his baseball jacket to Kyle that morning just after the first group had left for the airport.

The bus engine was running as the last of the luggage was loaded, and Father Paggi and Mother Ana Maria stood outside the convent making sure everyone was on board. The accident had affected everyone, especially Jeremiah, who felt responsible for the brace letting go. After close inspection, it was obvious to everyone that the bolts and cotter pins had rusted. The good news was that Kyle had only suffered a severe concussion and some lacerations to his forehead requiring stitches. The prognosis was good, and he would be released from the hospital within days. Father Paggi now focused on getting the remaining students on the bus and on their way to the airport in time for their flight. After Finn loaded the last piece of luggage, he turned to Father Paggi.

"I don't know how I can thank you enough. It's been an honor to be here and something I will never forget. Both you and Mother Ana Maria did a great job organizing and supporting this fellowship. I promise I will stay in touch. May the Lord be with both of you, Father."

"And may the Lord be with you, Finn. It's been a pleasure, and don't forget to write me a letter and give me an update on how things go at the Vatican. I am sure they will be supportive. If the Vatican doesn't work out, send me a wedding invitation."

The late fall was still pleasant in Florence, but as the season ended it had gotten chilly. Lately, during the misty fall nights, the moon had shone on the streets and refined their shabbiness into something ineffably strange and mysterious. The Arno still swept along without a sound, and the pale tenements hung above it like a challenge to their architecture. Street cleaners were out more frequently now, sweeping up hickory and oak leaves. In some ways, Florence remained richer in pictures, and its history impregnated the neighborhoods with decorative detail and glowing forms. Even the San Marco and St. John Fisher neighborhood projected a feeling of melancholy and Florentine splendor.

As Father Paggi and Mother Ana Maria stood together in front of the convent, the St. John Fisher bell tolled. It was bittersweet. The fellowship had come to an end and all the students, with the exception of Kyle, had returned home. The most recent report from the hospital indicated that Kyle was recuperating from his injuries and could be released earlier than expected. Father Paggi placed his arm around Mother Ana Maria, as he often did, demonstrating his affection and support. He thought back to the earliest meeting that was held more than a year ago where the idea was first hatched, and they then decided to write a proposal to seek the financial support needed from the Vatican. Along the way, there were hurdles and minor setbacks, but together they endured.

The fellowship had accomplished the first phase of the overall project. The luminosity of the images was back to near original condition. The second phase was to expand the museum to include the upstairs rooms and all the dorm wing cells. As they walked slowly towards the convent entrance, Father Paggi turned to Mother Ana Maria.

"Well, they're off and let's pray they have a safe trip home. I'm off to the hospital to check on Kyle, but I just want to say that you did a great job on this project, and Florence will always be proud of what's been done here."

Mother Ana Maria's eyes watered up. She was proud of her fellow Sisters and the hard work they demonstrated over the past eight weeks. Gone was the interpersonal bickering and complaining. For her Sisters and herself, this would be something they would never forget. She smiled at Father Paggi.

"I'll check the flight arrangements for Kyle. Let me know how he is doing when you return."

64

The second flight of students from Florence to Detroit took off on time with everyone aboard and landed in Detroit ten minutes early. A day earlier, Finn had made a quick call to his family letting them know his flight plans. His family was eager and excited to see him after an absence of more than eight weeks. They were waiting for him in the luggage area when he stepped off the escalator. His brother held up a large sign that read, "Welcome Home Finn."

There had been only one lengthy call home over the eight weeks, and that was when he talked with his mother about having met Olivia and what it meant to his future. She had been supportive his whole life and had weathered his ups and downs. His parents had had some time to digest this change in his life, but right now, all they could focus on was the excitement of his return.

There were hoots and hollers as everyone competed to hug him first. This was a large Irish Catholic family who loved their prodigal son. Finn was equally excited to see everyone as he worked his way through his siblings until he finally reached his mother. He had missed her more than anything and could not wait to feel her embrace. She would be the one to whom he would confide his situation with Olivia and his plans to take a position at the Vatican. As always, he knew she would deliver the message to his father in a way that he could not refuse. As he hugged her, he whispered in her ear.

"Does everybody know?"

"No, just your father. I have missed you, Finn."

By the time they reached the house, his grandmother had set the table for a feast. She had been cooking all day and loved it when her grandson came into the kitchen.

"Hello Nanny! I see you're cooking for everyone, just like the day I left. How are you? I have missed you!"

Finn had to bend down to hug his grandmother who had not changed from what seemed like his earliest recollections. The small, slightly overweight, cheerful woman with white hair and a smile that lit up the room always cooked with a pint of Guinness not far away. As the dinner was served, Finn began to talk.

"Okay, so you have heard a lot, but something else incredible happened, along with enjoying the fellowship. I met a wonderful girl."

His oldest sister quickly said, "But Finn, you're studying to become a priest."

Finn's parents were quiet as they observed everyone's reactions and expressions. The young girls were animated and crazy about the idea. His brothers were quiet and didn't say much. Everyone was surprised. This was a family earthquake, a ground-shaking event that affected everyone. Finn's oldest sister turned to her mother and asked.

"Mom, did you know about this?"

"Well, he called me about three weeks ago and told me about Olivia and his plans. I told your father, and we talked about it. We just want what is best for each of you, and if God has a new plan for Finn, then we are happy for him, but I wanted all of you to hear it from him, not us."

Finn spent much of his dinner conversation explaining the fellowship work at San Marco, the discovery of an ancient box, meeting Olivia and the arrival of Pope John Paul II to Florence.

"The people at San Marco weren't positive the Pope was coming until a couple of weeks before his arrival. Once we had confirmation, everyone was so excited. Apparently the Vatican helped sponsor the costs of the fellowship, and the Pope was particularly fond of Fra Angelico's frescoes. Mother Ana Maria had hired a part-time prep cook weeks before the Pope arrived, and it turns out he was planted by a right-wing conservative Catholic group called the Piagnoni. They are a small radical group of dissenters, mostly Dominican priests, who railed against the Pope's position on Vatican II. They had been mostly protesting, but now they were planning an assassination. I had seen this new person rehearsing his steps one night, and it looked suspicious, but apparently his paperwork had been checked and cleared. So after a tour of San Marco, we were all seated at dinner in a large room they called the refectory room, and this guy came out of the kitchen with a towel over a gun. I saw the gun barrel from where I was sitting and jumped him before he got to the Pope."

Finn's family couldn't believe what they were hearing. His parents were floored by the story, and everyone at the table had questions. His father blurted out, "It sounds like a spy novel!" and then his mother. "Did the gun go off Finn?"

"It did, but the bullet went into the wall."

"My God! You could have been killed, Finn!"

"Well, I guess so, but it was just an instinct. Anyway, the church has offered me a position in Rome working for Cardinal Federico Lombardi. He heads up the media relations for the Vatican."

Finn's mother interrupted. "But what about Olivia?"

"I know. It's been hard to sort this out, but I told the Vatican I would give this a try. They have arranged for me to start immediately. In fact, I have a ticket to leave for Rome tomorrow. I need to talk with Olivia. It's hard, because we started making plans to get married…and now this."

Everyone suddenly got quiet, and they could tell there was some apprehension in Finn's voice. He was obviously torn. Because he had already talked with his mother about his feelings for Olivia and leaving the seminary, she was surprised.

"You told me you love this girl, right?"

"I know Mom. I fell in love with Olivia, but an offer like this is so rare, I think it's worth a try. So, I need to get over there, meet her mother, and talk with her some more."

The dinner had lasted more than two hours, and everyone was happy to see Finn and hear about all his experiences. The children all had responsibilities for clearing and washing the dishes, and it gave Finn some time to talk privately with his mother and father. While everyone went to work, they walked into the living room and closed the doors.

After sitting down, Finn's mother said, "We will support you in whatever you decide. Just make sure you know what you want."

The mood in the house was joyous. Everyone was proud of Finn and now, more than ever, they wanted all the details. After doing the dishes, his sisters started with non-stop questions and their conversation went on and on until Finn looked at his watch and realized he wanted to make sure he had time to go over and see Olivia before it got too late. He asked his father if he could borrow the car, and within minutes he was on his way to Livonia. He held the steering wheel with his left hand, while at the same time, holding a map that was hand written by Olivia, something she had quickly given him the night before she left. He gradually followed the map and watched the addresses until he spotted a small, two-bedroom house in the middle of a small subdivision. He parked on the street.

Finn looked in the mirror and ran his fingers through his long hair. He was excited about seeing Olivia but nervous about meeting her mother. He wanted to make a good impression. He stepped onto the porch and rang the doorbell. It seemed to take forever before Helen came to the door.

"Hello? Can I help you?"

"Mrs. Gianetti? Is Olivia home?"

"She is in the backyard. Can I say who's calling?"

"Yes ma'am. My name is Finn McNelis. I am a friend of hers from the fellowship."

Helen looked at this beautiful young man a bit confused. "Come in Finn. She told me about you, but..."

The backdoor slammed, and they could both hear Olivia in the utility room at the rear of the kitchen.

"Olivia, you have a guest."

"Be right there."

As she walked slowly through the kitchen and into the living room, Finn said.

"It's me. Good morning, and how are you?"

Olivia put her hands up to her face, and then rushed into Finn's arms. He was surprised at her reaction. It was more than he expected, especially in front of her mother. And then she kissed him. Now Finn was shocked at her response. There was something happening here that he didn't understand. She was trying to talk through her tears, but he couldn't understand her.

"Livi, what's going on?"

She wiped her face, and tried to calm down.

"We called the convent from the airport and they said there was an accident. Rosario said someone wearing a sport coat had fallen and was seriously injured. I assumed it was you." She wiped away more tears and tried to calm herself as Finn began to explain.

"I didn't know that. I mean... I didn't know that you had called. No one told me, but it was hectic around there, and everyone was busy. It's true, there was a terrible accident. I had given Kyle my baseball jacket that morning, and he was wearing it when the scaffold came down."

"And you're all right?"

"Yes, of course. Look, I am fine. Now I realize why your Mom looked so confused when I told her my name was Finn."

Helen sat listening, not far away. She was happy for her daughter and now anxious to meet and get to know Finn.

"How was your trip?"

Finn started laughing. "Great. I just came from my parent's house where I have been telling everyone about you. They all had a ton of questions."

The phone rang, and Helen left the room. Finn's face changed.

"Livi, what we talked about that night in the garden, about me working at the Vatican. I had to make a decision before I left Florence."

The color drained from Olivia's face.

"I gave them my decision that I would accept the position. I wanted to talk with you and tell you that night. I want you to know how much I wanted to start a new life with you, and now this."

Olivia had trouble responding, but finally cleared her throat and said softly.

"This is an incredible opportunity. I wouldn't want to marry you and have you always wondering if you made the right decision. Do you know what I mean? You have to take it. I understand that."

Finn had wanted nothing more than to look into her eyes again, and now he could hardly force himself to look at her.

"This has all happened so fast. But I want to try this and see how it feels…do you know what I mean? But no matter what, I love you Livi."

She stepped away from him and wiped her face dry with her sleeve.

Finn asked, "Will you return to your order?"

"No."

Olivia felt completely calm now. When her mother returned to the living room, she introduced Finn properly in the way she had rehearsed for days. Helen then asked about Kyle.

"So how is Kyle, and what happened?"

"Kyle volunteered to go up and loosen the braces. As he climbed up, he grabbed on to a brace that broke loose. He suffered a concussion and some cuts to his head, but he should be home in a few days."

Finn turned to Olivia and asked, "How was your flight?"

"It was terrible. I was sure something had happened to you and we couldn't get information. I'm so relieved that you're alright"

"I talked to my family about the job offer in Rome, and they thought it was exciting and a great opportunity. The Vatican has already made my flight reservations for tomorrow afternoon."

Olivia worked hard to conceal her emotions, and Helen made up an excuse to leave the room.

"Wow, that soon? I thought it would take a while, and we could have some time together."

"I did, too. But the position has been open for a while, nearly six months, and they are anxious to get it filled. I'll be able to come home to visit, and maybe you could visit me there."

"We'll have to see. I need some time to sort things out, but I am happy for you Finn. You're going to do a great job."

Finn reached out and held Olivia close. With her head buried in his shoulder, she started crying, and Finn said softly, "I am sorry about this. Everything has happened so fast. It's hard for both of us."

Olivia wiped her eyes and stepped back. "I haven't had time to process all of this. I haven't even talked with my mother about how things have now changed, so I have to do that first. It feels as though my life has been turned upside down – twice! I guess I need to pray."

Finn pulled her close and kissed her on the forehead. "I still love you, Livi, more than ever. That has not changed."

65

Finn sat at his gate having arrived an hour ahead of his departure time. He hadn't slept well. As he closed his eyes, he thought he might be able to take a catnap. He thought maybe that would help, but when he closed his eyes, all he could see was Olivia's face and the look in her eyes when they'd parted.

Finally, his flight was called, and he got in line with his boarding pass. He noticed a couple of young nuns dressed in Felician habits. From where he was standing, he couldn't see their faces clearly, but it reminded him of Olivia and Vanessa when they first met at the convent. *Had that been only two months ago?*

Finn managed to sleep on the overnight flight and wiped his face with a warm cloth as the wheels touched down in Rome. It was as if he hadn't left Italy. Although the flight was perfect and all the arrangements were in place, Finn was as confused as he was excited.

He was to be employed at the Vatican, carry on with his seminarian studies, and work for people close to the Pope. He had never been to Rome, Italy's largest and most populated city. The only knowledge he had of the city was via a couple of PBS programs and his uncle's photographs while he was stationed in Rome during World War II. As a child, he would listen to his uncle tell stories about the rise of power by the Italian fascist, Benito Mussolini, and how much his uncle loved Italian women.

It took forever to disembark the aircraft. When finally he rode down the escalator, his backpack slung over his shoulder, he saw a man dressed in a black suit holding up a sign that read 'Finn – Vatican City.'

The first few days at the Vatican were a whirlwind. Much of his time was spent going through a thorough orientation that started with getting him settled into his dormitory accommodations, then continued as a tour of the Vatican grounds. Introductions were made to those who worked at the Holy See, and he registered for his seminarian classes. He soon realized that people from all parts of the world came to the Vatican to study, and he was placed in the Institute for Advanced Catholic Studies as a second semester sophomore. He had been in Vatican City four days before he was summoned to meet with Cardinal Lombardi for the first time.

As Finn left his small dorm room located on the fifth floor behind the Vatican Museum, he marveled at the diversity of religious apparel. Priests from various orders, friars and monks all wore different "uniforms," and the nuns wore either black habits, white starched dresses, or blue uniforms, all representing different orders.

The Cardinal's office was located in the Palace of the Governorate on the second floor. Finn approached the building, noticing the Swiss Guards posted in uniform on each side of an insignia identifying the various Cardinal offices.

66

A week later, Olivia went to Madonna University for several appointments. Her mood was dark and gloomy. She had managed to get through the initial group meeting the sisters had after returning to Detroit, but could not find the energy to share her impressions. The hardest meeting was with her advisor, Sister Ariel Modera, where she had to explain why she would be leaving the Felician order.

Her advisor had brought in her Mother Superior, hoping to convince Olivia to stay on and give her decision more time. The discussion went on behind closed doors for more than two hours, where Olivia found herself alternately crying, confessing, and pleading for forgiveness. But she was determined to terminate her path towards becoming a sister. In the end, the final arrangement was that she would be allowed to finish her studies but she would have to work in the Madonna pre-school as compensation for her college expenses. There were more papers to sign than when she entered the order, but as it neared the end of a long and emotional afternoon, she came to the realization that the decision to leave the Felician order was complete and now behind her.

Both her advisor and her Mother Superior gave Olivia a hug and wished her well as she closed the thick oak door to a small conference room. It was one of the hardest things she had ever done. As she walked slowly down the long shiny hallway, she felt empty. She stopped at the open chapel doors, and then walked down the aisle to a pew where she knelt on the riser. She bowed her head and began to pray.

She needed a life jacket. She asked God for forgiveness. She asked God for understanding, especially for what she had put her family through with her decision to leave the order. At home, her mother lay in bed with a mild case of pneumonia. Olivia prayed for her grandmother who was beside herself over her inability to dissuade Olivia from leaving the order. She prayed for Finn and asked that God help him sort out his life. After an hour alone in the chapel praying, she crossed herself and quietly left the chapel.

Vanessa had been back at the convent and carrying on with her studies. She was on her way to the bookstore when she saw Olivia leaving the chapel and ran to catch up to her.

"Olivia! Hey! Wait up?"

Olivia was caught off guard, but seeing Vanessa felt good.

"I just had my termination meeting, and I feel pretty awful. Got a minute? Can we talk somewhere private?"

They both knew of a small study room just down the hall that was seldom used. Olivia began their conversation before they reached the room.

"I've been here all afternoon explaining my decision to leave the order. I met with Sister Ariel and Mother Superior."

The room was open as they entered and closed the door behind them. There was a light film of dust on top of the table and two chairs. Although these small study rooms were needed when the convent was operating at full capacity, it was obvious the room had not been used for a while. Out of habit, Olivia kept her voice low.

"So I guess you heard it wasn't Finn who fell from the scaffold. It was Kyle. Finn had given him his baseball jacket, and that's where the confusion came from. When Finn got home, he came over and…"

Olivia's eyes welled up, and her voice failed her for a moment. Then she continued and told Vanessa about Finn's job offer and his decision to take it.

Vanessa put a gentle hand on Olivia's shoulder. "How can that be? After all your plans, and leaving the order?"

Olivia started crying so hard she had to cover her face with her hands.

Vanessa opened her small purse and rummaged through to find some tissues.

"How did you leave it with him?"

"I told him he should take the position and give it some time, that I didn't want him always to be wondering what it would have been like. Do you know what I mean?"

"Maybe he will discover he doesn't want that life."

Olivia wiped her face and blew her nose with the soggy tissue.

"Oh sure," Olivia said. "He's living on the Vatican grounds, working with the Cardinal and going to school in Rome. Who wouldn't want that life?"

"There is so much you don't know Olivia. Things could change overnight. You need to clear your mind, pray, and use work and family to distract you from this. Use your friends, too. I'm here for you."

"Thank you for being here with me. I needed to talk with someone, and I'm so glad it's you."

Olivia looked at her watch. "I need to get home and help my mother, but I'll still be taking classes and working here in the preschool. Can we visit?"

The two stood and embraced before leaving the small room and heading off in different directions. In the parking lot, Olivia realized that Vanessa was a very close friend, someone she could trust, and she thanked God for Vanessa.

67

Cardinal Lombardi sat at a desk that looked more like a glass conference table. The windows against the south wall stretched from floor to ceiling and looked out over the Vatican gardens. The Cardinal was dressed casually in khaki pants, a black shirt with a traditional white collar, and a red kippot on the back of his head.

"So you're Finn?" the Cardinal said, his strong voice reverberating on the high ceilings. "I remember you. You're the young man who saved the Pope's life in at San Marco. Welcome to the Vatican. I'm glad you're here. I needed somebody in this position. I understand you're going to resume your priesthood studies while you work here for me."

"Yes, your Eminence."

"Well good. I am assigning you to work with Angelo Bersonti. Have you met him yet?

"Not yet, your Eminence."

"Enough of that 'your Eminence' stuff. You don't need to use the formal address with me. Of course, if you should come in contact with the Pope, then it's always 'your Holiness.' Bersonti is the editor of the L'Osservatore Romano and will give you your assignments. I head up our communications efforts, but you won't have direct contact with me. Bersonti's a good fellow, and I'm sure you will learn a lot from him. I will see you now and then, but all of your daily contacts will be with Angelo. Are you familiar with our newspaper?"

"I have looked at it a few times, mostly since I have been here in Rome. Before that, I would sometimes take a look at it on-line."

"Well, that's a start. He will gradually work you into the way we cover events and slowly give you work that may seem small, but everyone has to gradually work their way up to writing full page articles. Do you like to write?"

"Yes, sir. I wrote for our seminary newspaper for a while, but as you know, I was away in Florence."

"You'll do just fine. Let me know how you're doing now and then, and good luck with your studies. I have to run. I'm late for a meeting. Nice meeting you again, Finn."

Over the next several months, Finn moved around in the various departments, which included the publishing house, the archives, and the press office and ended up in a small office at the Vatican Press Service. It was there he wrote articles on the Pontifical acts, the College of Cardinals, and a very long series on the struggle for religious freedom in third world countries. Along with the editor, Finn took an extended trip to Bulgaria, Poland, and Rwanda, where he did extensive interviews with a group of African Bishops.

In Rwanda, he found prisons overflowing due to political protests that were often accompanied by late-night arrests by soldiers of the new regime and arbitrary executions of those merely accused of being with the former Hutu militia. Finn wrote an article for the news service where he reported that "many Rwandans, both Hutu and Tutsi, say they are afraid to drive at night because so many cars are stolen at gunpoint by men in uniform."

The travel and writing were good experiences, and there were times when he loved the work, but attending his seminary classes gradually became less interesting, and he found himself extremely interested in writing and journalism. When he was assigned to cover the sex scandals that were beginning to plague the Catholic Church, he saw a side of things unfamiliar and uncomfortable.

Just as the Pope's health began to decline, allegations emerged of physical and sexual abuse in large cities in the United States. Pedophile priests were moved around from parish to parish in large cities like Boston, Philadelphia, and Los Angles. Finn was assigned to help cover the Bernard Law case, where the Archbishop of Boston was shown to play a role in protecting priests accused of abuse. Finn traveled to Boston to cover the trial of John Geohgan, who was convicted of indecent assault and battery for improperly touching a ten-year-old boy. Geohgan was sentenced to ten years in prison.

Finn's editor liked his work, especially the way his writing represented the Vatican's positions. The work began to take its toll on Finn after he wrote an article for the L'Osservatore Romano on the case of Reverend Paul Shanley, who was convicted of raping a minor and sentenced to fifteen years in prison. The most worrying element of the story was the church cover-up. The idea of becoming a priest was becoming less and less attractive. He was happiest when he was back in his dorm room, surrounded by the serenity of the Vatican grounds, reading books and occasionally listening to a baseball game.

68

The Vatican Museum cafeteria was always crowded at lunch, partly because the seminarians were given free meals. Recently renovated, the cafeteria next to the museum bookstore was a destination for all Vatican tours. Finn looked forward to his walk through the Vatican rose gardens before arriving for lunch. Although he usually sat with other seminarians, his schedule was changed that morning, and he arrived at the cafeteria late. As he sat alone at a small table against the windows, he noticed a young mother struggling to manage her three young children. As the mother drew closer with three children in tow, he could see she was expecting a fourth. They sat a couple of tables away, and she gave each child a small treat and had them take a seat. The oldest child, a girl of six or seven, ignored the mother's offer and was in and out of her seat as the mother did the best she could to keep them all together. The eldest girl reminded Finn of his youngest sister when she was that age, long dark hair and beautiful features except her mannerisms were odd. Before long she was out of her seat and walking in Finn's direction. As she got closer, her angelical face and green eyes seemed to glow. She was obviously in a world of her own and did not hear her mother calling her back.

"Elizabeth…Elizabeth, come back this way."

As she walked toward Finn, she used her hand to touch each arm on the cafeteria chairs in a ritual that could have been playing or counting, but something told Finn it was deeply sub-conscious. As she passed Finn, she made no eye contact.

"Hey there. How are you?" said Finn gently as she passed by.

The young girl ignored Finn's question as well as distant calls by her mother. Finally, her mother pulled herself up from her seat, leaving the children unattended, and chased down the girl, grabbing hold of her hand gently and walking her back to where the children were seated.

Visiting the museum with three young children was a balancing act. Each child vied for its mother's attention in one way or another. The younger boy pulled on his mother's skirt asking for another treat, while the one-year-old started crying. In only a few minutes, the oldest girl was once again out of her seat and walking in Finn's direction. As she drew alongside him, she stopped and looked, not at him, but beyond him toward the cafeteria windows. From the corner of his eye, Finn could see her mother getting up from her seat.

Finn spoke to the girl quietly. "Hey, I think your mom's looking for you."

When she got to Finn's table, the mother looked to Finn first and smiled, then gently grasped the girl's arm.

"Come on, Elizabeth, let's not bother the nice young man. Let's get back to our seats. I am sorry. I hope she's not bothering you."

Finn smiled. "She reminds me of my youngest sister. How old is she?"

The mother glanced back nervously to make sure her children were in their seats.

"She just turned seven. She loves to explore. There's so much stimulation here."

"Well, you have your hands full. Have a great time, Elizabeth."

The girl acted as if she did not hear Finn's voice and continued to count the clouds outside the cafeteria windows. The mother was gentle with her daughter, and Finn detected some protective behavior on her part. "Thank you. I think we'll be alright. Come on Elizabeth. Let's find our seats."

Finn had seen a child very much like this at St. John Fisher school in Florence once. Father Paggi told him they were in the process of evaluating her for a mild form of autism call Asperger's Syndrome. The young five-year-old boy could not pick up on social cues and lacked inborn social skills, such as being able to read others' body language, or start or maintain a conversation. The boy did not like changes in his routine or taking turns talking. He was unable to recognize subtle differences in speech tone, pitch, and accent that altered the meaning of what was being said.

The mother began to walk her daughter back in the direction of her siblings, who by now were quietly playing, when suddenly Elizabeth broke loose from her mother's grasp and ran back to Finn. As she reached his chair, she came close and looked directly into his eyes before whispering, "You need to follow your heart."

Finn was taken back. "Excuse me?"

By now the mother was clearly exasperated and had decided to leave the cafeteria. She rounded up Elizabeth once again, apologizing to Finn, and herded the children out.

Finn watched as they moved along, wondering what had just happened, when the girl turned her head in Finn's direction and said again, "You need to follow your heart." He could not hear her clearly but could easily make out the words, and then finally he saw her shaking her head from side to side. She was saying no.

69

At the end of each school day, Olivia always spent time picking up toys and materials before she started organizing her plans for the next day. She put the tables back in order and upended the chairs on top. The three- and four-year-olds in her preschool class of twenty-three never failed completely to exhaust her by day's end. She looked forward to that afternoon time when she could enjoy the silence and unwind.

Autumn in Michigan was coming to an end, and there was a cool sharpness to the air. Most of the colorful leaves had fallen from a row of sugar maples along the rear of the school property. Dressed in the traditional blue pleated skirt and white blouse, she stood looking out through the large vertical windows at the university campus. Students, including Felician sisters, dressed in their brown habits walked along the brick walkways to their cars. Olivia loved the fall colors. It was as if nature had finished using its paintbrush and was now preparing for a long winter sleep. Although the sun was trying to break through the overcast day, small light flakes of snow sporadically tumbled through the air.

She reflected on the fact that it had been a difficult year, with her mother's illness and her grandmother's passing. And even though there were many conversations, Olivia was never completely sure she had reconciled with her grandmother.

She suddenly noticed something out of place in her field of vision, and then realized it was a reflection of a person standing in the classroom doorway. Afraid to turn around, she looked again at the reflection in the window and reached out to touch it. Outside, snowflakes stuck to the window momentarily and then blew away. She could see the large reflection of herself and then inside the image was a person, a young man, standing in the backlit doorway.

He hadn't wanted to startle her. Finn could feel his heart race as he stood in the doorway. His fleece jacket came to his waist, and he wore his old blue jeans, the same ones he'd worn the entire time in Florence. He stepped forward. "Olivia?"

Olivia took a deep breath and turned to him.

"Are you home for a visit?"

"No."

"I haven't heard from you in months," she said quietly.

"I've been traveling. My last trip was to Rwanda..." he trailed off, then continued. "You said I needed to find out what it was that I wanted to do with my life. So I did."

Finn moved closer and drank in Olivia's face. Her beautiful green eyes shimmered with a film of tears. Finn took a few steps closer.

"One day at lunch, there was a sign. Maybe it was from God, I don't know. But I left Rome yesterday evening right after I submitted my withdrawal notice from the seminary. My plane landed this afternoon, and I came here directly from the airport."

As Finn spoke, he looked into Olivia's eyes, then down at his feet, then back into her eyes. Tears rolled down her cheeks.

"Now, looking back, it was a mistake accepting the Vatican position and it took several months...for me to understand that. I have always loved my Catholic faith, but I now realize... I want to be with you... and raise a family. I now know the priesthood is not for me. When I met you, it was like a light shone down and lifted me. Your grace touched my heart. It took the words of a child to point me in the right direction."

Olivia wiped the tears from her face.

"I didn't want to prevent you from taking advantage of a great opportunity. I wanted...what was best for you. If being here is truly what you want, then I could not be happier, and God willing, our lives will be changed forever."

They each stepped closer toward each other until they first embraced for a minute and then Finn kissed Olivia gently, and then again.

"I love you Olivia, and this is what I want. You are what I want. I know that now, better than ever. It's as though I was being tested by temptation and survived stronger. Forgive me for ever doubting that this is what I want."

During the year in Rome, Finn kept a small velvet bag on his dresser and now pulled it from his jacket pocket. Inside was a petite antique gold ring with a small Pave diamond. Finn had kept the ring that his mother had given him after his return from Florence, and before the sunshine moved behind a cloud, he took it out and offered it to Olivia.

"It probably needs to be resized, but will you take this ring Olivia? I love you, and I want to spend my life with you. Do you remember my promise?"

The falling snow, soft and pristine, collected on the windowsill as she took the ring and slid it gently onto her finger. It was a perfect fit.

70

A year later, back in Florence, investigations into the attempted assassination and a full-blown public trial eventually found its way through the courts, but this did not occur until nearly a year after Pope John Paul's historic visit to Florence and San Marco. By that time, it was hard to put the two events together. The evidence gathered against Daresh Oldani was not enough to produce proof of a conspiracy. The Piagnoni had done an expert job at covering their tracks, and the prosecution could find no evidence connecting Oldani to their organization. Documents obtained through Interpol and the CIA, years later, could not come up with conclusive evidence making the link to a conspiracy.

Daresh Oldani was convicted of attempted murder and sentenced to life in prison without the possibility of parole. The trial only lasted four days and received very little press. At his trial, he did not take a stand in his own defense, and, as a result, he was not subjected to any cross-examination. A year later, Pope John Paul II visited the prisoner who described himself as a mercenary with no political orientation, although he was known to have been a member of the Piagnoni organization. Pope John Paul II asked people to "pray for my brother, whom I have sincerely forgiven."

Meanwhile in Florence, Father Fitzpatrick and Monsignor Delsoni sat on the interior balcony at San Lorenzo having a glass of Red Breast Irish Whiskey on ice as, once again, summer came to an end and leaves had fallen. They sat together and reminisced about the incident at San Marco. The light from the balcony was fading as a pink pastel sky grew dark red. Father Fitzpatrick had spent his time providing continued security for the Pope on papal visits to North and South America. It felt good to be off and in Florence for a few days of rest. It had been two months since Cardinal Guiseppe Gellini had passed away. Franco Delsoni had donned the title of Auxiliary Bishop, awaiting the Vatican's decision on who would become the new Archbishop of Florence. Franco placed another log in the small fireplace when there was a knock at the door. He shrugged his shoulders at Jonathan, then scuffed to the door in his fleece-lined slippers and turned the brass handle. The door creaked open to reveal Father Stephen Paggi holding a manila folder. Grey hair was starting to fill in at his temples.

"Come in, Stephen. We were just reminiscing. Did you bring the papers?"

"I have them right here, signed, sealed and now delivered. I hope I am not disturbing you. There was no one at the desk, so I let myself in, hoping I would find you."

"It's perfectly fine. I've been expecting the final paperwork. It's just me and Father Fitzpatrick having a drink. Come in and join us."

Stephen placed the folder of documents on the table and said.

"I know it's been a while, but now that the trial is over, the final registration papers from the Ministry of Cultural Affairs Office are complete, and that formalizes the procurement of the antiquity. Photographs of the actual box and copies of all the documentation are in the folder and should be filed here at San Lorenzo for safe keeping."

"What box?" asked Jonathan Fitzpatrick.

Stephen looked at Franco and raised his eyebrows, realizing that very few people knew about the discovery of the box at the Duomo restoration. Franco explained.

"While the students were doing renovations at San Marco and the Duomo, there was a very old wooden box discovered in the renovation debris. The box contained documents written by Girolamo Savonarola and a sketch. Just recently, authorities concluded that the sketch was a da Vinci."

Stephen jumped into the conversation.

"Also recently, because of the discovery of the lost mural by da Vinci behind the existing Giorgio Vasari mural, we realized that it matched the sketch in the box. So gradually, the parts of the puzzle have come together. There was some fear in the minds of art historians that the lost mural would cast da Vinci in an unfavorable light. But that has not been the case. In fact, the new mural, a majestic painting of Mother & Child, is quite magnificent, soon to be placed on view for the public. Can you imagine the tourism? A newly discovered work by Leonardo da Vinci?"

Franco finished his drink and added.

"And, regarding the box, we couldn't make 'the official announcement' until we had the authorized registration papers in place. Not even the Vatican knew."

Fitzpatrick laughed. "Apparently not! We didn't know a thing! Florence keeps providing the world with surprises. And you're right, Stephen. Tourism will skyrocket. Who knows, maybe the Pope will want to come back…ha…here we go again."

Stephen finished his drink, and Franco poured him another. Then Stephen said.

"There's more…"

Franco's eyes widened, and Fitzpatrick laughed.

"Do you remember the ancient document that was found when they raided the Piagnoni safe house? The document was the De Ruina Mundi."

Franco sat up. Stephen continued.

"The De Ruina Mundi predicted that he who finds the box would someday change the world."

Franco asked. "Are you referring to Finn?"

Fitzpatrick added, "I remember him. The kid who loved baseball. He left the Vatican without much notice after working there for less than a year. Can you believe that?"

Stephen leaned back in his chair.

"Finn married one of the Felician Sisters from the restoration fellowship. Well, she was a Felician novice. They're expecting their first child, but you're right. He was the one who discovered the box. It's all documented in these registration papers. In fact, Finn was contacted and provided a legal deposition. If the prediction in the De Ruina Mundi is accurate, who knows what he will do?"

Franco laughed. "Well, he did save the Pope's life!"

Jonathan joined in the laughter. "More likely, he is destined to become the next... baseball commissioner."

CPSIA information can be obtained at www.ICGtesting.com
Printed in the USA
BVOW07*2206050914

365385BV00001B/16/P